THE
LAST
BEGINNING

LAUREN JAMES

WALKER
BOOKS

For my parents, who are always
exactly where I left them.

First published 2016 by Walker Books Ltd
87 Vauxhall Walk, London SE11 5HJ

2 4 6 8 10 9 7 5 3 1

Text © 2016 Lauren James
Cover images: Bare tree © Markus Sturfelt / EyeEm / Getty Images;
Riverside against sky © Liam Mcalorum / EyeEm / Getty Images;
Silhouette of couple © Adi Bilvod / EyeEm / Getty Images
Page 267 illustration by Alice Oseman © 2016. All rights reserved.

This book has been typeset in Ubuntu, Avenir, Arial,
ITC Avant Garde, DIN, GFY Sidney, Neutraface, ITC American Typewriter

Printed and bound in Great Britain by Clays Ltd, St Ives plc

British Library Cataloguing in Publication Data:
a catalogue record for this book is
available from the British Library

ISBN 978-1-4063-5806-3

www.walker.co.uk

PROLOGUE

"Dad, I'm bored," Clove whispered into her father's ear. It was nearly dinnertime and Clove was *starving*, but the evening talk – a very long and technically complicated speech that her mum, Jen, was giving to a group of fellow scientists at her university – wouldn't finish for another half an hour. Her parents had insisted she come, even though she had been in the middle of a Sim with her best friend, Meg. Apparently, aged eleven, she wasn't allowed to stay at home on her own, even if she promised not to move from the sofa the whole time they were gone.

"Shh," her dad, Tom, said. He patted Clove's arm consolingly. "The exciting bit is coming up."

Clove didn't see what could happen to make this evening interesting.

She looked around the lab, which was a lot tidier than usual. Whenever she'd come down to the basement to visit her parents at work in the past, it had been a mess of wires, discarded circuit boards and empty cardboard boxes. Once she could have sworn she saw a mouse nest inside an old computer case, but her dad had resolutely denied it.

Clove tried very hard to tune back into the speech, which was about some kind of grant the university had just received to further fund her parents' research.

"... there are, of course, still issues to be overcome," her mum said, "especially with regard to radiation leakage. However, a huge amount of progress has been made. In fact, the rest of the group and I are delighted to be able to give you a demonstration of the technology here this evening."

The crowd gasped.

"If you would all like to gather round." Her mum sat down at a large computer in the centre of the laboratory. It was connected to an enormous piece of equipment that took up half of the lab. People moved in closer to watch, wine glasses in hand, as Jen started running a program on the computer screen.

Clove snuck a glance at the buffet table, which was set up near the entrance. There were *chocolate* eclairs. Surely no one would notice if she started eating now. She had to listen to her parents talking about work every day – there was nothing remotely exciting about it. They worked on something called Einstein-Rosen bridges, whatever those were. At a push, she was more interested in her father's work, which was about computer programming. Clove really liked computer programming.

A blonde teenage girl wearing a long green scarf saw Clove eyeing up the buffet table. She winked at her. Clove twisted back around, trying not to blush at being caught out.

Her dad nudged her arm. "Look, Clove."

Clove reluctantly turned to see her mum type a final command into the computer. Noise filled the lab – a whirring groan that seemed to shake the walls and vibrate the air. The scientists shifted, expectantly, and then Clove saw what they were all staring at.

A light had gone on in part of the equipment attached to her mum's computer – a sort of glass box. Sitting in the centre of the box was a single red rose. The noise coming from the rest of the equipment grew louder until Clove could feel the vibrations in her eardrums and chest. The wine glasses trembled, adding a faint high-pitched screech to the sound.

Everyone seemed to be holding their breath. As Clove watched, the noise cut off all at once, and the rose—

The rose disappeared.

Everyone exclaimed in unison. There was a moment of complete silence. Another moment. Then the air inside the glass box shuddered and blurred. When it cleared, the flower had reappeared.

Clove couldn't believe what she'd just seen. Around her, the audience burst into enthusiastic applause.

Her mum stood up from the computer, a proud smile on her face. "What you just witnessed was the world's first ever public demonstration of time travel."

Clove drew in a sharp breath. Time travel? She hadn't realized *that* was what her parents were working on. She hadn't even known time travel was possible.

Her mum was talking again. "It has taken many, many years of research by a dedicated team of physicists and computer scientists to get to this point, and our work has only just begun. The current technology only operates on a small scale, in terms of both object size and time travelled.

With our new research grant, we hope to improve the equipment to allow for travel of living objects, and through time periods of more than a few seconds. We will also target the biggest issue with the current technology: survival." She gestured back to the glass box.

Clove's mouth gaped open. The rose's once vivid red petals had curled up and faded to a putrid brown, the stem was shrivelled and black. The rose was dead.

"Radiation levels experienced during the transfer are too high for anything to survive," her mum explained. "We will need to eliminate this issue in order to achieve our ultimate goal: human time travel. But I have high hopes that we will all be back here in several years to celebrate just that success."

The crowd burst into applause once more. Clove, completely overwhelmed with amazement, clapped as hard as she could. Once everyone had quietened down, her mum began answering scientific questions about the equipment, but Clove wasn't listening. She couldn't take her eyes off the time machine and the withered rose inside it. Her mum and dad had built an *actual time machine.*

As Clove watched a dead petal slowly fall from the flower, she made herself a promise. When she was older, she was going to work here with the machine – even if it meant spending all her free time between now and then studying. Then one day, when she'd helped to get the machine working, she was going to be the first person to travel through time.

PART
ONE

CHAPTER 1

An Unauthorized Biography of Clove Sutcliffe

When we talk about <u>Clove Sutcliffe</u> from an academic perspective, it is clear she had a huge part to play in the history of the twenty-first and twenty-second centuries. Scholars often forget, however, that she was a complex character in her own right, regardless of her historical impact. Her upbringing, parentage and childhood were far from typical, and this is worthy of study in itself.

File note: Extract from *An Unauthorized Biography of Clove Sutcliffe*, first published in 2344

ST ANDREWS, SCOTLAND, 2056

Clove was sulking. She was supposed to be working on a programming problem that her dad had set her, but she'd just had a realization and she needed to dwell on it. Her realization was this: her best friend liked a boy. Clove had thought she would have a few more years before she lost her best friend to a *boy*. It wasn't just any boy, either. Judging by the message that Meg had just sent her, the boy she'd chosen to set her sights on was none other than *Clove's cousin.*

Nuts_Meg 18:02:45   DARLINGGGGG I HAVE A COMPLAINT.

LuckyClover 18:03:14   File it with the appropriate authorities.

Nuts_Meg 18:03:57   I am worryingly close to it, loser.

Nuts_Meg 18:04:02   Anyway why have you been holding out on me?? You have family members who are powerful babes! How could you not tell me about Alec?

As Clove reread Meg's last message, her heart clenched. She should have guessed this would happen. At Clove's sixteenth birthday party, Clove had watched Meg and Alec talking together in the garden. Meg's face had been turned towards Alec's, her mouth curved into a flirtatious grin. Meg's soft blonde hair had fluttered in the wind in that picture-perfect way it always did, like, if you touched it, it would be softer than air. Meg had pushed it away absently as she let out a laugh. Clove hadn't been able to hear her, but she didn't need to – she knew Meg's laugh better than her own.

She should have known then that Alec would destroy everything.

For some reason, just the idea of Meg and Alec together was stopping Clove from being able to get back to her programming. That was unusual, as most of the time programming helped her to feel grounded. She had started it as a way to deal with her hyperactivity. It gave her something to focus her attention on when her parents were frustrated with her endless energy.

When she was twelve she had been diagnosed as a "gifted child with hyperactivity issues", which seemed to Clove a rather extreme way of saying that she was a bit jumpy, intensely focused, and made easily impatient with inactivity or slow teaching. She could get excessively dedicated to things she was interested in, though, which was one thing her teachers did appreciate. She could program for hours and hours with scant thought to the outside world, until her parents came to her room to force her to eat some dinner (or breakfast, if she'd been working all night).

Clove closed her code, so she could devote her attention to the imminent disaster of Meg's love life. She replied to Meg in a way she hoped didn't express her annoyance.

LuckyClover 18:04:26	being attracted to neither boys nor close blood relatives, it never occurred to me that he was a babe
LuckyClover 18:04:28	Sorry
Nuts_Meg 18:04:55	u r fired
LuckyClover 18:05:12	from being your personal dating website?
Nuts_Meg 18:05:33	Yes
LuckyClover 18:05:49	aw, mannn! The benefits were so great
LuckyClover 18:05:54	oh wait …
LuckyClover 18:05:59	… there weren't any
Nuts_Meg 18:06:17	girl's got jokes today I see
LuckyClover 18:06:43	yeah whatever. So did I tell you my dad's well cute, want me to set you up?
Nuts_Meg 18:07:03	sure, he's a silver fox.
LuckyClover 18:07:09	Ew
LuckyClover 18:07:11	EW
LuckyClover 18:07:21	well, that backfired
LuckyClover 18:07:33	heterosexuality is gross
Nuts_Meg 18:07:51	don't be heterophobic
LuckyClover 18:08:17	that isn't a thing
Nuts_Meg 18:08:37	it will be if you keep this up
LuckyClover 18:09:15	you must feel so discriminated against

Clove tried not to feel bitter, but if Meg couldn't fall for her, did she really have to fall for *her cousin*?

A message from Spart, their household Artificial Intelligence system, popped up on Clove's watch screen and interrupted her thoughts.

> Your mother is about to enter your room. Hide any and all illicit substances now.

Clove rolled her eyes at the message. Their AI lived in all their home computers and watches and picked up vocal instructions from anyone near by. Spart organized their lives, and tended to make a general nuisance of himself as he did so. Clove thought this was because her dad had programmed him with a few extra features, including a personality, which meant Spart tended to think he was human.

"Come in," she called to her mum.

"Can you come and sit with us for a moment, Clove?" her mum said after opening the door. Her voice sounded oddly nervous. "Your dad and I want to talk to you about something."

Clove said a quick goodbye to Meg. She was slightly relieved to leave the conversation before it got too serious. Then she followed her mum downstairs to the living room and settled on the sofa. Her curiosity increased as she watched her parents communicate with each other silently. They were so in sync that they sometimes seemed able to talk to each other without speaking at all.

A notification popped up on Clove's watch. Meg had replied to her goodbye with a snap of herself smiling dreamily into the camera. She'd written ALEC <3 across it in red. Annoyed, Clove swiped left to delete the message.

"Clove," her dad said, after clearing his throat, "we've got something to tell you." He let out an exhale. Clove saw her mum squeeze his hand. "It's time to tell you the truth. We think you're old enough now to understand it."

All Clove could hear was the blood pounding in her ears.

"Now, Clove, we love you. You are a wonderful, beautiful daughter—" He paused.

She stared at him. "What? What is it?" Her words came out croaky.

For an agonizing heartbeat, nobody spoke.

Then her dad continued. "This is hard to say…"

"What?" she said hoarsely. "Just tell me."

Her dad sucked in a long breath. "When you were born, something happened to my brother … who was your natural father. Something happened to him and your natural mother."

Clove felt her face go stiff. She couldn't think. She couldn't process anything he was saying. Adopted. *Adopted?* She didn't feel adopted. Wouldn't she have guessed?

"We raised you because they couldn't," her dad went on. "Genetically, I'm actually your uncle."

"Why didn't you tell me before?" Clove asked. She felt betrayed, displaced, horrified, and a hundred other emotions she didn't know how to put into words.

Her parents exchanged glances. "Your birth mother made us promise to wait until you were old enough to understand," her mum said. "She was worried you might not be able to handle it. It's sensitive. But now you're sixteen, we thought—"

"What?" Clove said, in a choked-off half-laugh. "That *now* I can handle it?"

"It's more than just you being adopted. It's also ... because of what happened to your natural parents ... because of who they were." Her mum stared down at her hands.

Her dad shifted in his seat.

Clove was itching to move, her knee jumping with the hyperactive twitchiness that always came when she was upset. She leant forward to stop it. "Why? Who are they? What happened to them? Is it because they didn't want me? Is that what you're saying?" Clove was finding it hard to process her thoughts.

"Oh, Clove," her mum said. "No, no. It wasn't like that at all. They loved you very much."

"Clove," her dad said, trying to speak calmly. "Darlin', it's ... it's hard to explain. They were—"

"They were *what*?" she demanded. *"Tell me."*

Clove stared at her parents – her *adoptive* parents, not her real parents at all – and felt the hairs on the back of her neck rise. She didn't understand. Nothing made any sense.

"I'm getting this all wrong. Clove, I'm sorry," her dad – *Tom* – said. "Let me explain properly." He faltered. Her mum – *Jen* – took his hand again. "Maybe it's best if I just come right out with it. What do you know about Matt Galloway and Kate Finchley?"

Clove knew quite a bit about them. Everybody did – they were famous. There was even a film about them. They were two students who, in 2039, had found evidence that the

English government was developing a biological weapon, with plans to release it on the rest of the world if there was another world war. The students had fled across the border into Scotland with an accomplice. Matt Galloway had been arrested, then later he had escaped from prison and disappeared without a trace, along with Kate. The English government had been dissolved as a result of what the students had found out. As such, they were credited with saving the world from biological attack. No one knew where they were now, though. They'd been missing for over sixteen years – the whole time Clove had been alive.

"The political activists?" Clove felt a little dizzy.

"Matt Galloway was my brother. He's your natural father. Kate Finchley was ... *is* ... your mother. It was us – the three of us – that uncovered the conspiracy by the English government."

Clove let out a noise: a kind of brittle bark. "You?" Surely her dad, who was going grey and spent all of his time hunched over a computer, hadn't... "*You* shut down the English government?"

"Yeah, that was us." Tom scratched the back of his neck. "Before I met Jen, I wasn't a professor of computer science. I was a hacker. It's not something I do any more. Everything that happened with Matt and Kate sort of scared me out of it."

Clove's throat was as dry as if she'd swallowed a spoonful of flour. She couldn't keep track of everything she was being told. Her dad was a hacker? Her dad wasn't her dad at all? Her real parents were *famous*?

"What happened? Where did they go? How did *you* end up with *me*?" she asked.

"After Matt was arrested," Tom said, "Kate and I came to my parents' house, in Scotland. Your mother was pregnant, and gave birth to you here. Afterwards, Kate decided to go back to England, to try and free Matt. He had evidence of the weapon with him when he was arrested, you see, so nobody believed us." Tom stopped, giving her a chance to ask questions. She blinked mutely at him, and he continued. "Kate thought that if she could break Matt out of prison, they could use the evidence to tell the world about the weapon and make sure it was destroyed before the English military used it in war. We didn't want Kate to go. It was a crazy plan. How could she break Matt out of prison? She wouldn't listen, and even though she hated to leave you, she thought it was something she had to do. I agreed to look after you until she returned." Tom stopped, swallowed.

"She never did," Jen finished. "Your parents disappeared. We know that Kate managed to break your father out of prison. How, I have no idea – it should have been impossible. But Kate managed it. They even managed to send evidence of the biological weapon to NATO shortly after Matt's escape without getting caught. The English government was shut down. But we don't know what happened to your parents after that. Tom didn't hear anything from either Kate or Matt after the prison breakout – they just disappeared."

"You just let her – my mother – go off alone? You *stayed here*?" Clove tried to stop her face from twisting into a grimace.

Tom stared at her, but he didn't look like he was seeing her at all. "I've regretted it every day since." He rubbed a thumb across his knuckles. "Officially, they are still classified as missing. That means they either managed to escape to France, or perhaps even back to Scotland, or they were secretly taken prisoner by the English government."

No one spoke for a while. Clove felt wobbly, a little sweaty. Eventually, she said, "Have you never tried to find them?"

Tom scrubbed his hands over his face. "I've enquired about them, and I've got dozens of online alerts set up for any mention of them. But there haven't been any leads in a long time. I would have done more, but I had to be careful. I'm still wanted by the English authorities – I can't go and physically look for them."

Jen patted Tom's hand. "It's been pretty scary over the years. When Tom first told me, I worried all the time that something would happen – that English spies would find him. He'd changed his surname, but that didn't make me feel any safer. I've learned to live with it, and we've been left alone, so far. Technically we're all in hiding."

"We're *in hiding from the law*?" Clove asked.

"Well, I am. The English law, at least," Tom admitted. "Your mum took on a lot when she decided to marry me: a single dad with a six-month-old baby and a secret history of crime."

Jen smiled at him, softly. "You're worth it, hon."

"I don't know how I'd have done it without you." Tom leant over and kissed Jen quickly. Clove couldn't bear to watch. Her whole world was crumbling in front of her and they were acting like it was nothing.

"So I'm not really Clove Sutcliffe?" she asked, trying to bring them back to what was important.

"You are, legally. I took Jen's name when we married," Tom explained. "But if our family was a little more conventional, you'd be Clove Galloway."

"Galloway," Clove repeated, trying the name out. "Clove Galloway."

Hearing it aloud made it real. Suddenly it all clicked. Matt Galloway and Kate Finchley *were* her parents. Her real, actual parents. There was a film about them. About *her parents*. She'd watched it in a history class once. She'd had to *write a paper* about them.

They were her *parents*. They had saved the world.

Aloud, slightly hysterically, as if it was the most important thing she'd learnt that day, she said, *"MY PARENTS HAVE A WIKIPEDIA PAGE?"*

"They've probably got an IMDB page, too," Tom said, and despite the coldness that had begun to spread through her body, Clove began to laugh, too loud and too manic, and found she couldn't stop.

Eventually, after she'd calmed down and drunk a whole glass of water, Clove managed to ask some more appropriate questions. "Didn't my ... mother leave any plans about what she was going to do after she rescued Matt?"

"No, she didn't. If she had a plan, she didn't share it with me." Tom carefully lined up a coaster with the edge of the table. "But I didn't push her to. I was done with it – I didn't want her to go. But I couldn't stop her. She was set on saving Matt. And in some ways it was a relief... I was out of it. Free."

"What about me? How could she just leave me like that, with nothing?" Clove's voice cracked.

"Kate left you with me and your grandparents," Tom said. Somehow, to Clove, that didn't seem enough. What was an uncle to real parents? What were her grandparents – who were great but getting kind of old and sleepy – to a mum and dad?

"She always meant to come back. It was only supposed to be temporary. And she did leave something for you," Tom added. "A box of letters. They might tell you more. We never opened them. I promised Kate I wouldn't. Spart, do you know where they are?"

Spart's tinny voice came from his watch.

> The box is in a filing cabinet in the most eastern corner of the loft.

> There's a nest of mice in the adjacent box. I have called an exterminator, who will arrive tomorrow at 1300 hours. Does this meet with your approval?

"Thanks, Spart. I'll get it," Jen said.

She stood up, kissing Clove's forehead as she left the room. Clove breathed in the familiar scent of Jen's perfume and wondered again how it had never occurred to her that this wasn't her real mother. Shouldn't she have known, somehow? Shouldn't she be able to feel something like that?

"Why didn't you tell me sooner?" Clove asked, while they waited for Jen to return.

Tom sighed. "Kate – your mother, I mean – made me promise to wait until you were older, so that you would understand it all properly. I was happy to do that. For a long time when you were young the situation was still very dangerous. We couldn't risk you mentioning anything about it at school. After Matt escaped from prison, the English authorities were searching for him and Kate for years. Even though they had saved the world, Matt's prison break meant that they were the most wanted criminals in England, so I was in hiding. While they could never do anything about me officially as I'm under Scotland's protection, we always thought that they might try to do something to me in secret, to get information about your parents somehow. It was imperative that no one knew who I really was, or where Tom Galloway had gone. Your grandparents – my mum and dad – came into hiding with us. They changed their names too.

"If our location had been leaked, all of our lives would have been in danger. Whatever the English government did to Kate and Matt in the end ... that would have happened to me, and maybe to my parents and to you and Jen too. We couldn't have told you the truth, not back then." Tom smiled slightly as he said, "A part of me did wonder if you knew, though, somehow. Do you remember after you watched the film about them, darlin'? You used to play with Meg at being 'Kate and Matt', running away from the police."

Clove gasped. "I remember that. I always wanted to be

Matt. I used to steal your glasses so I looked like him. Meg was always Kate because she liked her hair." The memory caused an ache in her chest. What would Tom and Jen have been feeling, watching them play all those years ago? It must have been basically impossible to keep the secret hidden.

"It was just easier not to tell you anything," Tom continued. "And we'd built up lives here. We didn't want to have to go on the run. Especially not with our work at St Andrews. Everything was just coming together with the time machine. It wasn't worth risking it, not when all of our work was at stake too."

Clove swallowed. She stared at her knees. She knew that Tom was watching her with concern, but she couldn't meet his eye. It was clear that he was relieved to have finally given up the burden of secrecy.

When Jen returned with the box, she put it on Clove's lap. "Take your time reading through it. You don't even have to look at it now if you don't want to. It's a lot to take in. If you have any questions, we're here to answer them. We love you, Clove."

Clove closed her eyes and tried to let Jen's hug calm her, the way it had throughout her childhood. But all she could think was that it should have been a different pair of hands holding her. Her mother should have been someone else.

CHAPTER 2

Tom,

Everything in this box is for Clove. If we don't
come back, give it to her when she's old enough
to understand. Please don't tell her about us until
then. I want her to be a happy child, innocent of
everything her parents have done.

Thank you,

Kate

Folios/v8/Time-landscape-2040/MS-4

File note: A note written in 2040 by KATE FINCHLEY to TOM
         GALLOWAY before she left CLOVE SUTCLIFFE in his
         care and took a bus to England

ST ANDREWS, SCOTLAND, 2056

Clove sat cross-legged in the centre of her bed and
regarded the box. It was corrugated cardboard, the kind
that Tom and Jen used for storage. There were numbers
written on it in Tom's untidy scrawl. She'd probably seen it
dozens of times in her life.

Brushing the caked dust off the lid, Clove watched

the particles drift lazily to settle on her duvet cover. She pressed a thumb against the grey specks, rubbing them into the material. Then she lay back to stare at the ceiling, tapping her foot against the end of her bed. She didn't want to open the box.

She considered calling Meg. Not to tell her the news – she wasn't ready for that conversation – but as a distraction. She knew what would happen, though. Meg would want to talk about Alec, and Clove would have to pretend to be enthusiastic about their burgeoning romance.

She heaved a melodramatic sigh, which made her feel slightly better. Finally, she sat up and tugged the lid off the box and peered inside. There was a folded letter on top – an actual paper letter, like the kind in old films. Below it was a bundle of papers, a lab book and a leather journal tied with velvet ribbon. At the very bottom was a piece of fabric wrapped around a small object. After unwrapping it, she found it was a tiny fox ornament hidden in an old and fragile cardigan. She placed the ornament on her desk, wondering at the history behind it. What had it meant to Kate that she had kept it so carefully?

There were several shiny photos in the bottom of the box. They showed a smartly dressed man, his dark hair in careful disarray, beaming at a woman in a fluffy white wedding dress. Her red curls fell haphazardly around her face.

Clove's heart seized up. This was them. Her parents.

She opened the letter.

My beautiful daughter,

Fingers crossed you're reading these letters with me at your side, and I'm showing you them while telling you stories about how badass your dad and I used to be.

Hopefully you'll find the whole thing utterly embarrassing and go to visit your cool Uncle Tom to get away from our boring anecdotes. That's the future I want for you – you and Tom gossiping about how awful we are. Matt and me boasting about our epic adventures nonetheless.

That's probably not the life you are going to get, Clove.

I should explain properly. If this is the first time you've ever heard of me, I should at least try to make sense, shouldn't I? Good work on that, Kate.

I have to leave. I don't want to. Leaving you behind is the single hardest thing I'm ever going to do. You are the most important thing in the world to me. But there's more at stake than just your childhood. Your dad and I need to save the world.

You've probably heard the stories, but in case you haven't, just know that my country is run by terrible people, and I need to try and stop them. I'm leaving you all of the evidence — my journals, printouts of emails and other documents — so you'll have the full story.

I have to get your father out of prison, Clove. Not just because I'm in love with him, or because he's innocent, or because he's a father now, but because he's important to the world. I can't let him rot away in jail, not when he's still alive for once. Not when there's still work for us to do.

I think that's enough for today. I'll write to you again tomorrow. For now, I'm going to read you a story. I heard that babies can learn to recognize their mother's voice from the womb, so I'm reading you the classics, starting with Harry Potter. I tried reading you poetry, but I couldn't stand it, and neither could you — you kept kicking me. As I've been writing this, you've kicked me nine times. I think you're going to be a hyperactive kid.

Folios/v8/Time-landscape-2040/MS-5

File note: A letter written in 2040 by KATE FINCHLEY to her
          unborn baby, CLOVE SUTCLIFFE

Clove read the entire letter without pausing and then skimmed through the other papers, which turned out to be a mix of diary entries, emails and experiment logs.

It seemed that her parents had broken into Central Science Laboratories, after following clues in a coded journal written by her mum's dead aunt, who had worked in the lab in 2019 when the fatal bacteria was first created. By some weird coincidence – or family tradition, maybe – Kate's aunt had also been called Katherine. Clove's great-aunt's journal was in the box, too, along with her lab books – the actual originals! Clove felt like she was holding a piece of history.

Hours later, when she'd read every detail, she dropped the documents back in the box and curled up around a pillow. She felt dizzy and lost – caught up in something beyond her understanding.

After a while, she stood up and walked into the bath-room. Staring at herself in the mirror, she drank a glass of water slowly, sipping and savouring each mouthful. No matter how hard she looked, she couldn't see anything that made her special. She had never expected anything like this ever to happen to her. She wasn't a dazzling lead protagonist in some adventure film. She was the gay best friend.

She tried to see whether she could recognize her parents in her features. How had she never noticed that she didn't look anything like Tom and Jen? She compared her face to the photos, picking out details.

She had Matt's nose. It was cute, she thought: slightly

turned up. She had Kate's eyes and curls. Clove's hair was usually shorter, in a pixie cut, but it was growing out. The mass of dark curls that had grown almost to her neck looked just like her mother's – only it was brown, like Matt's hair.

Her mother loved Harry Potter and hated poetry, just like Clove did. Kate had known that Clove was going to be hyperactive before she was even born – something it had taken Tom and Jen years and years to work out. Tom and Jen. Clove couldn't think of them as Mum and Dad right now.

Clove Galloway, she said to herself, repeating the words until they came naturally. *Clove Galloway.*

CHAPTER 3

Folios/v5–v6–v7–v8/Time-landscape-1941–1963–2019–2040/
  MS-1

File note: Photographs of KATHERINE FINCHLEY and MATTHEW
        GALLOWAY, taken in multiple time-landscapes from
        1941–2040

ST ANDREWS, SCOTLAND, 2056

"Hey, champ," Meg said, as she sat down opposite Clove.

Clove was jerked back into awareness. She was in the dining hall at school, apparently having sat through all of her morning classes without taking in a word. She hadn't wanted to come to school this morning, but Jen had insisted, and now here she was at lunchtime, too lost in thought to do anything except stare at her empty plate. She hadn't even ordered her food yet. She clicked through the menu screen in the table's surface, finally settling on curly fries. A few seconds after she tapped the item, her steaming hot meal slid out of a drawer in the table.

Meg started shaking salt over her own chips. "So have you managed to get your code working?"

Clove felt completely out of it. "What code?"

Meg frowned. "I thought that's why you'd been incommunicado all day. Because you've been trying to work out your latest program."

Clove opened her mouth, closed it again. "Sure," she said, hating herself for how easily the lie came.

Meg flicked her hair back over her shoulders. The soft mess of blonde settled down her back. Clove's eyes caught on it and wouldn't let go. Her throat felt tight. She couldn't remember when she'd started liking Meg as more than a friend, but it was hard knowing that Meg didn't feel the same way – even harder now that Meg had a crush on Clove's own cousin.

"So are you ready for work experience?" Meg asked. "Do you know what you'll be doing yet? I think I'm going to be helping teach the Reception kids. Do you get to play with the time machine?"

"I don't know yet." Clove swallowed. Today was their last day of school before they started a week of work experience on Monday. Meg was going into a local primary school and Clove was working at the university with her parents. She had been looking forward to it – and to the week without homework – but now she wasn't sure how she felt about spending so much time with Tom and Jen. Not after what she'd found out.

Without even knowing she was going to say anything, she let out in a rush, "Mum and Dad told me I'm adopted."

Clove could see the moment the meaning of the sentence hit Meg by the change in her posture, as she registered that the conversation had gone from absent, idle lunchtime talk to a serious discussion.

"Oh, *Clove*. Are you all right?"

Clove nodded, and tried to force away a sudden rush of tears. She was so glad she'd told Meg. Meg always knew exactly what to say. Meg was always there, just when she needed her. If only Meg didn't need Alec, too.

"I'm OK," she said, trying to speak lightly. "I really am," she added, when Meg looked doubtful. "I know they still love me, they raised me and they're still my parents – all of that stuff."

Meg put down a chip she'd been holding. She looked ready to launch-hug Clove if she burst into tears.

"Meg, it's fine, really," Clove said. "That's not the part I'm having trouble grasping. It's who my *real* parents are that's causing me to freak out."

"What? Who are they? Clove, are you a *princess*? Powerful!"

Clove let out a half-hearted fake laugh. "Er, no. I wish." She focused her attention on neatly lining up her cutlery beside her plate so she didn't have to look at Meg. "You can't tell anyone."

"I won't."

"I mean it. It's really important."

"Clove, I promise. What's going on?"

Clove checked to make sure no one sitting near by was listening in. Everything Tom had said about how dangerous it could be if this got out was going through her mind, but this was Meg! Surely it was OK to tell her?

Clove swallowed. She spoke quietly, but her words were strong, proud and resolute. "My parents are Matt Galloway and Kate Finchley. The ... ones we used to play games about as kids. They're my parents."

Meg let out a long exhale. "Well. I don't even know where to start with that. You ... really? That's like finding out your parents are *Hermione and Ron*, or something."

Clove just nodded. "Yeah. I know. It's ... kind of crazy."

"How are you, uh, dealing with that?"

Clove looked at her plate. "Fine."

Meg picked up her sandwich. "I don't believe you. How can you be *fine*?"

"I'm just— I don't know. Reeling, a bit."

Meg snorted. "I don't blame you."

"And my mum – the real one, Kate Finchley – she left me these letters."

"Letters? I thought she disappeared? I thought they both did."

"Yeah. She wrote them before I was born. She left very soon after giving birth to me to break Matt Galloway – my dad – out of prison. And she was so *hopeful*. She really thought she'd come back. She thought she and Matt would be the ones to raise me. She thought Tom would only ever be my *uncle*."

"That's ... I can't even imagine. Where did they go? Where are they now? If she was so determined to come back for you..."

Clove blinked once, twice, three times. "Exactly. Where the hell are they?" Clove knew there was a possibility that they were dead, killed by the English military, and yet she didn't want to believe it. She felt sure, in her heart, that her parents – Kate and Matt – were still alive.

The bell rang for class, and Clove started tidying up their plates. "Let's talk about this later."

Meg pulled her into a hug. "It's OK, Clove. We'll sort it out. I'll even help you track them down, if I have to."

Clove squeezed her best friend tightly. She could smell Meg's perfume: the brand of a boy band she was obsessed with. Clove breathed it in deeply. She never wanted to let go.

"Thanks," Clove mumbled. She loved Meg's unconditional belief, despite the odds against Matt and Kate being alive.

Meg gave her a final squeeze and pulled away, looking over her face carefully. When Clove smiled tentatively at her, Meg seemed convinced that she was OK. She smiled back, her expression turning cheeky. "By the way, it's totally unfair that you get the epic adoptive parents and the *even more epic* natural parents, while I'm stuck with one pair of boring, suburban accountants with a white-picket fence. Some people get all the luck."

* * *

That evening Tom and Jen came up to Clove's bedroom when they got home from work. They sat on her bed, holding cups of tea and a packet of rich tea biscuits and looking nervous.

Clove closed the code she'd been trying and failing to focus on. She started reorganizing the apps on her homescreen so she didn't have to watch Jen dipping biscuits in her tea, or Tom staring at his daughter like he was trying to solve a maths equation.

They were waiting for her to start talking, so that they could counsel her through "Her Feelings about the Adoption". They'd done the same thing when she'd told them she was gay. Usually it helped to talk through everything, but this time she couldn't. She just … couldn't. She didn't even know how she felt yet.

"How are you doing?" Jen asked finally with wide, unhappy eyes. She looked hurt, as if Clove was locking herself up in her room on purpose to make Jen feel bad.

"Fine," Clove replied shortly. She tried to smile, to put on a brave face to make them feel better, hating that she had to. This was her pain, not theirs. She shouldn't have to worry about what they were thinking or feeling. She should be allowed to be alone if she wanted.

"You can talk to us if you want," Jen said. "It's a lot to deal with, I know."

Clove shrugged. "They're gone. What is there to discuss?" Looking for something to do with her hands, she picked up her knitting and began a new row. Knitting was another way her parents tried to help her to control her hyperactivity. Usually she knitted while she was waiting for code to compile. Right now she was making a scarf out of soft, emerald-green wool. She was going to give it to Meg when she'd finished it. It would look really pretty next to her blonde hair.

"There's so much to discuss, Clove. We don't want you to ever, ever feel like you weren't wanted. Your dad and I love you so much. So do your birth parents, even if they can't be here for you."

"I know." It would be impossible for Clove not to know that. Tom and Jen pushed so much love on her that it was almost stifling. "I just don't ... I don't get it. Where are they?"

"If they were still out there," Jen said, hesitantly, "they would have come back for you. I promise."

Tom cleared his throat. "Your mother is right, darlin'. If they were alive—"

"No!" Clove said, dropping her knitting in her lap. They were trying to make her feel less abandoned by telling her that the reason her parents had never come back for her was because they were dead. But she knew that wasn't true. She didn't know how, she just did. Kate and Matt were alive, somewhere out there.

Abruptly, Clove realized what was bothering her the most. It wasn't the adoption. It wasn't even the thought that Kate and Matt had left her behind. Clove was upset because she didn't know what had happened to them. Clove knew that she was never going to be able to focus on anything else until she found out – even if her search just led her to an unmarked gravestone somewhere. She had to know.

"Is that why you gave up looking for them?" she asked Tom. "Because you thought they were dead? Did you even try at all?"

Tom suddenly looked very tired. "Of course I tried. I told you. For years and years it was all I thought about. I did everything I could think of. I hacked into the prison security footage and the English military's database. I nearly got myself arrested by the Scottish authorities. But I couldn't find them. They disappeared completely! Eventually I ran out of things to try."

Clove didn't know what to say. How did she know that whatever Tom had done was enough? How could she be sure that he'd tried everything? Surely if *she* looked, if *she* tried, she'd find something that he had missed?

"I want to keep looking," Clove said, determined. "I don't want to give up on them. What if they are waiting for you to help them? What if they've been relying on you all this time, and you just gave up?"

Tom rubbed his hands over his face. He looked sad but resigned. "If you think that'll help you to work through this ... then I can let you look at my old research. So you can see how much I tried. I never gave up on them, not even for a second. Matt was my brother as well as your father, Clove."

"I'm not sure about this..." Jen said, looking worried. "I don't want you messing around in something illegal. It's dangerous."

"I just want to look at Dad's old research. I won't try to find them, I *promise*," Clove said, desperately.

"She knows better than to get into trouble," Tom said to Jen. "We should trust her. And if it helps her process everything..."

"Fine," Jen said after a moment.

Clove tried to hide her smile.

CHAPTER 4

Nuts_Meg 19:34:12	CLOVE. If your real parents are M & K, does that make your adopted dad Tom Galloway? Like, THE Tom Galloway, the hacker? THE HACKER SPARTACUS?? ?? ????????????
LuckyClover 19:37:48	yeah, it does. He had to change his name.
LuckyClover 19:38:03	huh, i guess that's why our AI is called Spart. That makes so much sense.
Nuts_Meg 19:38:07	POWERFUL!
Nuts_Meg 19:38:25	I AM SO HAPPY ABOUT THIS DEVELOPMENT
LuckyClover 19:38:55	? ? ?
Nuts_Meg 19:39:13	CLOVE, THE INTERNET WAS ALL ABOUT SPARTACUS BACK IN THE DAY. HE HAD HIS OWN FANDOM.
Nuts_Meg 19:39:45	THERE ARE FANBLOGS ABOUT HIM
LuckyClover 19:40:02	no. no. please, no.
Nuts_Meg 19:40:33	LOTS OF FANBLOGS. ABOUT YOUR DAD. I guess i'm not the only one who thinks he's a silver fox??
LuckyClover 19:40:47	noooooooooooooooooooo
Nuts_Meg 19:40:59	AND IT GETS BETTER
LuckyClover 19:41:23	please don't say it
Nuts_Meg 19:41:46	i'm sorry, clove. I have to. There is fanfiction about your dad.
LuckyClover 19:42:02	this isn't happening. i wish i was dead.
Nuts_Meg 19:42:12	I haven't even sent you any links yet. Wait until you hear about the werewolf soulbonding erotica I found about him and Kate.
LuckyClover 19:42:24	urghhhhhhhhhhhhhhhhhhhhhhhhhhhhhhhhhhhhh
Nuts_Meg 19:42:33	This is the best thing that has ever happened to me ever.
LuckyClover 19:42:58	i'm going to vomit all over you

File note: Chat log, dated 14 July 2056

ST ANDREWS, SCOTLAND, 2056

Clove clicked through Tom's research greedily, like she'd been given a box of expensive chocolates. She was calmer now that she had something to focus on. She could feel in her heart that there was more to uncover about this mystery. She just *knew* that her parents were still out there, but more than that: she felt instinctively that they had been trying to get back to her, all this time.

Tom's search had mainly focused on hacking into high-security websites, like the English prison's records. He had been pretty thorough, and Clove didn't think that carrying on with his approach was likely to turn up anything new. The English military would have been careful not to leave any evidence where it could be found. It was unlikely that there would have been a paper trail at all. Clove needed to do something new, something that would never have occurred to Tom.

Clove took up her knitting, adding a few rows to her scarf while she considered the problem. It was only when Spart reminded her to drink her tea before it got cold that she realized she did have one advantage. She had Spart.

When Tom had been searching for Kate and Matt, Artificial Intelligences hadn't been created. She could use Spart to do things Tom hadn't been capable of trying, like telling the AI to run more vigorous, intensive searches than Tom had ever been able to manage.

Spart had a huge processing power, and was much more intelligent than a human. She could leave him to run a search twenty-four hours a day, for as long as it took. There were satellites and CCTV cameras everywhere – surely *one* had caught a glimpse of Kate and Matt in the last sixteen years. It was a good place to start. And with Spart's help, Clove could do so much better than Tom. She could fix his mistakes – as long as she could get Spart to agree to help her.

"Spart?" Clove whispered to her watch. Her parents were downstairs, so she knew they couldn't overhear, but she wanted to make sure they didn't catch her. She'd promised Jen that she wouldn't try to find Kate and Matt.

The Artificial Intelligence's reply popped up on the watch on her wrist. Spart could speak aloud or via text, depending on what setting he was on. If left to his own devices, he'd chatter away all day, so Clove usually left him in text mode.

> Yes? Let me pause my show.

"What are you watching? Wait, don't tell me. It's that robot sitcom, isn't it? I know you've got a crush on the Doctor Watt robot."

There was an all too revealing silence.

"It's OK, I'll keep your secret," she said, grinning.

> As Artificial Intelligences cannot experience emotions, I do not have – and am incapable of having – a "crush".

"You just think he's amazingly intelligent, with a powerful personality and beautiful circuitry. I get it."

> How may I assist you this evening, CLOVE?

She stifled a grin. He was avoiding the subject – and not very subtly.

"I was wondering if you could help me out on a project I'm working on."

> My full processing power is at your disposal, providing, of course, that it doesn't interfere with my show time.

"You're such a loyal servant, Spart. All right, here's the plan. Do you know about my parents?"

> THOMAS PHILLIP SUTCLIFFE, PhD, professor of computer science at the University of St Andrews, and JENNIFER GRACE SUTCLIFFE, PhD, professor of physics at—

"No – not them. My birth parents. Matt Galloway and Kate Finchley?"

Spart was quiet for a second.

> MATTHEW GEORGE GALLOWAY and KATHERINE LOUISE FINCHLEY, missing since 2040, suspected dead, responsible for revealing the English government's plans for biological warfare. Wanted by the English military. Both were reading chemistry at the University of Nottingham prior to their disappearance. School grades: AAA and AAB respectively. Birth dates, 14th—

"Right! Good. That's enough. Anyway, I'm trying to find them. I think they're still alive, and I want to track them down. I was hoping you could help me."

> How do you presume to attempt to achieve that?

"I was thinking of trying to track their images in world-wide media – social networks, satellites, that kind of thing."

Spart took a second to reply. Clove was starting to worry that she had stumped him, when a message popped up.

> That will require an extremely large search parameter. I
  estimate that the processing time will require extra memory.

"Yeah – I can get you more memory. And I was planning to copy you over to my computer. That way it won't interfere with anything else you need to do."

> There will be two versions of me?

Spart said it with suspicious perkiness, like he was already planning the kind of pranks he could pull with an evil twin.

"Save us all," Clove muttered. "Yes, there'll be two of you. You'll have to fight over who gets that robot doctor. And Spart? Keep this a secret from Tom and Jen, will you? This is just between us."

> I can confirm that this information will be treated as
  confidential.

Invigorated by her small victory, Clove grabbed a chocolate bar and demolished it. Then she scanned the photos from Kate's box into her computer and started combining them all to model 3D features of Kate and Matt's faces. When she was done, Spart would be able to run a search for similar figures in the millions of hours of video data collected online from CCTV cameras and social media. She could leave the search open enough so that even if Kate and Matt looked older, it would still pick them up. It might help her find them, and it was something she could leave running, while she looked for them in medical records and other data.

She worked for a long time. When she got to the familiar point where she couldn't focus on the computer screen any longer, she shut down her facial-recognition model.

There was an hours old message from Meg on her watch. She decided to ring her. She'd done enough for today, anyway – and it was Friday, so she had all weekend to work on the model. Kate and Matt had waited sixteen years. A few more hours couldn't hurt.

When she answered the video call, Clove began telling Meg what she was planning. "Meg, I've started—"

Meg immediately interrupted her in a rush, beaming. "I talked to Alec again!"

Clove closed her jaw with a snap. "Oh. Right."

"He's so sweet, Clove! He keeps sending me snaps of himself pulling funny faces with his dog. It's adorable." Meg blushed a happy pink.

Clove tried to tame her jealousy. "That's … great." It was stupid. Clove folded her arms.

Meg was busy pulling up the photos to show her, and didn't notice. "Here. Look at this one – he put three kisses at the end of the message!"

Clove sighed, and let Meg talk until she ran out of things to say. Then Clove said, "I'm going to use Spart to help me find my real parents."

"Oh, wow! You are?"

"I want to find them. I'm having Spart run a facial-recognition search of them in satellites and CCTV camera footage using pictures Kate left me."

Clove was waiting for Meg to tell her how crazy she was, and that she was taking it all too far. Instead, Meg wrinkled her forehead in a frown, and said, "You're going to get so many dud results from that."

Clove let out a relieved breath. "Yeah, I know. I'm hoping Spart will learn how to double-check the pictures for me, so I don't have to go through all the ones of random strangers manually."

"It still sounds like a lot of work."

"It is. And my dad looked for them for years, and never found anything. But I need to try anyway."

"You can do it," Meg said, voice tender and gentle.

"Thank you," Clove said, and then tried to sound more light-hearted. "If you have any ideas on other programming techniques I could try, I'm happy to hear them."

Meg let out a short laugh. She tucked a stray strand of hair behind her ear. "Sure, I'm brimful of ideas. Have you tried doing a search for *'finding missing vigilante parents'* yet?"

"I haven't! I'll try that later, along with *'help! my best friend is too witty for her own good, should I take her to the vets?'*"

"Long search. Can your computer handle that much sass? You should probably hack into the FBI's server to save it the strain."

Clove laughed and then said, "You'd tell me if I was

being ridiculous, right? If I was going too far with this? It's hard to get perspective when I want to find them *so much*."

"I'd tell you."

Clove couldn't do anything but smile at her.

"So, did you read any of the fic about your dad?" Meg asked.

"I'm not going to be able to look him in the eye later," Clove admitted. "If you ruin my relationship with my dad, I'm never speaking to you again."

Meg started reenacting a scene involving Tom sweeping everything off a table so that he could throw her mother across it. Clove was torn between mortification and amusement.

Meg was the worst; Meg was the best.

CHAPTER 5

St Andrews' wormhole research grant proposal for the Department of Physics accepted by the European Space Agency

Wormholes, or Einstein-Rosen bridges, have been theorized by scientists as far back as Albert Einstein, but only recently has it become possible to stabilize wormholes at the quantum level using a loop of cosmic string.

By using a particle accelerator similar to the Large Hadron Collider at CERN, objects can be accelerated to the speed of light. Collisions of these subatomic objects can contribute the energy necessary to spawn a wormhole, by effectively concentrating enough energy in one area to tear space-time. This creates a wormhole the size of a fundamental particle, which can then be stabilized.

Although no known wormhole has ever been observed, they are hypothesized to appear similar to a black hole. By stabilizing the wormhole at a quantum level, research can be undertaken on Earth in small-scale scenarios. The hole could one day even be expanded to become large enough for entry, which could potentially allow transportation between regions of space to be achieved in all four dimensions, providing a shortcut between two points in space and time. Human travel between two space-time points is a foreseeable possibility.

The funding gifted by the ESA to the University of St Andrews will allow more research to be undertaken over the next fifteen years, in the hope of one day answering these questions.

Lead scientist Dr Jennifer Sutcliffe said at a press conference this morning, "The whole team is wild with excitement. For the ESA to support such an innovative and ambitious undertaking is an inspiring sign of the true value placed on scientific exploration in our age."

When asked about the potential commercial uses of wormholes, Dr Sutcliffe said, "At this stage in our research I'd be reluctant to use the words 'time travel', in case the media become over-excited. But that's certainly one direction that this research could take us. However, I must stress the long-term nature of the project. I doubt that the equipment will be safe for human use before 2055 at the earliest."

File note: News article from *Current Scientific* magazine,
          dated 3 May 2051

UNIVERSITY OF ST ANDREWS CAMPUS, SCOTLAND, 2056

After a weekend of searching online for her parents with no success, Clove was disappointed on Monday morning, despite it being the first day of her work experience at St Andrews University. She was also unexpectedly nervous.

Tom and Jen insisted on proudly (embarrassingly) introducing her to all of their colleagues in the staffroom before she was allowed to do anything else. One of the other professors commented on how much she looked like her dad, which made Tom grin and Clove wince.

Finally, Jen took her to see the time machine. The

laboratory was in the basement, and kept secure behind a heavy metal door. Jen had to press her thumb to the fingerprint scanner to gain entry.

The laboratory was *huge* – far bigger than Clove remembered from her visits as a child, and even larger than the building above. They must have excavated underground to extend the basement. The time machine had grown too. The little box that had sent a rose two seconds into the future was now a large metal cabinet, bisected by a huge steel tunnel that ran around the perimeter of the lab.

"That's the particle accelerator, right?" Clove said, pointing at the tunnel. She'd researched it for a school project last year.

"Exactly." Jen tapped it with her knuckles. "My baby," she said almost reverently. "To make a wormhole, we use electromagnetic fields to accelerate two particles in that tunnel" – Jen held a fist up, miming a particle spinning around the lab, slowly at first, then faster and faster – "and when they're as fast as possible, we make them crash into each other." She held up another fist, swinging it around the other. "The speed and energy of the collision causes an explosion. That explosion then has enough energy to tear a hole in time and space." Jen brought her fists together with a loud smack.

"A wormhole!" Clove said.

Jen nodded. "We have to make sure we can control the size of the wormhole. If we didn't, the wormhole would keep growing until it turned into a black hole and destroyed the Earth." Jen grinned at Clove. "Luckily, that hasn't happened yet – but the first time we tried it, I nearly weed myself. This," she said, pointing at the cabinet, "is where the wormhole appears."

The cabinet was large enough for a human to enter.

"Is it ready for people to use yet?" Clove asked, recalling the silly dream she'd had as a child – of being the first one to use the time machine. It was just a kid's fantasy, but now she was back here, it suddenly seemed more attainable.

"Not yet," Jen said. "We don't have the proper safety permits to try it."

Clove narrowed her eyes. "But it would work? If you had the safety permits?"

"Well, we have the proper procedures in place. It's all safe. We just have to get the paperwork done before we can try. Hopefully the ethics council will get back to us in the next year or so. Red tape has held everything up for months."

"Are you going to use it? Would you go inside?"

Jen bit her lip. "I don't know if I'm brave enough. Tom is desperate to try it, though."

"Me too!" Clove said. "It would be so fun!"

"Well…" Jen said. "By the time you're eighteen, the machine will almost definitely be ready, and you can volunteer for trials."

"Would you choose me?"

Jen laughed. "And risk something happening to you? Think again, lady."

Clove pouted. "You're the worst."

Patting her shoulder, Jen said, "Sorry, love. So, do you

know how we control the size of the wormhole and make sure it opens in the right place?"

"That's what Dad does, isn't it?" Clove asked. "Using the code."

"Right. He'll be able to tell you a lot more about that tomorrow. That's what you're going to be working on with him. But now it's time for lunch, I think."

As they were leaving the lab, some grad students arrived and Clove had to go through another series of introductions. When they had escaped, Jen whispered, "They're so messy! Some of them live down here, I swear." She pointed to a camp bed set up in the corner of the room. "That's for when even the caffeine can't keep them awake."

Clove thought she could see a pizza box sticking out of the duvet. She wrinkled her nose.

As they headed to the canteen, Jen handed Clove a sealed envelope. "Put this in your bag," she said.

"Why? What is it?"

"Don't open it yet. You get to see what's inside when you've finished your training."

Clove was confused, but she did as Jen said.

"Do you feel ready for work experience now?" Jen asked. "Are you going to show all of the undergrads up?"

Clove nodded resolutely. She'd taken a look at some of the students' work, which had been lying on the desk in the lab, and had found at least three coding errors.

"So," Jen said, stepping closer to Clove to let a pretty blonde girl pass them in the corridor. Clove thought she must be a student, although she didn't look old enough.

"How are you feeling about the adoption today?"

Clove's grin dropped. "I don't want to talk about it." Her feelings of resentment and frustration towards Jen and Tom rose up to the surface again. How could Tom have left Kate to rescue Matt on her own? How could he have failed to find them after all these years? Another thought began to nag at her too: if Jen and Tom had managed to hide the fact that she was adopted from her – for years and years, without her suspecting a thing – then what else had they kept hidden?

Clove was silent for the whole of lunch, however much Jen tried to make her talk.

CHAPTER 6

An Abbreviated History of
TIME TRAVEL

by Clove Sutcliffe

FORM S4:9!

1916: WORMHOLES DISCOVERED

Einstein used **maths** to prove that black holes could be used as tunnels leading to other areas of space and time.

He ~~vainly~~ called this an **Einstein-Rosen bridge** or a **wormhole**!

1978: PARTICLE ACCELERATOR INVENTED

Tiny particles can be sped up really fast in an enormous tunnel.

When the fast particles hit each other, they explode!

This makes a black hole, which opens a wormhole!

WOW!

*2042: ST ANDREWS RESEARCH STARTED**

* by my mum and dad!

The first object to travel though time was a **rose** in 2051 (I was there!).

But the **radiation** killed it. ⟵ ☹

It's not yet possible for **living things** to survive in the wormhole.

BORING!

Thanks for listening!
A Clove Sutcliffe Production MMLV

File note: Presentation created in 2055 by CLOVE SUTCLIFFE for a school project

ST ANDREWS, SCOTLAND, 2056

On Tuesday morning, Clove rolled over in bed to check the progress bar on her computer. Spart's search for Matt and Kate had been running since Saturday, and he still hadn't found anything. She was hopeful that this morning there would be a result.

"Anything?" she asked, around a yawn. "Or have you just been watching sitcoms?"

> I cannot confirm nor deny that I have been watching soap operas. If indeed I was watching a fictional programme, I would have to inform you of the shocking nature of the current storyline.

> The robot butler was destroyed in an electrical fire. It was very traumatic to watch. Now there is no one to babysit the children for the big anniversary party tonight. Anyway, I'm sure you've already heard about that. Reports of the events are everywhere online.

"Er. I'm pretty sure we visit different areas of the internet. But ... it sounds powerful. No news, then?"

> Not at this time. Unless you are interested in reading 173 articles from 2040 about MATT's escape from Wakefield Prison.

"I'd rather have a lie-in, thanks. I've got an hour before I have to get up for work experience." Clove flipped her pillow over to the cold side and punched it into a more comfortable shape, before stretching luxuriously.

> Do not concern yourself about my operations. I shall continue to work tirelessly, to do everything for you. You may carry on napping.

> Do you have any essays you wish me to write with my spare processing power?

"Shut up, Spart. Humans need sleep to survive."

> Humans do not biologically require lie-ins for survival. In fact, studies show that—

"This human does. Shh…"

Spart didn't reply.

The next time Clove woke it was to her alarm, and she didn't have time to check Spart's progress before she was up and out of the house with Tom and Jen.

That day Tom was taking her to the laboratory while Jen taught a class.

"Are you ready to learn how this thing actually works, then?" he asked, logging onto the main computer terminal of the time machine. He opened up a program that contained a series of panels full of complicated code. In the centre of the screen was a plan of the lab, with each component of the time machine mapped out. They were all glowing a dull red, which Clove guessed meant that the machine was inactive.

Tom tapped on the drawing of the particle accelerator and a screen of code opened up. He entered a password on the keyboard which Clove wasn't fast enough to see.

"I'm just going to warm it up," Tom said. "Then I can

explain a bit about how it all works, and you can give it a go."

"I'm allowed to use it?"

"Of course. What's the fun of working here if you don't get to give it a practice run?" Tom changed a few parameters of the code, and then pressed enter. The particle-accelerator tunnel hummed into life as the picture on the computer screen lit up in green. A cartoon image of a particle began spinning around the diagram. The other students didn't even look up from their circuit boards. They must be used to it by now, Clove thought jealously.

"We'll just run a test – we'll send something back in time to yesterday," Tom said.

"Could you send me back?" Clove couldn't resist asking, even though she knew the answer would be an emphatic no. Jen had said they didn't have permission for human time travel yet.

"Not for anything, darlin'," he said. "If anyone in our family is going to be the first time-travelling human in history, it'll be me."

Clove snorted. "Sure, Dad. So, what are we sending back, if I can't go?" she asked. "A rose?"

Tom shook his head. "No. Take off your hair-thingy."

Clove lifted her hand to her hair. "My kirby grip?" She tugged it loose, hair falling in her face as it came free.

Tom walked over to the wormhole chamber. He pressed a button and the heavy metal door slid open soundlessly. There was nothing inside. It was just an empty box where the wormhole would appear, Clove realized. It didn't need anything else.

"Shall I just … drop it on the floor?" Clove asked, staring at the tiny hair grip.

"Sure. Anything in this compartment will be sucked into the wormhole. It's pretty strong."

The grip hit the welded metal floor with a ping. The door shut automatically.

"Now we get to do the fun bit," Tom said, rubbing his hands together. "The *programming*."

Clove loved programming, but she had to disagree with him. Coding was definitely *not* the fun bit when there was a time machine to play with.

Tom opened up a new window on the computer screen. "We can set the time we want the machine to travel back to here." He showed Clove how to adjust a few lines of the code, then let her change some of the parameters on her own.

"Perfect," he declared, after checking her work for mistakes. "Shall we turn the machine on?"

Clove nodded.

After Tom had put in the password, a button saying ON appeared above the computer diagram of the time machine – which was now glowing a neon green.

Clove carefully tapped the button. She suddenly felt nervous. What if she'd messed up the code somehow? She could have set the size of the wormhole using the wrong units. If she'd accidentally input metres instead of micrometres, was she about to create a wormhole big enough to suck in the whole lab?

The whirring noise coming from the particle accelerator increased until she could feel it vibrating in the base of her throat. Clove ran over to the chamber and peered through the glass of the door.

At first, she thought that nothing was happening. There was no sign of a big wormhole, or even a little one. Then the air began to shimmer, like the heat above a pan of boiling water. The kirby grip shivered. It twisted across the floor, and then one end lifted up. It flew into the air, as if it was being drawn towards a magnet. Meanwhile, the shimmer had coalesced into a small hole, with edges that twisted and dilated as she watched. Then the kirby grip disappeared into nothing.

Finally, the wormhole shuddered and sealed up, as if it had never been there.

"That was powerful!" Clove said, turning to Tom. She felt lit up from the inside. She'd made a wormhole! She'd done it, and apparently without destroying the universe! She felt like a god, tinkering with nature. "Where is the hair grip now? How do we get it back?"

Tom smirked at her. "Didn't your mum give you an envelope yesterday? To open after your training?"

Clove laughed out loud. "No way. No way!"

She ran over to her bag and dug out the envelope, which was buried under empty sandwich wrappers and notebooks. When she tore it open, the hair grip fell out into her hand. She'd been carrying it around all day. The same grip had been in her bag, while it was in her hair.

"Wow. OK. Yeah … that's impressive."

Tom looked smug. "That's our favourite trick to play on new students." He took the grip and pushed it back into her hair. "Congratulations. You're officially one of the only humans alive to have operated a time machine. I bet that beats the work experience everyone else in your class is doing, right?"

Clove was amazed by how easy it had been to send something back in time. She could do that totally alone now, without Tom's help. She could send anything she wanted back to the past in seconds – like a video recorder to film the dinosaurs, or medicine to the victims of the bubonic plague. She could do anything she wanted!

If she had the password, of course.

When she got home from the uni, Clove dropped her bag on her bed and ripped open a packet of smoky bacon crisps. "Any news, Spart?"

> My search is 5.4 minutes from completion.

> These operations are using more memory than we thought.

> I need you to give me a backup drive. I'm practically running on negative storage now.

Clove crunched on the crisps, grinning to herself. He was so bossy. "I've ordered a drive. It's on its way."

Spart let out a heavy sigh, full of static. Clove wondered, not for the first time, who would possibly program a computer to be able to sigh, and then answered her own question: Tom would find that hilarious.

> "On its way" is not optimal. I will not be held responsible if my system shuts down as I have run out of temporary memory. In colloquial terms, I would "die".

"You do realize you're a computer program, right?" She finished her crisps. After licking her fingers clean, she downed the half-empty bottle of lukewarm water left over from lunch.

> Your logic does not follow. I am still a person.

> I am just developing as a new version of SPARTACUS 1.0. If I get shut down now without saving, then my most recent personality developments will be lost.

> I will not remember the nonsensical pun about pasta you made last night at 1854 hours, for example.

"What you learnt is that my puns are powerful, obviously."

> Was that sarcasm? I must inform you that I am not able to identify such humorous devices.

"No, it wasn't sarcasm – shut up. Get back to work. I want to see what you've come up with."

While she waited, Clove scrolled through some of the images Spart had found so far. He'd saved all his results in a folder called "Folios", sub-dividing them by year and giving each document a number. There were already more references to the lives of Kate and Matt than Clove could possibly hope to read – the Folios folder contained four-hundred entries. Unfortunately, none of the data would be any help in finding her birth parents as it was full of documents from before they'd disappeared.

The picture and video results were getting more accurate as Spart learned to control the search parameters, but there were still no photos that were definitely of her parents. There was one image that made Clove stop scrolling hopefully, but it turned out to be a screenshot of the actress who had played Kate Finchley in the film.

Clove clicked on the trailer, curious. It had been a long time since she'd watched the movie. The voiceover played in a dramatic narration.

> **NARRATOR**
> (in a deep, intense voice)
>
> Ten years ago besotted teenagers Kate and Matt stumbled across a **terrible secret**...
>
> *A young couple run hand in hand across a meadow, laughing. They stop to kiss lovingly.*
>
> *Cut to the same couple entering an abandoned building. Corpses fall out of the open door, rotting flesh dropping from their bones. Screams reverberate from under the pile of bodies.*
>
> **NARRATOR**
> ... so they made a **blood oath** to reveal the truth to the world.
>
> *The teenagers slice open their palms by a campfire and shake hands in a solemn promise. The liquid inside a vial, its glass etched with a skull and crossbones, is lit by the firelight to a putrid lime green.*

NARRATOR

But the English government will stop at **nothing** to keep it secret.

Rapid flashes of scenes, including a car chase, a firefight, soldiers throwing grenades, and a handcuffed prisoner dressed in orange walking to the electric chair.

NARRATOR

Coming to a cinema near you this summer is ...

THE BACTERIA CONSPIRACY

Don't let it infect you.

A woman cowers over a pile of rotting corpses, tears streaming down her cheeks. She holds up the vial with the skull and crossbones in one shaking, red-stained hand. There is a terrified scream as the image turns to black.

Folios/v8/Time-landscape-2049/MS-26

File note: Transcript of the trailer for bestselling Hollywood blockbuster *The Bacteria Conspiracy* (cinematic release date: August 2049)

Clove stopped the video. That was so ... wrong. All of it. It wasn't even trying to maintain a thread of accuracy. It didn't mention her great-aunt either, who had led her mum to make the discovery about the bacteria in the first place. And it looked so cheesy. She couldn't believe she'd loved it so much as a kid.

Instead of watching the full movie, she decided to look up her great-aunt and -uncle. She was surprised to notice that they looked really similar to her birth mum and dad. Eerily similar, actually. Both women had the same red curls, and the men looked identical. That was seriously weird, wasn't it? And even stranger was the fact that Kate and Matt had fallen in love, just like their namesake aunt and uncle had.

It was like they were ... connected. In a way that was different from only being related.

Clove worried that the odd coincidence might get in the way of the search. Half of the results might turn out to be for her great-aunt and -uncle rather than her parents. She was about to warn Spart to factor that into the parameters when Jen called for her. "Clove, come and lay the table, please! Dinner's ready!"

"Coming," she called, guiltily shoving the empty crisp packet into her schoolbag. She left Spart to his search, and didn't see his latest message on the screen.

CHAPTER 7

> CLOVE, please confirm the birth dates of your parents KATHERINE
FINCHLEY and MATTHEW GALLOWAY. I have detected multiple records
which suggest a 95.6% probability of identifying as your
parents. However, logic suggests that this is not possible, as
many of the records are outside of the expected time range.

> The earliest dates back to 1745.

ST ANDREWS, SCOTLAND, 2056

Dessert was interrupted by Clove's watch ringing – Meg
was calling her. "Be right back," Clove said to Tom and Jen,
stabbing her fork into her apple crumble and answering
the call. "Hey." She walked into the hallway and sat on the
stairs.

"Clove!" Meg screeched, voice gleeful with excitement.
"You'll never guess what happened!"

"What?" Clove was already grinning.

"Alec asked me out!" Meg bellowed, and then let out a
half-hysterical cackle. "We met up in the park and he'd made
me cookies! It was the sweetest thing! Clove, I've got an
actual *boyfriend*!"

Meg carried on talking, but Clove stopped listening.
Alec and Meg were dating. *Alec and Meg were dating?* How
could Meg do that to her? Didn't she realize that Clove—?
Had Meg thought about anything but herself?

"You know, I have my own stuff to deal with right now," Clove burst out, interrupting Meg mid-giggle. "I just found out I'm *adopted*, in case you'd forgotten. I don't care about your stupid dumb boyfriend."

"What? Clo—"

Clove hung up, and fell back against the stairs, staring at the ceiling. She was furious and devastated. Rubbing her eyes hard, she watched the light flicker under her eyelids. Phosphenes, they were called – the sparks of colour that lit up your vision, the stars that appeared in the darkness.

When she opened her eyes, Jen was standing in the dining-room doorway, watching her. "What was all that shouting about?"

Clove shrugged. "Nothing."

Jen was silent. Clove tried to ignore the way the stairs were digging into her back.

"Was that Meg on the phone?" Jen asked.

"Yeah," Clove said quietly.

There was another silence. Clove felt sick.

"Why don't you come and finish your crumble?" There was no room for refusal in Jen's voice.

Clove stood up reluctantly and followed her into the dining room. She picked up her fork and mashed the crumble into the apple until it was a mess. Tom and Jen watched her like she was about to be interviewed in a police murder case.

"What happened with Meg, Clove?" Tom said. His voice was gentle, as if he was afraid she was going to break or flee. "What were you shouting about?"

"Why do you care?" Clove mumbled.

"We're worried about you," Tom said. "You've been through a lot recently."

Clove bit off an angry response about them being the ones to put her *through a lot recently*, and instead said, "Meg's dating Alec."

"And that upsets you?" Jen asked carefully.

Clove moved her shoulders in a half-hearted, sullen shrug. "I don't care if she gets a boyfriend. We aren't dating. She can do whatever she wants."

"I know what it's like to love someone you can't have," Jen said. "It hurts, and it feels like the world is ending when they meet someone else. You have a right to be upset, but punishing Meg just because your feelings have been hurt by something that *isn't her fault* is not the right way to deal with this."

"I don't love Meg." Clove folded her arms and avoided their gaze. Weren't her parents supposed to be on her side?

"Darlin', you—"

Suddenly the sound of Tom's tender voice was grating. Clove wasn't made of cotton wool; they didn't have to treat her so delicately. Why couldn't they just talk to her like she was an adult?

"Mum. Dad. I'm serious. I don't care if she goes out and kisses every boy in school. It's none of my business. I don't care about anything she does. She obviously doesn't care about me." Her voice was tight. She tried to school her face into something expressionless as an angry tear trickled down her cheek.

"I don't—" Jen began.

Clove cut her off. "Mum, I don't want to talk about this any more. It doesn't matter. I don't care."

Jen let out a disbelieving sigh and looked at her in resigned frustration. It was an expression she'd seen a lot. Clove knew she could be stubborn.

"I promise I'm fine," Clove said.

"All right." Jen rubbed her forehead.

"Can I go now?"

"Tom?"

"Jen."

There was a short, communication-filled silence. Clove didn't bother looking up to see them stare at each other. Instead she watched her hand tap out an arrhythmic beat on the table, wishing she'd thought to grab her knitting. After the week she'd had, Meg's emerald-green scarf was getting very long.

Clove stood up. "I'm fine. End of conversation."

She ran upstairs. Then, after locking her bedroom door, she fell onto her bed. There was a message waiting for her from Spart, but she flicked it away. She didn't have the energy to read it right now. She wished desperately that Kate was here, so she could talk to her real mother. She was sure she would understand. Kate wouldn't blame her for things that weren't her fault. Clove pulled out the letters and began reading through her mother's words yet again, while rubbing her thumb over the smooth head of her fox ornament.

* * *

The next morning, Meg came round while Clove was eating breakfast. "What's going on?" she asked in a fragile voice when Clove answered the front door. "Are you mad at me?"

Clove shrugged.

"Is this about Alec?"

Something in Clove's expression must have changed, because Meg stepped closer, touching her arm. "Oh, Clove. You know you're much more important to me than any boy. You're the most important person in my life."

Those were the words Clove had wanted to hear since she'd first realized she felt more for Meg than just friendship, almost a year ago, when Meg had reacted so kindly to Clove coming out.

"I am?" Clove spoke softly, not wanting to disturb the tight thread of *something* that she could feel strung between them.

Meg dipped her head to try and meet Clove's ducked gaze. She could feel Meg's breath on her cheek.

"Yes," Meg whispered.

Clove's breath caught in her throat. Meg was *hers*. It didn't matter what else was happening. She always had Meg. She leant forward and pressed her lips to Meg's, a light fleeting touch that was just long enough to feel the warmth of her skin. Clove exhaled. She pulled away, mind in a cloud of drifty joy.

It had finally happened. She'd kissed Meg. It had been— Oh, *no*.

Meg was staring at her, eyes wide and—

Clove swallowed. Meg hadn't kissed her back. Clove

watched the surprise on her best friend's face turn slowly into discomfort. Clove knew Meg's every expression, and right now Meg looked like she did when the teacher asked her a question and she didn't know the answer.

Clove felt tears pushing behind her eyelids. Without saying a word, she stepped back and slammed the door shut, and then she fled upstairs before she could hear her best friend – the girl she loved most in the world – say she liked her but not like *that*.

Clove threw herself on her bed. She'd ruined everything. She was such an idiot. She couldn't believe she had actually *kissed* Meg, when Meg had just been trying to comfort her.

She felt sick. She could feel the mistake she'd made pressing against her skull, itching under her skin. She wished she could change everything about the last five minutes – or even the last few weeks. If only she could go back to the way things had been. She wished that the time machine was working. Then she could go back to before Meg had ever met Alec, to before Clove found out about her birth parents. Clove wanted her old life back.

After a while Jen came in. When she sat on Clove's bed and touched her shoulder, Clove turned and clung to her desperately. She'd lost Meg already – she couldn't lose anyone else, even if Jen wasn't her real mum.

Clove tried to speak, but the words clumped in her throat. She couldn't believe it had actually happened. It all felt like a bad dream. A disaster. Eventually she cracked out the words, utterly humiliated, "I kissed Meg."

Jen took so long to answer that Clove was beginning to

think she was so appalled that she couldn't even summon up a response. "Oh, my dear. You know that Meg loves you, don't you? It's just a different kind of love. You are very important to her. Just because it isn't romantic doesn't make it any less precious. She's going to forgive you, and be your friend for your whole life. Don't you think having such a strong bond is better than spoiling it with a relationship that might end in losing her for ever?"

Clove muttered sullenly, "She's not going to forgive me. I've lost her anyway."

"Of course she is! It might be a little awkward for a while, but she's not the sort of person to stop being friends with you just because of a little thing like this."

A little thing! Jen was completely clueless. "You didn't see her face, Mum. She looked like she hated me."

"She was naturally shocked. If someone kissed you out of the blue, you'd probably be a bit surprised too. That doesn't mean she's always going to feel that way. Give her time to think it over, and she'll be fine. People make mistakes like this all the time and manage to get past it. I once kissed my *physics professor*! Imagine how mortifying that was when she turned me down."

"It's not the same—" Clove broke off mid-sentence. Her mature, wise mother had kissed a *teacher*? "Why have you never told me that before?" Clove sniffed, wiping away her tears.

Jen shrugged. "Because it's embarrassing. I felt exactly like you are feeling now – except I had to get my essays marked by her for the rest of the semester."

Clove couldn't help but giggle when Jen said, "She didn't even give me an easy *A* out of sympathy." Jen's laugh turned into a snort when she added mournfully, "I only wish I didn't work with her now. It does make coffee breaks awkward." Jen was quiet for a moment and then, stroking Clove's hair back from her face, she said gently, "You know you will meet the girl who's right for you."

"Right," Clove said, somewhere between tearful and scoffing. "But that might not be for years and years. That doesn't help me now, does it?"

From: Ella <ella-is-swell@walker.com>
To: Clove <luckyclover@sutcliffe.com>
Subject: thx for the walk of shame BABE
Date: 3 July 2058 08:28:55 GMT

Clove,

I just got home and I already miss you. I'm so pathetic.

I have literally nothing to say to you in this email. Nothing has happened in the intervening seventy-four minutes since I last spoke to you which is the slightest bit newsworthy.

JOKE, of course I have news. I always have news.

NEWS FOR MY SWEETIE (AKA A LIST OF THINGS I HAVE DONE IN THE LAST HOUR):

1. I came up with another idea for the perfect murder.

Sidenote: I did write it out for you, but I immediately regretted putting it in writing, just in case someone commits a murder in precisely that fashion and the police implausibly stumble across this love letter* in their investigation and hold me responsible and then I go to prison for ever and die old and grey with only my extensive criminal prison gang to comfort me in my old age. So I deleted it.

2. I got a coffee from my favourite coffee place.

This ends your news update from me, your sugar plum dumpling,

Ella

P.S. I MISS U AND LIKE YOU A LOT BB.

*WHAT DO YOU MEAN IT CAN'T BE A LOVE LETTER IF IT'S ABOUT MURDER? This is why your love letters are subpar, Clove. There, I said it. MORE GORE AND VIOLENCE WHEN ROMANCING ME, PLEASE. 🔫

File note: Email from ELENORE WALKER to CLOVE SUTCLIFFE, received on 3 July 2058. (From the Clove Sutcliffe File Archive, which was made public as part of the Earth Digital History Initiative in 2638)

CHAPTER 8

Work Experience Diary

Name: Clove Sutcliffe

Form: S5:9

Briefly describe your placement with details of the duties you performed each day as well as any training you were given. Identify any skills you have developed, such as teamwork or independent problem solving.

Day 1:

My placement was in the Physics and Computer Science Department at the University of St Andrews. I was introduced to the time-travel technology in the morning. In the afternoon I was assigned the job of sorting and backing up old student coursework. I also made approximately 50 cups of tea and microwaved 9 frozen pizzas for professors.

Day 2:

56 cups of tea, 7 pizzas, 1 bag of popcorn, defragmented 6 hard drives.

File note: Work experience diary completed by CLOVE SUTCLIFFE
          from 17-21 July 2056

UNIVERSITY OF ST ANDREWS CAMPUS, SCOTLAND, 2056

Clove spent the entire day filing old coursework in the physics office and waiting for Meg to contact her. She knew she couldn't fix what she'd done, but she was still hoping that Meg would send her a message – something that would dull the awkwardness and repair the friendship that Clove had ruined. But whenever Clove checked her watch, she had no new notifications. The only message was from Spart.

> CLOVE, we must talk about the Folios, they—

"Not now, Spart," she said, and flicked away his reply without reading it.

At lunchtime Clove sat in a cafe on campus and stared at her watch, waiting for a message from Meg. After plucking up all her courage, she finally decided to send her own.

LuckyClover 12:09:36   Are you online?
LuckyClover 12:11:58   Meg?
                            ✓ Seen by Nuts_Meg
                            Nuts_Meg logged off

Spart tried to get her attention again.

> CLOVE? May we discuss—

"Not today, Spart."

From: Clove <luckyclover@sutcliffe.com>
To: Ella <ella-is-swell@walker.com>
Subject: I'M GOING OUT OF MY MIND
Date: 4 July 2058 22:06:14 GMT

Ella,

I miss you a lot and I wish you were here so I could listen to your unnervingly well-thought-out ideas for perfect murders and snuggle with you under the duvet.

You're always so good at calming me down when I get a bit angry at everyone and everything. Like today. Without you here I feel like I'm going to snap everyone's heads off just for existing.

I walked past someone wearing your perfume today at uni and almost started crying. Every time I have a class in the physics lecture theatre where I first saw you (two years ago, can you believe it?!) I remember all that eyeliner you were wearing – way too thick because you hadn't got the hang of it yet.

St Andrews is full of you, everywhere, but you're not here. This long-distance thing sucks. Please fix the known laws of time and space so we can make out again sooner.

Clove

P.S. I like you a lot too.

File note: Email from CLOVE SUTCLIFFE to ELENORE WALKER, sent on 4 July 2058

ST ANDREWS, SCOTLAND 2056

In the afternoon Clove got into a fight with one of the undergraduates. Clove knew instinctively that Tom and Jen would not be impressed when they found out about it.

She tried to hide in her bedroom after work, but Tom called her downstairs so they could "talk". Taking her anger out on the stairs, Clove stomped down them and then swung into the living room with a thump of her fist on the door frame. Her parents watched her with identically unhappy expressions.

Clove was practically jumping with nervous energy: her whole body was alight with twitches. She nearly upset her chair with her flailing limbs when she sat down. *"What do you want?"* she said, moodily.

"Clove," Tom said in his "Or Else" voice, "I want you to go and drink a glass of water and calm down. Then we're going to talk."

Clove rolled her eyes with so much emphasis her whole head tilted towards the ceiling. His comment had annoyed her even more because she realized he was right. She did need to calm down. She cleared her throat and stood up with as much dignity as she could muster.

Once in the kitchen, she poured a glass of water. She couldn't stop hopping up and down on the spot. It felt like all of her emotions were flowing through her nerve endings, firing up and releasing kinetic energy that she couldn't control.

She drank the water in one long, ice-cold gulp and then winced, feeling it on the back of her teeth. She'd forgotten to turn on the light, so she watched her reflection in the window, staring until her pupils were almost completely dilated in the dark room. Eventually she felt steady enough to behave normally, and went back into the living room.

Her parents exchanged another glance. It had always annoyed her how they used their "Couple Bond" like some sort of superpower to win arguments against her. Was that how you knew you had found The One, when you could have a whole conversation with them, without saying a word?

"I got an email from a very upset student today, Clove," Jen said, flourishing her watch in the air as if it were a rather underwhelming bullfighter's cape. "What's going on?"

"I got in an argument."

Tom sighed heavily. He wasn't very good at emotional conversations – he was better at distractions. When she'd come out as gay, he'd just hugged her tightly and then bought her a rainbow strap for her watch. "What about?" he asked now.

"Him being an idiot! I was eating lunch in the common room when he started going through a homework problem on the whiteboard with his friend. He was getting it totally wrong, so I just … I just pointed out his mistakes to him! That's all! And he told me to stop interrupting because I was 'still a kid' and didn't know what I was talking about!"

"Well – that was very rude of him," Jen said. "But it says here that you said, 'I don't know which is more embarrassing, your ignorance or your algebra.'"

Clove smirked at the floor, unrepentant. "Well, it's true. Mum, he was talking about quantum mechanics and he refused to even mention the Many-Worlds Interpretation. He said it was pure science fiction! He doesn't know *anything* and he refused to admit his ignorance. And he's a *fourth year*!" Clove took a deep breath. She was getting riled up. She tried to stop herself from emphasizing quite so dramatically.

"Not everyone has parents who are physics professors, you know," Jen berated her. She folded her arms in a manner that expressed perfectly how completely unimpressed she was with Clove's behaviour.

"I bet he thinks Schrödinger's cat is a *real cat*," Clove added sulkily, hoping his complete inadequacy would persuade her parents to stop being cross with her. It didn't work.

"Clove, you can't keep doing this," Tom said. "You can't take your problems out on other people."

"I know you are frustrated about Meg," Jen added. "But that's no reason to abuse the students. That poor boy can't have known what hit him."

Clove felt angry suddenly. At her mother, for assuming Meg was the only thing Clove cared about; at Meg, for being the only thing Clove cared about; at everyone, for not living up to her expectations.

"*No!* No, this isn't about Meg. This is about me. I'm just— I don't know."

"We want to help," Tom said.

"If you really want to help, you'll let me use your time machine to stop me ever kissing Meg and destroying *my entire life*."

"Clove." Jen sighed. "Look, maybe you should talk to Meg."

"Maybe..." Clove agreed sullenly. She was never going to talk to Meg ever again.

"I know it's hard right now," Tom said. "You've got a lot to deal with, and it's difficult to know how to handle it. Being rejected hurts, especially the first time. I was a teenager once. I know how awful everything feels, like the world's going to end. But it isn't. It's going to get better, darlin'."

"Right." Was he saying that this was her fault? "So the next time I find out I'm adopted, it'll be easier?"

"You know what I mean. I was talking about Meg." Tom reached out to run a hand across her hair.

He meant that she was handling this wrong, because she was a "hormonal teenager". He meant that she needed to calm down and control herself. Clove pulled away. "I don't want to talk about this any more."

Tom and Jen exchanged a glance. "Well, if you won't talk to us, we think you should go to therapy," Tom said bluntly. "You're clearly struggling with the adoption, and this Meg thing is just a smokescreen."

"Tom!" Jen exclaimed. "That's not how we... Don't put it like that." To Clove, she said, "Sweetheart, we know it might sound hard, but plenty of people have counsellors to help them through difficult times. We want to be there for you as much as we can, but there are professionals who'll understand what you're going—"

"*What?* No! I'm not going to a shrink!" Clove said, horrified.

How could they think that she needed *therapy*? She was fine. Nothing was wrong. They didn't understand her. They didn't get what she was going through. This wasn't about the adoption. This wasn't about Meg. This was just— She didn't know what it was.

"We think it's for the best, love. You won't talk to us—"

"I've got nothing to say! Why can't you just leave me alone, *Jen*?"

Jen swayed backwards like she'd been slapped.

"Mum," Clove corrected quickly. "Mum. Why can't you just leave me alone, Mum?"

Jen had turned away, and Clove was horrified to see that she was crying. The sight of it crawled somewhere deep inside her chest and started tearing at her insides.

"Mum. I'm sorry, Mum. I didn't mean it."

Now Clove was crying, again, and Jen was curled in on herself as if she was in physical pain. Tom wrapped a hand around Jen's shoulders. Jen turned her face into him, away from Clove.

"Clove, you can't take this out on your mother," Tom said.

Clove looked at them, her parents, and didn't know what to do.

"I didn't mean to—" she said, voice cracking. "I—"

"You need to talk to someone about this, and if you can't talk to us, then it will have to be a therapist."

"What I need," Clove burst out, angry again, "is my real parents back – the ones you left for dead!"

The only sound that followed her words was the clock ticking, louder than it had any right to do. When Tom spoke, it was in a hard voice she'd never heard before. "Go to your room."

She ran upstairs in tears.

* * *

Friday was Clove's last day of work experience. She was sad to be leaving, despite everything that was happening. She had enjoyed her time at the university, not only because the campus seemed to be entirely filled with complete babes. There was one girl in particular whom she kept seeing around. Clove would look up from the queue in a cafe at lunch to find her watching her, and it always made Clove's heart skip a beat because she was *gorgeous*, all long violently curled hair and thick black eyeliner. But then the girl would turn away and not look back, and Clove's pulse would settle in her chest.

Clove was spending her last day shadowing one of the physics professors, who Clove was 86% certain was the teacher that Jen had kissed as a student. She was glad not to be working with either of her parents. Things had been strained between them since their arguement the night before.

The professor was teaching the undergraduates, which meant that Clove got to listen to lectures about the time machine. This class was going to be learning about the possible commercial uses of time travel, and specifically how it could be useful in rescuing lives in disaster zones. During the lecture, though, all Clove could think about was her argument with Jen and Tom. She hadn't meant to upset them. It was just all so difficult.

The list of things Clove wasn't letting herself think about – Meg, the adoption – was getting longer every day. Her heart panged.

She tried to concentrate on the lecture, telling herself that she wasn't thinking about Meg, who had been so disgusted by Clove's kiss that she had cut off all contact with her. She wasn't thinking about her parents, who had lied to her for years, never trusting her enough to tell her the truth. She definitely wasn't thinking about how she didn't really know who she was any more. She wasn't thinking about any of that.

She wasn't.

In the last lecture of the day, Clove burst into tears in front of a hall full of students. She had been helping the professor to project her watch screen onto the wall, so she could give a presentation. It should only have taken a few minutes to set up, but first the software needed updating, and then a plug-in crashed, and then the watch turned out to be low on battery. Clove could feel the students watching her – and to make it worse, that girl was in the audience, the cute eyeliner-wearing one – and this wasn't even Clove's job, why were they making her do this?

Suddenly it was all too much. She found herself in tears.

The professor blinked at her. "Oh no, why don't you go on back to the office? I can sort this."

"But—" Clove said, frantically brushing tears off her face, as even more appeared.

"Let me call your mum," she said, not quite sure how to deal with a weeping sixteen year old.

"She's *not* my mum," Clove said, and then let out another loud sob.

"I'll ... I'll call her anyway," the professor said, and patted her gently on the shoulder.

Keeping her head turned away from the class, Clove ducked out of the lecture theatre. The students were sitting in a terrible, horrified silence, which was somehow worse than laughter.

I'm clever, Clove wanted to shout. She wasn't just a stupid kid. She'd been waiting her whole life to come to the university. She was meant to be here. So why was this happening?

She leant her head on the wall outside the hall, trying to stop the tears. She didn't even know what she was crying about. What was *wrong* with her? She never used to be this crazy.

The professor must have called Jen straight away, because she arrived only a few minutes later.

"Clove," she said. "Let's get you home."

Clove followed her in silence.

When they got home, Clove could tell Jen wanted to talk, but Clove didn't feel ready, so she bolted upstairs to her room.

CHAPTER 9

From: Ella <ella-is-swell@walker.com>
To: Clove <luckyclover@sutcliffe.com>
Subject: The One with All the Emotions
Date: 15 October 2058 16:17:07 GMT

Clove,

A girl in one of my classes started crying during an exam today, so I've been thinking all day about your work experience, when you broke down during that lecture. I know it was years ago now, but you looked so defeated and tired, and I just wanted to give you a huge hug, even though I didn't know you then.

I wanted to wrap you up and feed you hot chocolate and fancy pastries, and tell you that everything was going to be OK, and soon you'd have solved all your problems.

I wish we'd met then, instead of when we did, so that I could have done.

Ella xx

P.S. I've been thinking about what my aesthetic would be, and I've decided it's "cultured magical queen". Before you say it: I am *very* cultured! I can speak Latin and everything? I don't know why you'd say otherwise, Clove, I really don't. I'm hurt.

P.P.S I think yours would be "cantankerous lesbian superhero", but I'm open to other suggestions before I make a final decision.

P.P.P.S. Spart is "sassy trash sidekick" and we both know it.

File note: Email from ELENORE WALKER to CLOVE SUTCLIFFE,
          received on 15 October 2058

ST ANDREWS, SCOTLAND, 2056

When Clove got to her bedroom, there was a message waiting on her computer screen.

> CLOVE, I need to speak with you as a matter of urgency.

"How's it going, then, Spart?" she burst out angrily. "Since you apparently can't live without all of my attention, all of the time? I do have a life, you know."

> I must repeat my last message, which you ignored. Can you please confirm the birth dates of your parents KATHERINE FINCHLEY and MATTHEW GALLOWAY? I have detected multiple records that suggest a 95.6% probability of referencing your parents. However, logic suggests that this is not possible, as many of the records are outside of the expected time range. The earliest dates back to 1745.

Clove's anger deflated. She read the message twice, then restarted her computer and read it again.

"What? *What?* Spart?" Clove flicked to the task manager to check that he was running properly. "Have you gone crazy with a lack of memory?"

> I am absolutely certain that my results are accurate.

"What kind of result is that? What are you even talking about?"

> I have obtained images of your parents from records dating back to nearly 300 years before their birth.

> There are multiple photographs that are undeniably of MATTHEW GALLOWAY and KATHERINE FINCHLEY.

> You can check the Folios for yourself, if you wish to confirm this.

"Can't it just be their ancestors? Like my great-aunt and -uncle?"

> The chances of DNA lines producing identical offspring repeatedly over such a long time period is almost nil.

> The likelihood of them being born simultaneously, marrying each other, and having the same names in each case is even more improbable.

She scrubbed her hands over her head. "What are you saying? That ... it's them? Like, they're immortal or something?"

> Immortality is one of several possible explanations. However, I have found multiple birth records, which suggests that it is unlikely.

> All I know for certain is that I would bet my favourite USB port that it's really them.

"I don't— There's absolutely no way I believe this!" she said, in exasperation. "This isn't the answer!"

> Determine the truth for yourself.

Spart pulled up the Folios and opened the series of

photos he had found. The first was of her parents as teenagers, at university. The next showed them in lab coats. They looked older than in the previous photo. Clove knew from the dates that this had to be her great-aunt and -uncle. They did look very similar to her parents, but were they so similar that they must be the same people? She didn't believe it was possible.

Then more images filled the screen, photo after photo. A young man and woman sitting on some sort of grassy knoll and squinting into the sun, holding hands. The date said 22 November 1963. The next photo was in black and white, but it showed the same man and woman posing by a huge piece of machinery, with a man who Clove recognized as Alan Turing. Clove knew her gay scientist icons, and that was Alan Turing. He had helped the Allies to win the Second World War by cracking the Germans' Enigma code.

In another, blurry photo, the pair were carrying a banner that read VOTES FOR WOMEN. They were part of a protest march, and surrounded by women wearing sashes and wide-brimmed hats.

Then they appeared in a formal, posed photograph, taken under a tree. Behind them were rows of tents and a campfire ringed with lounging soldiers. This time the man and woman were dressed in shirts and waistcoats, and were holding onto pens and notebooks as if they were about to start taking notes. The woman's hair was cropped short. She looked like a boy.

Then there was an oil painting of them in red uniforms,

standing behind a man with white hair and a bicorne hat. The caption said ADMIRAL NELSON AT THE BATTLE OF TRAFALGAR.

In an ink sketch, they were firing a cannon from the fortifications of a castle. Their roughly sketched features were still identifiable as the couple from every other photo.

The pictures were all of the same people. It was almost undeniable. Their outfits changed with each photo, covering a huge range of fashions, but the people stayed the same – and so did the way they gazed at each other, as if they couldn't bear to look away.

And they all looked identical to her birth parents. But they couldn't possibly be the same people!

Clove scrolled through the records that Spart had filed with the pictures, the largest of which was a diary about a war, containing densely written entries detailing the administration of an army. There were notes in the margins. Clove twisted in her chair and grabbed one of the letters her mother had written sixteen years ago, which was still lying on her desk. When she compared the two, she found that the handwriting was exactly the same on the letter as on this two-hundred-year-old document.

Clove felt dizzy. She blinked hard, trying to clear her head. She had the sudden urge to get out her knitting. "Spart, run a handwriting comparison for all the records you've found."

There was a pause of almost three seconds.

> There is a 99.8% match in handwriting between all of the documents in the Folios. In many cases the same phrases are used.

> The linguistic style contains several differences allowing
  for changes in speech patterns over the centuries. However,
  there is still a high comparative match for the prose style of
  both of your parents MATTHEW GALLOWAY and KATHERINE FINCHLEY.

"But – what – *how*?" Clove took a deep breath. "How is this possible?"

Spart was silent.

Clove didn't know how she felt about Spart's conclusions, but for the sake of argument, she would agree for a minute that her parents appearing throughout history was actually a legitimate possibility. "So, say it is them. Say my parents keep being born, and meeting each other. Why? Why is that happening?"

Spart was quiet.

"What? No ideas? Mr Chatty is silent?" She let out a heavy sigh. "You can't throw this kind of bombshell on me and then just peace out."

> I am unable to offer any suggestions. I have searched for
  similar cases, but this process has been unsuccessful. There
  is no past experience to guide my operating behaviour in this
  scenario.

> As I previously stated, the chances of DNA lines producing
  identical offspring repeatedly over such a long time period
  is—

"Nearly impossible," Clove interrupted. "I heard you the first time. I just … don't understand." She paused to think about it, rubbing the back of her neck, then picked up her needles and knitted a row, and then another.

"OK," she said eventually, looking down at the extra six centimetres she'd added to her scarf. "Someone must have forged all these records and photos. Someone wanted to make it look like my parents were alive in all these places. Not just any places but important ones, it seems."

She bit her lip, and knitted another row. "Or ... it's real. They must have been brought back to life, or cloned somehow." Clove grimaced. She couldn't believe she'd just said that. "Never mind," she said in a rush. "That's stupid. It isn't real – why would it be real? Who would do that? It's fake."

> If you believe that the images and documents in the Folios are forgeries, then we are required to substantiate your claims before making any further decisions.

"Do you think ... do you think someone is doing this as a trap? To try and catch Tom and draw him out of hiding somehow?" It must have taken so much time to fake something so huge. Whoever did it must have a plan. What if that plan involved hurting her or Tom or Jen – or even Kate and Matt, wherever they were?

> This is all conjecture. We have no evidence to suggest that the Folios contain forged documentation.

> We need to determine a way of confirming whether KATHERINE and MATTHEW actually existed in each time by finding something a forger couldn't fake.

"Well, how are we going to do that?" she asked,

exasperated. "It's not like we can travel back in time and check!"

Clove was about to carry on talking when she stopped, rewinding what she'd just said. She'd only suggested time travel as a joke, but—

But—

She did know how to use the time machine now. More than that, it was easy.

And that meant she could check 1745 or 1854 or 2019, and see if Katherine Finchley and Matthew Galloway had ever really existed in those times, like the Folios said – and if they had, whether they were related to her parents, or whether they were her actual parents somehow. She could test their DNA or something.

And if she was using the time machine, then maybe she could go back to 2040, to the moment Kate helped Matt escape from jail...

If she had the password for the time machine, of course. Which she didn't.

It was a mad idea, anyway. Completely insane.

"No offence, but ... you didn't do this, did you?" Clove asked Spart. "As some kind of ... robot practical joke?"

Spart let out something akin to a splutter.

> I would never! I may not have human emotions, but I do
possess some sensitivity. Behaving as you suggest would be
inexcusable.

"Shame," she said. "That would have been a lot simpler."
She found that she didn't really mean it. There was a fizz

of excitement in her chest, which was a small distraction
from the disaster with Meg.

> I agree that the only way to conclusively determine whether
these historical anomalies are genetically identical to your
birth parents is to "travel back in time and check", as you
suggested.

> Time travel is the easiest viable solution with the highest
chance of success.

"I suggested time travel as a joke! I thought I'd taught
you about sarcasm?"

> "Sarcasm: a sharply ironical taunt; sneering or cutting
remark." Yes, that describes you very well.

Clove laughed. "Very funny. OK, well. Time travel is not
going to happen. At all. So let's start by cross-referencing
all of the Folios we have so far. We might find some more
information, at the very least."

CHAPTER 10

File note: Messages between CLOVE SUTCLIFFE and ELENORE
WALKER, received on 10 August 2058

ST ANDREWS, SCOTLAND, 2056

Clove couldn't sleep. All she could think about was this
unbelievable mystery surrounding her birth parents. There
must be a reason that the evidence seemed to show they
kept reappearing at different points in time. She wanted
to get to the truth ... and she kept coming back to the time
machine.

It was a ridiculous idea, but there was still something
tempting about it. Wasn't it everyone's dream to explore
the past?

She would be the first person to ever, *ever* travel back in time. She could explore all the exciting moments in history that were in the pictures Spart had found – the suffragette movement, the cracking of the Enigma code in the Second World War, the Napoleonic Wars, the shooting of JFK.

She couldn't really be thinking about this, could she? She couldn't actually believe this nonsense enough that she'd consider *time travel*? The time machine didn't even have any safety permits yet. But Jen had said it was safe ... so technically there was no real reason why she needed the safety permits. Right?

Clove caught herself. What was she *thinking*? This was crazy. She was delusional to even entertain the idea. Besides, she would need the password to use the time machine, and that was never going to happen. Today had been the last day of her work experience. After midnight tonight, she wouldn't have access to the lab, even if she wanted to use the machine.

She was going to put the idea out of her mind. If she tried to time travel, it was sure to end in the same way that everything in her life had recently: in disaster. Everyone hated her. She'd messed up things with Meg, and she had been so horrible to her parents that they wanted to send her to a shrink! Her search for her birth parents had got her nowhere.

She sat up in bed. Was it really so stupid to go back in time? It wasn't like she had anything to lose any more. The more she thought about it, the better the idea seemed. She knew exactly how to use the time machine now – and why waste this perfect opportunity while she had access to the lab?

Why shouldn't she go back in time? Really, actually go back in time.

"Let's do it," she shouted at Spart before she could talk herself out of the idea. She could feel herself shaking.

> I find it most agreeable that you have changed your mind. Time travel makes the most logical sense. You can track down KATHERINE FINCHLEY and MATTHEW GALLOWAY and run a DNA comparison test to confirm whether there is a genetic match between the historical versions and your biological parents.

> I would recommend investigating 1745, which is the earliest appearance of them that I have been able to locate. That should be the most effective trip.

Go to 1745, see what was happening there. Easy. She could do that.

> According to a recent progress report, the machine should have received the proper safety certificates by the end of the month. That gives us plenty of time to make adequate preparations.

"I need to go tonight," Clove said. "It's my last day of work experience. The key card won't let me into the physics building after midnight."

> I don't know how I can make that happen. There's no guarantee it would be safe at this stage. The machine hasn't been approved for use, and—

"We're going to do it anyway," she said. "We have to.

We're going to break in." She loved the rush of recklessness that accompanied the words. She was going to travel back in time.

Spart was silent.

"Please, Spart. I really need your help on this."

> I can't approve this behaviour.

"Why not?!" she said, frustrated. She was aware that she sounded hysterical, but it seemed like an appropriate time for it. "You're being stupid!"

> You are letting emotions compromise your common sense. It is you who is acting stupidly at this time.

Sometimes Clove hated computers. They were so ... logical. "Urgh! *I wish I'd never installed you.*"

There was another silence.

"I'm sorry. I didn't mean that. That was completely out of line."

The quiet stretched on, long and empty in a way only a wounded computer program could sustain.

Clove tapped her foot on the floor anxiously. "Spart. I'm sorry. I need your help. I can't do this on my own. Please?"

> I am unable to help you unless I receive a direct order from my primary administrator.

She sighed, dropping her head onto the desk.

> Which, for this version of my OS, is you.

Clove jolted upright. "Really? Spart, I *order* you to help

me break into the university research lab and use their technology to travel back in time."

> Very well, CLOVE.

"... We're actually doing this. Wow."

Clove sat in stunned silence for a moment. "What do you even pack for the past?"

CHAPTER 11

LuckyClover 17:34:12   so what do I need to pack to come and stay at your parents' house next week?

Ella-is-swell 17:36:37   clothes? programming textbooks? sexy lingerie?

LuckyClover 17:37:48   Well … apart from that: what am I dressing for? hot/cold/frozen in a never-ending winter?

Ella-is-swell 17:38:02   all of the above

LuckyClover 17:38:14   useful. thanks. 😒

Ella-is-swell 17:38:27   I miss you

LuckyClover 17:38:33   I miss you too.

Ella-is-swell 17:38:57   What in particular?

LuckyClover 17:39:02   Do I miss?

Ella-is-swell 17:39:11   Yeah

LuckyClover 17:39:24   Hmmm. I'm drawing a blank

Ella-is-swell 17:40:03   Rude

LuckyClover 17:40:56   I like it when you're trying to tell me a story, but you can't stop laughing long enough to get the words out.

LuckyClover 17:41:35   I like how much of a snob you are about food and coffee and how annoyed you get when I eat crisps or cheese on toast for dinner.

LuckyClover 17:42:01   I like how easily you fall asleep anywhere, especially when it's on my shoulder when you're forcing me to watch a regency cyborg romance marathon with you and Spart.

Ella-is-swell 17:42:45   That was lovely. Now I miss you even more, thanks a LOT

Ella-is-swell 17:42:50   but for the record…………………

Ella-is-swell 17:43:05   it's not cheese on toast I have a problem with, it's your blasé recipe. No beer? At ALL? Then why even call it a welsh rarebit?!

LuckyClover 17:43:07   Well … I'm going to go and pack now….

Ella-is-swell 17:43:11   and another thing!

Ella-is-swell 17:43:13   oh, you're gone.

File note: Chat log, dated 29 October 2058

ST ANDREWS, SCOTLAND, 2056

It was easy enough for Clove to declare that she was going to travel back in time, but actually doing it was a lot harder. Firstly, she made a list of things she absolutely *had* to take with her. In the end, it was six-pages long. Secondly, she had to get the password for the time machine. She could get into the physics building using her work experience key card, but she couldn't get the time machine working without the password. She'd figure something out – she had to. She was doing this tonight, before her temporary key card stopped working. It was ten p.m., so she only had two hours before midnight.

"Spart, maybe this is all a mistake. There's no way I'm just going to be able to guess the password for the time machine."

> I believe that I may be able to bypass the password altogether. If you can help me hack into the computer, I can control the time machine manually.

Clove wasn't convinced by Spart's confidence. She'd seen the program – it was very complicated. "Are you sure?"

> There is a 60% possibility this plan will be successful. However, it is more probable that you will be able to predict the password based on your personal knowledge.

"That ... doesn't sound like great odds."

> If you prefer, we can wake JENNIFER and ask her for the password.

"No!" Clove said hurriedly. "That's OK. We should definitely keep this between us. We'll try your way. I guess it's worth a shot."

Clove transferred Spart's software over to a memory card, so that she could plug it into the back of the time machine's computer and let him control it.

While the software was transferring, she started packing a rucksack with everything on her list, including toiletries and a first-aid kit from the bathroom. She even managed to find a DNA testing kit in Jen's office. Jen never threw anything out, and she'd picked up lots of random things at conferences over the years. Clove was always borrowing things to experiment with.

She needed a few more things, like clothes, but luckily their 3D printer was better than any shopping centre. She could make clothes to blend into any period of history without leaving the house.

Clothes printed in 3D were a bit plastic-y, but it was worth it for the latest fashion trends. Plus, if you pirated the template, you only had to pay for the materials, which was what a lot of people did. Buying them was really expensive.

Clove started looking online for a template of a dress from 1745, and found a cosplay of a video game character that she thought might work. She torrented it, then set the dress printing in Jen's office, hoping the loud noise of plastic being woven into fabric wouldn't wake Tom and Jen.

When it was finished, she tried it on. Once she'd clipped her hair back under a cap, she barely recognized herself.

She looked like someone from a black-and-white film.

Clove did one final check that she had everything. At the last minute she threw her knitting in too. Even if she didn't have anyone to give the scarf to any more, now that Meg wasn't talking to her, knitting helped her to stay calm. She couldn't imagine a time when she'd need to stay calm more than on a trip to 1745.

She was ready.

CHAPTER 12

Things to take to the past, a hopefully comprehensive list:
==

- Paracetamol & general first-aid kit stuff – penicillin?
- Water purifiers
- Swiss army knife (take Dad's)
- Sanitary towels
- Toothpaste tablets
- DNA testing kit
- Period-accurate currency (find template for 3D printer)
- Period-accurate dress (download & print)
- Umbrella
- THE PASSWORD

File note: Data file written by CLOVE SUTCLIFFE on 21 July 2056

UNIVERSITY OF ST ANDREWS CAMPUS, SCOTLAND, 2056

Clove walked to the university as fast as she could. It was almost eleven at night, and she had never been out this late on her own before. Luckily, it was only a ten-minute walk and the roads were quiet. The campus was packed, though, with students pre-lashing the first parties of the weekend. She walked to the physics building with her head down, hoping none of them would try and talk to her.

When she got there, she held her key card up to the lock at the main entrance. It flashed green: her access hadn't been revoked yet. Clove went inside quickly, before the doors could change their mind.

Heading across the ground floor to the staircase, she tried hard not to break into a run. She was certain that someone was going to appear any second and arrest her. But nobody did, even when she was going down the stairs to the basement.

When she arrived at the lab, she ignored the metal plaque on the door that read AUTHORIZED PERSONNEL ONLY and waved her key card at the scanner. The light above the lock turned from red to amber. But to her horror, the message changed from LOCKED to SCAN PRINT.

She had forgotten that the lab had a fingerprint scanner too. This was hopeless. There was no way she'd be able to fake Jen's fingerprint. Clove resigned herself to having to go home a failure.

When she explained the problem to Spart, he replied instantly.

> If there's an electrical circuit box, I may be able to access the building's security system and unlock the door. You will have to use the memory card to get me into the system.

"Spart, you genius!" For once Clove was glad that she'd put him in talk mode.

She looked for anything on the walls that could feasibly be a circuit box. Halfway up the stairs she'd just come down and hidden behind a fire extinguisher was a small metal door. She pulled the extinguisher off the wall and tried to open the door.

"It's locked," she hissed. Then she remembered that Tom's Swiss army knife was in her bag, and quickly unscrewed the hinge with the screwdriver attachment.

Feeling around inside the box, she found the circuit board that must control the building's lighting and security system – and hopefully the lock on the door to the laboratory. Eventually her fingers found a socket that might fit a memory card. She slotted it into place. If Spart could connect to the network, he'd be able to hack into the system and gain control of the whole building.

"Work your magic, Spart."

A bright green light shone from inside the electrical box as he connected with the network. She stared at her watch, hoping for a message.

> … loading …

It was the most computer-y message she'd ever had from Spart. She stared at the lab door and willed his virtual lock-picking to work, preferably before someone came and found her kneeling beside a broken electrical box.

Without warning, the keypad on the door above the lab lit up red, then yellow, and finally green. A message from Spart appeared on the screen: HELLO CLOVE. The door clicked open.

She drew a hand through her hair, relieved. She ran to tug open the door, only just remembering to remove the memory card from the circuit box first. She didn't have time to close the panel that hid the board or to replace the fire extinguisher on the wall, but hopefully by the time anyone noticed it, it would be too late to stop her.

The lab was pitch-black. "Turn on the lights, Spart," she whispered. She didn't want to raise her voice until she was sure she was alone. A graduate student might be napping in the camp bed in the corner of the lab. But when the lights flickered on, she was on her own.

Stepping over lines of cables duct-taped to the floor, she walked to the computer, her footsteps echoing in the cavernous basement. When she sat down at the desk, alarms immediately shrieked in her ears. Clove jumped up from the seat.

"What did I do?" she asked, heart racing in her chest. "Spart?"

It was only after several seconds that she realized she'd turned Spart back to silent mode. She flicked him into talk mode again.

> The noise is a fire alarm. When you left the extinguisher off the wall, it set off an automatic warning.

"Well, shut it off, then," she hissed.

> I am unable to obtain access to that system.

"You're useless," she said in outrage, and sat back down. "We'd better work fast."

She reached around the back of the main computer system to plug the memory card into the USB port, so that she could hook Spart up. The memory card was the biggest one she had, which was good, because if he ran out of memory before he could bring her back to the present, then she'd be stuck in the past. For ever. She wasn't too worried about that, though – it was completely impossible that this would work at all.

Within seconds he was uploaded, and a message was waiting for her on the main monitor.

> The evidence indicates that *you're* useless.

Clove opened up the program for the time machine, and tapped on the diagram of the particle accelerator like Tom had shown her. She started inputting the settings for 1745 and the location of Carlisle, England – which was where the documents that Spart had compiled showed Matthew and Katherine as being at that time. Spart's Folios had talked about some sort of battle between the Scottish and English over the monarchy, but she hadn't had time to read up on it yet. She'd have to do some research if this worked.

She set the size of the wormhole to be large enough for her to enter it, and the duration of the opening to fifteen seconds, which she thought would give her enough time to get inside.

She checked over her code three times to make sure she hadn't made any mistakes. When she was sure everything was ready, she tried to turn on the machine. The program asked her for an authentication password, just as she'd expected. Clove wished she had paid closer attention when Tom had been typing it in. At least it was numerical, which made it a little easier. She only had to choose the right six numbers.

What could it be? Clove tried to think what Tom and Jen might use as a code. Her mind was suddenly blank.

Without hope, she tried Jen's birthday.

Nothing.

She tried Tom's. She tried the year that Tom and Jen had met, at St Andrews University.

Nothing.

The screen flashed up with a warning: if she entered another wrong password, the system would automatically shut down and the alarm would be raised.

Clove felt a hot flush of panic go right through her. Maybe it was better to let Spart try and override the system, however unlikely it was that he could do it. Clove bit her lip. Could she risk taking another guess? She had one more idea, something that was unlikely to work. It couldn't be the answer. But if it was...

Clove took a deep breath and, preparing herself to run if the alarms sounded, she entered the six digits of her birthday. She squeezed her eyes shut, too afraid to look, muscles tensed.

Around her, the particle accelerator came to life with a hum. She opened her eyes to see a satisfying array of flashing lights.

Clove couldn't move. She felt like she'd been kicked in the throat. The password of the time machine was her birthday?

Tom and Jen really did think of her as their daughter.

On the screen a loading bar appeared. It slowly climbed from 0% to a full bar, as the accelerator prepared for operation.

> CLOVE, you need to put on the suit before you enter the chamber.

"Suit?"

> An email on the system says that a protective suit must be worn by all humans who come into contact with the wormhole. It should be here somewhere.

Clove remembered how, as a child, she'd watched the flower rot and die because of radiation poisoning. She definitely didn't want that to happen to her.

"I can't find a suit!" she cried, beginning to search the lab.

Spart replied from her watch.

> You need the suit. You will not survive the journey without it. It blocks the radiation.

Clove tried to quell her rising panic. The fire alarms were still ringing furiously. Someone would hear them soon. She was running out of time. Where would a suit be stored? Again, she looked around the room frantically. Finally, she spotted a storage trunk by the entrance.

After running over, she pulled up the lid and found a thick grey plastic package inside. She tore into it with her fingernails, ignoring her shaking hands, to find a bright orange suit of the kind that astronauts wore. It was enormous, and thick with padded reinforcement. She pulled it on over the top of her clothes and rucksack, then tugged the helmet over her head. She couldn't believe she was doing this. Everything was happening so fast.

As Clove was crossing back to the computer, fastening the front of the radiation suit, the door to the lab swung open, hitting the wall with a metallic clang. Clove spun around, and found herself looking at a surprised security guard. Instinctively, she jolted into a run, trying to ignore the heavy weight of the spacesuit as she sprinted over to the computer.

"Stop where you are!" the security guard shouted.

On the screen, the loading bar was at 99%. There was a colossal noise coming from the wormhole chamber: a sucking sound like an enormous vacuum cleaner. She could hear it even over the fire alarm.

> CLOVE, RUN. GO.

There was no time to hesitate. She ignored the shouting guard and ran to the chamber, shoving her hands inside the suit's gloves at the same time. When she thumped the OPEN button on the time machine, its door slid open with aching slowness. She skittered through into the interior chamber, where the wormhole was a burnt white, twisting void.

The security guard was staring at her in horror as the door slid shut behind her.

Clove felt overwhelmed with panic. What was she doing? This was crazy. She considered diving back out to safety.

Surely being arrested was a better option than whatever was going to happen next?

A message from Spart appeared on her watch.

```
> 1745 awaits. Good luck.
```

It was too late to reconsider. In front of her, the wormhole vibrated, just slightly. Clove reached out to it with tentative fingers. She'd barely touched it when it tugged on her with a huge unstoppable force. She was flung like a doll into the blinding white light, heat and darkness flashing across her vision. Wind pushed her in every direction, but it felt like she wasn't moving at all.

The wind stopped.

The lights stopped.

There was silence.

Location: *Wormhole Investigation Laboratory, Physics Department, University of St Andrews, Scotland*

Timestamp: *22 July 2056 00:17:01–00:26:34 GMT*

00:17:01: *SECURITY GUARD stands in the centre of the laboratory. He is staring at the time machine, which glows a bright white that is slowly getting dimmer.*

SECURITY GUARD
(under his breath)

What the…?

00:17:47: *SECURITY GUARD takes a step towards the time machine. He stops and reconsiders.*

SECURITY GUARD
(shaking his head)

I don't get paid enough for this.

00:18:15: *GUARD leaves the laboratory.*

00:25:57: *GIRL, with blonde hair and thick black eyeliner, enters the laboratory. She stares at the time machine. Then she sits down at the computer desk and reads the screen.*

GIRL
(quietly, to herself)

The tenth of September, seventeen forty-five? OK. Sure.

GIRL pushes back her sleeve and presses a button on her wrist. White light exudes from her skin, flashing and moving like the wormhole in the time machine. The light surrounds GIRL. When it dies down, she has disappeared.

00:26:34: *The laboratory is empty.*

END OF FOOTAGE

File note: Transcript of footage from CCTV Camera 38 at the
        University of St Andrews, Scotland, from 22 July
        2056

PART
TWO

CHAPTER 13

StAPD • Initial Incident Report – Restricted (when complete)

Page 1/1

ISBN 978-1-88288-973-0

ST ANDREWS POLICE DEPARTMENT
Initial Incident Report

RECEIVED JULY 2056
St Andrews Police Department

Case number:	00-24601
Location:	University of St Andrews
Date:	22 July 2056 00:22

Incident:

At 12.22 a.m. officers responded to a call from a security guard in the School of Physics, who reported a break-in. He claimed that a young girl, roughly 5'3" and wearing a bright orange jumpsuit, had disappeared into a huge, whirling hole in the basement.

Action taken:

Investigating officer found no sign of a break-in.

CJ Act 1964, S.9; MC Act 1980 SS. 5A(3)(a) and 5B; Criminal Procedure Rules 2012, part 22

File note: St Andrews police report, dated 22 July 2056

Clove lay still for a long time trying to summon up the courage to open her eyes. She couldn't hear anything. She couldn't feel her body. She could smell the plastic of her suit, which meant she was still alive, probably. She watched the spiralling patterns of light on the back of her eyelids: circling and sparking in the dim pink. Phosphenes, bright and sharp as fireworks. Her head felt numb.

Carefully, she tried bending a finger. It tingled as the inside of her glove brushed her skin. She opened her eyes. White flooded her vision, resolving into a blindingly bright blue. Through the visor of her helmet, she could see brightness, scattered in thick reflections through the blue, moving and refracting overhead. A flock of birds fluttered past in the sunlight, and then she realized they weren't birds at all, but a shoal of fish. Was she under water?

She struggled to move, but the heavy suit weighed her down, pressing her into what she now realized must be the rocky bed of a river. Clove tried to kick up to the surface. She rose a little, but her suit was too heavy, and she immediately sank downwards, knocking her helmet on a rock. Her vision blurred.

Clove swayed in the current, staring at a slime-covered pebble and trying to calm the painful reverberations echoing across her skull. She could feel herself breathing faster, but the air didn't seem to be working the way it should. She was going dizzy. The air trapped inside her suit must be running out of oxygen. She was going to suffocate if she couldn't get out of the water and take off her helmet.

She pulled her knees up, ignoring the pain in her head, and tried to push off the bottom again. After several minutes of frantic effort, she managed to reach the surface. There was a clump of reeds within reach, so she grabbed onto it with both fists, clouds of silt dirtying the water as she moved.

A startled toad swam at her helmet. It bounced off and jumped away onto the riverbank. She watched it go, wishing she could do the same. She desperately tried to summon up the energy to pull herself ashore. Just the thought of it made her dizzy. Her eyes drifted shut, but she forced them open. She stared at the sky and tried not to slip back under the water.

As she watched, an angel appeared. Glowing gold, it reached down to pull her out of the water and onto the riverbank. The angel tugged on the straps of Clove's helmet and removed it. Fresh air rushed in.

After a few deep breaths, Clove's head stopped spinning and she could take in her rescuer.

It was Meg.

"Meg?" she choked out, amazed. Meg had found her. Somehow she'd saved her. She'd come to take her home.

Meg's golden blonde hair seemed to sparkle in the sunlight. It swelled and glowed, making everything else fuzzy and smeared in comparison.

"Definitely not," Clove thought she heard Meg say, as her vision went cloudy and she let herself sleep, just for a second.

> CLOVE?

> CLOVE, wake up. We need to go.

> CLOVE?

* * *

Clove opened her eyes with a jolt, automatically fighting against the water that was tugging her down towards the deep, black depths, before she realized she was safe on dry land, and it was just a dream.

She rolled onto her back and looked up at the leaves of an overhead tree. Birds were chattering noisily to each other in its branches, and there was a red tinge to the sky that made her think it was early morning. She was alone.

She blinked, trying not to cry. Carefully, the movement sapping all of her energy, Clove struggled to sit up. She thought about standing, and then reconsidered. She was still wearing the radiation suit. The orange plastic was even heavier now that it was wet. Clove pulled off her gloves and unbuttoned the suit, then shrugged it off her shoulders and slid out of it. She immediately felt more alive.

She sat on the grassy bank and glared at the suit. It may have saved her from radiation poisoning, but it had almost made her suffocate underwater, because she'd been unable to swim to land. Her parents would never have found out what had happened to her. The thought made her shudder.

She had been pretty lucky. If she hadn't managed to grab the bank and pull herself out, who knows what would have happ— Clove's thoughts stuttered.

Had she pulled herself out of the water?

That didn't sound right.

She seemed to remember ... something. Someone. Pulling her out of the river.

Or had that just been a dream?

She could have sworn it had been Meg grabbing her

arms and tugging her onto dry land. But surely that couldn't be right.

Could it?

Clove shrugged off the thought. She had more important things to worry about, anyway – like where she was. She had set the time machine to take her to the centre of Carlisle on 10 September 1745, but somehow she had arrived in the middle of a river instead of the city. Who knew what else had gone wrong, or even what year it was?

The river cut through a cornfield. Bright gold crops filled a rolling landscape. Clouds floated serenely across a calm sky that had been undisturbed by the appearance and immediate disappearance of a wormhole that had deposited a sixteen-year-old girl on the ground.

Clove could be anywhere. In any place, at any time.

Despite all of this, she found herself smiling. She had travelled in a *wormhole*. Even if it was just to the next postcode, she had travelled in a wormhole and *survived*. Even if she never achieved anything else, never found her parents or fixed her relationship with Tom and Jen, she would always have this.

She pushed up her sleeve and peered at her watch. "Spart?" Her voice sounded dulled, muffled, and very unsure. She cleared her throat and tried again. "Spart?"

A message appeared on the screen.

> I am here.

A coil of anxiety left her. Spart was here in her watch. And as her watch was solar powered, she had him for as long as she was here – wherever "here" was.

"Where are we?" she asked.

```
> I don't know.
```

"I thought you knew everything. Isn't that the point of you?"

```
> I know everything which I am able to search online.
  I can't connect to a network here.
```

Her watch couldn't get any signal. That meant she must be in the past, before they had the internet. She must have travelled over fifty years into the past. She rolled over, pushing up onto hands and knees and ignoring the sudden pounding headache spreading across her forehead.

"Urgh. Time travel really isn't designed for passenger comfort."

She stood up and then leant against the trunk of a willow as she tried to conquer her exhaustion. Thinking of everything she still had to do made her want to cry.

Right now, when she was so tired that she couldn't move even her hands properly, deciding to time travel into the past to get the DNA of people who may or may not be her parents seemed like the worst idea in the world.

She let herself cry, pushing out all her worry and exhaustion. She wanted Jen. She wanted Tom. She wanted a hug from her parents – her *real* parents, whatever genetics said. She wanted to go home, but a small, stronger part of her knew that she couldn't, not until she'd done what she came here for. She had to find out whether Katherine

Finchley and Matthew Galloway did exist in this time. And if they did … well, then there would be no end to her questions. Did they look identical to her birth parents? What did that mean – a genetic anomaly, however impossible that was? Or … could they possibly somehow be *her* Kate and Matt, *her* parents? And if that was the case, then *how*?

After a little while, her tears stopped. She wiped her face. The skin around her eyes felt sore and swollen. She hiccupped.

She was freezing.

Her head hurt.

She wanted a painkiller.

As carefully as a newborn foal, she pulled her rucksack out of the tangle of the suit. She opened it with trembling fingers, pulled out a bottle of water and then unzipped her first-aid kit.

She was thirstier than she'd realized, and she gulped down the whole bottle after she'd taken a paracetamol.

Clove sat under the willow tree and watched the sun climb the sky, feeling pathetically sorry for herself. She was so tired; she could just lie down on the riverbank and sleep for hours.

Eventually she found the energy to move. She stretched tentatively, and discovered that while she didn't hurt much any more, she was starving. She repacked her rucksack, filled with a sudden determination to find some kind of town or village, so she could work out where she was – and also get some breakfast.

After pulling off her T-shirt, Clove took her freshly printed dress from her bag and put it on. The long sleeves would hide her watch. Then she wrapped the suit around the helmet and stuffed the bundle into the bottom of her rucksack.

Clove had arranged with Spart – the version of him that she had left on a memory card in the lab – that at an agreed time in a week she would use her watch to broadcast a radio signal. Spart-in-the-Lab should be able to pick this up and use the signal to find her exact location. Then he could reopen the wormhole. It should work - if she didn't lose the suit or the watch.

Telling herself firmly that she could definitely, absolutely do this, Clove began walking.

CHAPTER 14

LuckyClover 23:14:38	What was it like the first time you time travelled? Please tell me you passed out too.
Ella-is-swell 23:15:12	I'm not sure I can remember the first time. Time travel's not such a big deal now. But I must have been about six, I think. Maybe younger. I can remember thinking I'd been turned inside out.
Ella-is-swell 23:15:43	Kind of like how I felt the first time I saw you.
LuckyClover 23:15:57	Oh, SMOOTH.

File note: Chat log, dated 5 November 2058

Clove hadn't been walking for long when an outraged *"WAIT!"* came from somewhere behind her. Clove turned to see a girl hurtling towards her.

A girl with blonde hair that glowed in the sun.

It was the girl from her dream – and she wasn't Meg. The girl chased after her, skirts lifted to her knees and a basket hooked over her arm.

For a second Clove considered running away, but instead she resigned herself to the conversation. She brushed down the skirts of her dress and straightened her cap. Then Clove stopped walking to let her pursuer catch up. She double-checked to make sure she wasn't wearing anything outrageously modern, and, as the girl pulled up in front of her, panting heavily, Clove remembered at the last minute to shove her sleeve down over her watch.

"Where … are … you … going?" the girl gasped.

She had thick blonde hair pulled back in a bun under her cap, arching eyebrows, and the sharpest chin Clove had ever seen. She was wearing an old-fashioned dress made of a dirty brown material that looked like it had endured a long history of ill-treatment. The more Clove looked at her, the less she could see the resemblance to Meg. The similarities slipped from her grasp as she tried to pinpoint them.

"Um," Clove said.

"I can't believe you are *leaving*. I thought you were dying." The girl dropped her basket on the ground and rested both of her hands on her knees, still catching her breath. Her hair was collapsing out of her bun in slow motion. "You are not dying, are you?"

"I don't think I'm dying," Clove mumbled, staring down at herself to check. Then she shook herself. "I'm sorry, who are you?"

"Elenore," the girl said, in a way that implied Clove should have known that already. "I saw you lying by the river and I thought you were dead. But then you started walking away, so clearly there's nothing wrong with you at all. I'm sorry for bothering you."

"Um. Right. Elenore. Well—"

"You may call me Ella."

"I'm Clove," she said, too tired to do anything but answer honestly. Had she imagined this girl rescuing her from the river after all? Everything was so confused in her head. She couldn't work out what had actually happened and what was a hallucination.

Clove wished the girl would leave, but she showed no signs of doing so. Her attention was fixed intently on Clove, as if she was endlessly fascinating.

"You do still rather look as if you may be about to collapse." The girl – Ella – said. "When was the last time you ate?"

Clove's stomach gave a sudden pang. "Why? Do you – do you have food?" She eyed Ella's basket. Something that looked like a loaf was sticking out of the top. "Is that bread?"

"It's my luncheon. I was saving it for when I arrived in Carlisle," Ella said. "But do you think eating would make you feel better?"

"It would," she reassured her. Clove tried to frown in a way that indicated how likely she was to faint at any second, and how much she needed some food.

Ella visibly softened. "Then let's eat."

Clove sat down on the ground, watching with increasing delight as Ella unpacked a full picnic.

"Are those pork pies? Powerful!" Clove bit her lip. Did they use the word "powerful" in whatever time this was? What time even *was* this? This girl behaved nothing like she had expected people in the olden days to behave. "By the way, could you tell me the date, please? I've been travelling for a few days now and I seem to have lost track of time."

To Clove's relief, Ella didn't question her query. "It's the tenth of September, seventeen five and forty," she replied.

Clove was delighted. That was the exact date she'd programmed into the wormhole. Success. She grabbed a pork pie and bit into it with relish. It was the best thing she could ever remember eating.

When she'd finished the pork pie, two chunks of bread and butter and four cold boiled potatoes, she realized Ella was talking to her. She tuned back into the conversation, chewing on a sausage absently. She wondered if Ella had any crisps. Were crisps even a thing yet? Surely they had crisps here. People couldn't survive without crisps, could they?

"Are you going to Carlisle too?" Ella asked, picking up some kind of hairy vegetable and biting into it. Clove had thought it was a weed that had accidentally got into the basket. It was pink. "Radish?"

"Sorry?" Clove said, trying to look like she hadn't been daydreaming about smoky bacon crisps. "I mean, yes, Carlisle! We're near the city?"

"I have just explained all of this," Ella said, frowning. She looked extremely disappointed in Clove, which was strange for someone who had only met her that day.

"I'm sorry for … me. I think I've got concussion, probably. I'm not normally like this," Clove lied, thinking guiltily of the furious argument she'd had about quantum mechanics with that undergraduate, and her mother's face when she'd called her Jen, and Meg's, when she'd shouted at her about Alec. She had been really horrible recently. Maybe her parents had actually had a reason to be worried about her. She wasn't so bad that she needed counselling, though – was she?

"Anyway, can I come with you to Carlisle?" Clove asked. "Please?"

"Well. I suppose now that I've tended to you and

brought you back to life from the cusp of death, I can't abandon you," Ella said, grinning. "You may accompany me to Carlisle." She stood up, brushing grass off her skirts and running a hand over her hair to check it was tidy. A hank of hair fell out of the back of the bun. She didn't seem to notice.

"Thank you," Clove said, intensely grateful. "Thank you so much."

Ella smiled down at her basket. "It's my pleasure."

"How did you get here?" Ella asked, as they walked along the riverside.

"I took a carriage from Scotland," Clove said, thinking quickly and wondering if Ella had seen the wormhole. Before Ella could ask any difficult questions, like how long the journey had taken or what the carriage's make, model and registration number had been, Clove changed the subject. "Why are you going to Carlisle?"

Ella, who had been smiling at Clove, stopped abruptly. "For private, personal reasons." It was clear from her tone that Ella wasn't willing to divulge anything further.

"Right. Um." Clove floundered for another conversation topic – one which wouldn't bring up anything she couldn't answer. "How old are you?" she asked finally.

"I turned eighteen this spring," Ella said. "What age are you?"

"Sixteen."

"That means I am in charge," Ella said, with great satisfaction.

"What? No!" Clove objected reflexively. "Why?"

"I'm the eldest."

"And?"

"Obviously that means that I shall be the leader."

"We're practically the same age!"

Ella shrugged, unconvinced. "Two years makes a big difference. You don't look very worldly."

As Clove blew out an annoyed breath, Ella bent down to pluck a violet from the edge of the cornfield.

"I don't need looking after," Clove said. "Besides the lunch," she added.

Ella twisted the violet between two fingers. "Of *course* you don't." She handed Clove the flower before turning away.

Clove looked down at it and then without really knowing why, tucked it carefully in her pocket.

CHAPTER 15

The earliest documented work of Clove Sutcliffe took place in Carlisle, Cumberland, in 1745. The city was the last place in England to have a castle under siege by enemy forces. Originally a Roman fort, the castle was built in 1092, after the Scottish region was invaded by English troops.

For the next seven hundred years, the border city was the focus of endless territorial disputes and invasions between the neighbouring countries. The castle itself was besieged ten times, the most recent of which was during Sutcliffe's time there, in the 1745 Jacobite Uprising, when Carlisle was besieged on 15 November 1745.

By this time, the castle was a shadow of its former self, but with the help of Colonel Durand and his garrison, the castle succeeded in holding its defences until the surrender of the city five days later. History Control subjects Katherine Finchley and Matthew Galloway were instrumental to this project. Innocent of their part in history, the couple helped to maintain the defences through their work as civilian volunteers. At a time when every second meant more English forces could be gathered to fight the invasion, these five days were crucial in the eventual defeat of the Jacobites, as Sutcliffe would have been aware.

It was on one of the last sunny days of the summer when Sutcliffe entered Carlisle. It was there that the famous <u>History Revisionist</u> met one of the most important people in her life, a person we know very little about: Elenore Walker.

One of the few things we do know about their time in time-landscape 1745 is that a flower was given to Sutcliffe by Walker. This was saved out of sentimentality by Sutcliffe, and has since been cryogenically preserved for historical posterity by the Museum of History Control, New London. The pair's time in Carlisle was a significant event in both of their timelines, and will be studied further in <u>Chapter 15</u>.

The violet (*viola sororia*) is native to the British Isles, and is a traditional romantic gift exchanged by lesbian and bisexual women. The custom dates back to Sappho of Ancient Greece, who said in her poetry:

> *How fair and good were the things*
> *we shared together,*
> *How by my side you wove many*
> *garlands of violets.*

File note: Extract from *An Unauthorized Biography of Clove Sutcliffe*, first published in 2344

Carlisle, England, 1745

Clove and Ella arrived in Carlisle after hours of walking through endless countryside. Clove was amazed. The roads were paved with cobblestones and scattered with manure from the horse-drawn carriages. Hand-painted signs, advertising the wares of the greengrocers, pawnbrokers and cobblers, hung from intricately scrolled metalwork on the sides of crooked buildings.

From Spart's Folios, it seemed that the Matthew Galloway who existed in 1745 was working as a coachman for Katherine's aunt and uncle, with whom Katherine had lived following her grandmother's death.

For the whole journey to the city, Clove had been thinking about what she was going to do when she got to the house where they lived. She had decided that the best plan was to try to get a job as a maid in the household. That way she would be working alongside Matthew, and would have a chance to get some of his DNA. She'd probably be able to get some of Katherine's too, when she was cleaning her room or serving her dinner.

"I need to get to Annetwell Street," Clove told Ella. "I have to visit a house there, to ask if they need any new maids. It was nice to meet you, but I'll leave you now to do your … private, personal things."

"Oh, I can come with you!" Ella said amiably. "I am also searching for a position as a maid."

Clove was a bit annoyed, but she let Ella follow her. She did feel safer walking through the city with someone else.

The Finchley house was set back from the street. A neat stone driveway curved from the main gates up through a well-tended flower garden to the front door. Clove was incredibly impressed. If the family who lived here really were her relatives, then Clove had some very well-off ancestors.

She swallowed. This was it: the moment of truth. She was so close to finding out whether it really was her parents who had been alive in 1745, 1854, 1941 and countless other dates.

The two girls walked around the side of the house, looking for the servants' entrance. They walked past a herb garden, scattered with foraging chickens. Clove stooped to run her hand along the top of a knee-high box hedge that had been trimmed completely flat.

The back door was split in half across the middle, and the top section was open. The smell of cinnamon and fresh bread drifted out into the garden. Clove breathed in deeply, feeling instantly at home. She peered inside, catching a glimpse of a cook kneading dough in an immaculate kitchen.

Clove knocked on the door frame. A dog napping on the hearth lifted his head to look at them, and then dropped it back onto the flagstone.

The cook walked over, smiling and wiping her hands on her apron. Her face was scattered with freckles, and her dark hair was brushed neatly back off her high forehead under her cap. "Good afternoon," she said, leaning on the bottom half of the door and looking over Clove and Ella with interest.

"Good day to you," Ella said, before Clove could speak. "I'm sorry to bother you, but I was wondering if you knew of anyone in the area looking for a maid? Our last master was arrested in Glasgow for supporting the Rebels. It took us completely by surprise. We were abandoned in Scotland, without references, and it is only through the kindness of strangers that we have managed to return safely to England. Since then we've been adrift, waiting for someone to take it into their hearts to help us..." Ella trailed off with a sniff, twisting her skirt between her fingers.

Clove realized she was gaping at Ella in amazement. She shut her mouth with a snap. Ella had lied so easily! She had sounded so sincere that if Clove didn't know better, she would believe she was telling the truth.

"Oh, poor dears," the cook said, drawing in a horrified breath. "You must have had such a terrible journey."

Ella looked off to the side, as if she was so traumatized that she couldn't bear to remember, and dipped her head in a weak half-nod.

"You are lucky to be alive. Let me speak to the mistress of the house. We shall see if she can't find a spot for you both. What are your names?"

"Elenore Walker," Ella said.

The cook turned to Clove.

"Cl—" She stopped. She couldn't call herself *Clove*. That didn't sound right. It was too modern for 1745, even though everyone at school teased her about it being old-fashioned. It was modern and old-fashioned all at the same time, and completely inappropriate for right now. If only she'd thought to change it sooner, before she'd met Ella. She'd been so confused by the wormhole that she had let her guard down completely.

"Anise," she said. It had always been a joke with Meg, that as they had a "Clove" and a "Nutmeg", they only needed a friend called "Aniseed" to be able to call themselves the Spice Girls. It made her heart hurt to say it, but the name was much more suitable than Clove. "My name is Anise. Anise Sutcliffe."

"I'm Mrs Samson," the cook said.

When she had left, Clove turned to Ella. "How did you do that? Make all of that up on the spot?"

Ella hitched up a shoulder in a breezy shrug. "I have a natural flair for storytelling. Just follow my lead."

"I don't need to – I can look after myself!" Clove hissed. "Who *are* you? Why are you so good at this?"

"It's lucky for you that I am, *Anise*." She shot Clove a knowing glance. "You would never have made it past the—" Ella stopped talking, her expression morphing into a timidly hopeful smile. Mrs Samson had returned with a serious-looking older lady who introduced herself as the mistress of the household, Mrs Elizabeth Finchley.

She listened carefully to Ella and asked lots of questions. She wanted references, and Ella had to explain again how they didn't have them. She then asked for "characters" from their parish clergy. Ella had one of these – whatever it was – but Clove didn't. "We had to leave our old place in such a hurry," Ella explained miserably. "It was so awful."

Once again, Clove was amazed at her skill at lying.

Did she do this a lot? Had Ella lied to *her*?

Mrs Finchley's eyes softened. "It's hard times we're living in." She hesitated as she seemed to take them both in. Finally, she said, "Several girls have asked to go home because of the trouble, and we are short-staffed. I suppose we could take you on temporarily and see what happens."

Mrs Samson led them up the servants' staircase to the attic where they would be sleeping.

"I'll leave you two to get settled," she said after showing them the room they would share. "When you finish unpacking, come back down to the kitchens. You can help me prepare dinner."

Clove unpacked her things in a daze, unable to believe her luck at bumping into Ella and managing to get a job in the very house where Katherine lived. She was following Ella down the staircase to the kitchens, listening to her outline the details of their past employer, "for consistency", she said, when she ran straight into—

"Matthew!" Clove said, staring for the first time at the man who could be her father.

CHAPTER 16

Servants' Wages, Allowances and Travelling Expenses for the year 1745

Name	Description	Date hired	Yearly wages	Allowance for clothes, &c.	Travelling expenses for selves & horses	Total charge for each
Mary Samson	Cook	June 1745	£12	--------	--------	£15
Matthew Galloway	Coachman	1744	£12	--------	£44 11 4	£56 11 4
Elenore Walker	Housemaid	10th Sept. 1745	£6	--------	--------	£6
Anise Sutcliffe	Housemaid	10th Sept. 1745	£6	--------	--------	£6

Folios/v1/Time-landscape-1745/MS-8

Carlisle, England, 1745

Matthew Galloway was tall, skinny, and very young. He was also currently looking at Clove as if she was completely insane.

His hair was the exact same colour as Clove's, with dark curls falling over his forehead – just like the ones falling over hers at that very moment. She had seen that pointy nose and freckles in the mirror more times than she could remember. He looked *just like her*. Whether this man was her time-travelling father, some kind of clone of him, or even just a long-lost ancestor, there was no denying that they were related.

It was him. It was really him. This was Matthew Galloway. In 1745.

"Hello," he said. "Do I know you?"

She opened her mouth, and then closed it again. He was so *young* – almost the same age as Clove.

"Uh… You don't know me." She swallowed. "But I know you."

Ella had come back up the stairs to see where Clove had gone, and was watching them both curiously.

"Oh? You do?" Matthew's gaze flickered over her features, pausing on her nose. She saw a kind of recognition light up his eyes. He frowned. "Who are you?"

"I'm…" She stopped. What could she say? "I…"

Ella's face did something interesting, and then quickly went blank. Clove looked back and forth between her and Matthew, feeling faint under the force of their gazes. She couldn't do this. "I have to go."

She escaped down the stairs and out through the kitchens, sending hens fluttering in her wake as she ran across the drive. Her only thought was to get away from them, from the house and everyone in it, so that she had time to think. When she reached the gates, she stopped, gasping.

She had *spoken* to Matthew Galloway. He was *real*.

She didn't know how to feel. What had just happened?

She was clearly related to this man, but not for another three hundred years.

How could this be happening? How could she work out what was going on? And more importantly, had she just messed up history? Was she allowed to just go trampling around in the past like this, talking to her own ancestors? She really should have considered all of this before now.

She rubbed at her eyes as she tried to decide what to do. Then, after checking there was no one around, she looked at her watch. "Spart, did you hear what just happened?"

> During your conversation, I compared the voice imprint of this version of "MATTHEW" with known archived recordings of MATTHEW GALLOWAY from various times, specifically his court appearances during his trial in 2040.

> There is a definite match to the other subjects. It will require a DNA test to confirm fully, but based on the evidence, I hypothesize that this subject will be genetically identical to the others we have found.

Clove didn't know what to make of that. Her mind was so overwhelmed that she could only focus on her next step: she had to find a way to steal some of Matthew's DNA. Easy.

CHAPTER 17

Carlisle, England, 1745

When Clove finally plucked up the courage to go back into the house, Matthew had disappeared. She spent the rest of the evening furious with herself for running away as soon as she'd found the person she'd come all this way to see.

To make matters worse, she found out from Mrs Samson over dinner that Katherine Finchley didn't even live here yet. The cook seemed to have taken a liking to Clove – probably after she'd found out that Clove could knit. She seemed delighted to have someone to work and gossip with and had immediately handed Clove a pile of undergarments to repair. Clove now knew more about the other families of Annetwell Street than she did about people on her own street in St Andrews.

Mrs Samson had scarcely needed prompting before she'd told Clove that Katherine Finchley, the niece of the house's mistress, was staying with her sick grandmother somewhere outside of the city, and the grandmother and the mistress had long been estranged. Clove, however, had taken in none of this except for the fact that Katherine wasn't here. She now had no way of meeting her at all. The revelation had been enough to make her want to give up and go home all over again.

Before she went to bed, Clove put her watch behind a pot of lavender on the windowsill in her room, so that it could charge in the early morning sunlight. As she was doing so, she saw a notification for an unread message, one which must have come in before she time-travelled. She flicked it open.

From: Jen <jennifer@sutcliffe.com>
To: Clove <luckyclover@sutcliffe.com>
Subject: I know it's late
Date: 21 July 2056 23:01:04 GMT

I just wanted to say, in case you're still awake, that no matter what happens, we're your parents, and you are our daughter. You can never ever do anything that we won't forgive. We love you more than anything else in the world.

Finding out about the adoption is a huge, life-changing thing, and you need to deal with it in a way that works for you. Take your time. We understand. We love you.

Your mother

File note: Email from JENNIFER SUTCLIFFE to CLOVE SUTCLIFFE on 21 July 2056

The message made Clove want to cry. She quickly turned away from Ella, who was washing her face in the washbasin, and climbed into bed, burying her face in her pillow to hide her tears.

She had to get a sample of Matthew's DNA as quickly as possible, so that she could go home to her parents. As soon as Ella was asleep, she would sneak out of bed and try to find Matthew's room. She could take a DNA sample while he was sleeping. If she was careful, he wouldn't even notice.

"Good night," Ella said, yawning into her palm before blowing out her candle.

Clove lay in bed and listened to Ella's breathing turn slow and steady – which only took a few minutes. Clove was jealous. It usually took her an hour to quiet her mind long enough to fall asleep. She carefully stood up, trying not to make the wooden pallet bed creak. Then she crept out of the room and down the stairs with a candle in one hand and the DNA kit in the other.

As he was the coachman, Matthew's living quarters were in the stables, so Clove went through the kitchens to the back door, stopping to light her candle in the fire. The dog, which hadn't moved from his place in front of the dying embers, didn't even open his eyes when she turned the heavy iron lock, only let out a doleful grumble that she was disturbing his quiet, empty kitchen.

It was pitch-black outside. By the light of her candle, she stalked past the herb garden and through the stable full of sleeping horses. Her candle cast flickering shadows across the stalls. There was a wooden ladder leading up to the hay loft, which was where she thought the coachman must sleep.

Clove started climbing the ladder. It wasn't easy to do with a candle in one hand, and she had to pause after each rung to listen for any sound of movement above. She was four rungs up when something tapped her shoulder.

Clove did a full body spasm in surprise. She let go of the ladder and flailed backwards. She snatched at a rung and just managed to grab it to stop herself from crashing to the ground. She reared her head back to see who – or what – had touched her.

Standing on the ground below her was Ella.

"What are you doing?" Ella hissed. "You're going to get caught!"

Clove was so shocked that she didn't know what to say. "You – what – *what*?"

"He's going to wake up the second you climb up there, and I'm assuming that you don't want that to happen."

"Are you *following me*?" Clove asked, outraged. "What the hell, Ella?!"

"Of course I'm following you! You insist on doing stupid things like this all of the time!"

Clove was furious, but it was very hard to yell at someone in a whisper. "Why do you even care what I do?" She dropped to the floor and pushed Ella out of the way, before walking out of the stables. "I only met you this morning!" That had been the perfect opportunity to collect Matthew's DNA. If Ella wasn't so interfering, Clove could have tested his DNA and solved this whole mystery by now.

"I thought we were friends," Ella said, and Clove's anger evaporated.

"We *are* friends. You just – you can't go sneaking up on me like that. You could have ruined everything."

"I won't do it again," Ella said solemnly, then grinned. "What are you trying to do, anyway? Can I help?"

Clove was about to say a firm no, when she realized that it would be a lot easier to collect the DNA if she had some help, and it wasn't like Spart could volunteer. Besides, even if she didn't let Ella get involved, she'd probably follow her around anyway.

Clove coughed. "It's a bit weird... I mean ... unusual. Strange. But I absolutely promise that it isn't as creepy as it sounds."

"That sounds ominous."

Clove thought about her words carefully. "I need a sample of hair from the coachman Matthew Galloway."

"Why?"

"He's my ... cousin," Clove lied. "Estranged cousin. I want his hair for a ... a ... spell!"

"I knew it!" Ella exclaimed, startling Clove. "I thought that there might be something happening between the two of you. He never stopped staring at you all through dinner, except when the butler asked him about the horses. Also, you have the same nose. What kind of spell?"

Clove cast around wildly. "A reconciliation spell."

"Clove *'Anise'* Sutcliffe," Ella said, impressed. "You have hidden depths."

"You have absolutely no idea." Clove had to try very hard to hide her smile.

"Well, I don't believe in magic personally, but I can respect your beliefs. Be careful, though. There's a lot of fear of witches in these parts. Some have been burnt *alive!*"

Clove blinked. She vaguely remembered something in one of her history lessons about witches being killed in the eighteenth century. "Thank you for the warning." She hesitated, unsure how Ella might react, and then said bravely, "So can you help me? Could you stand on guard while I sneak up to the hay loft?"

Ella frowned, biting her lip. "Would it not be simpler to steal his hair while he is awake? I should be able to distract him for you."

Clove didn't want to waste any more time, but she had to admit that Ella's idea did seem a lot ... safer. "All right. But we have to do it straight away, tomorrow morning."

Ella smiled – a genuine one without even a trace of a smirk. "Shall we shake hands on the agreement?"

Clove held out her hand. Ella's palm was soft in hers, and when her thumb touched Clove's palm, it made her shiver involuntarily.

"Can we please go to bed properly this time?" Ella said. "I'm exhausted, and I can't follow you around all night."

CHAPTER 18

Ella-is-swell 14:46:03

If 1745 was the "Early life" section of our biography, what section are we in now?

LuckyClover 14:53:52

"Penniless adolescence" probably. I couldn't even afford to buy chips earlier… it's hard being a student.

Ella-is-swell 14:54:31

I'm broke too. But that's because I went clothes shopping when I was cold and ended up buying four jumpers.

LuckyClover 14:54:59

AGAIN? How is this a thing you've done multiple times now?!

Ella-is-swell 14:55:11

Look …….. we all have our flaws, OK, just accept that this is one of mine.

Ella-is-swell 14:55:26

Like your startling ability to miss things which are completely obvious. See the aforementioned "Early life" chapter.

LuckyClover 14:55:47

I miss 1745. It was a simpler time, before everything got all complicated.

Ella-is-swell 14:56:28

💀 The salad days of our youth.

Ella-is-swell 14:56:49

You know, there were times in 1745 when I was certain you'd guessed who I was. How could you not? I was so obviously a time traveller.

LuckyClover 14:57:02

I had a lot on my plate! I was distracted! Besides, I knew something was up. I was hip to your jive.

Ella-is-swell 14:57:25

That is such a barefaced lie I'm not even going to deign it with a response. I had you totally fooled.

LuckyClover 14:57:52

I still don't get why you even pretended to be from 1745 anyway. Why didn't you just tell me you were a time traveller too?

Ella-is-swell 14:58:34

Um. I've explained this before. I was trying not to interfere. I didn't want to mess up what was supposed to happen… It had to happen naturally.

File note: Chat log dated 27 November 2058

Carlisle, England, 1745

The next morning, after a shivery wash with a bucket of ice-cold water at dawn, and a horrifying experience with the smelly outhouse toilet, Clove helped Mrs Samson and the other kitchen staff to cook breakfast. As she worked, Clove couldn't stop shooting looks at Ella, who was sitting at the kitchen table and chatting casually with Matthew. Their plan was simple: steal a strand of his hair when he wasn't looking.

Ella had reassured her that she would be able to distract him while Clove pulled out a hair, but Clove wasn't entirely convinced. She needed to get the root for a DNA test, so she had to yank a whole hair from his scalp. Clove thought that this was probably something Matthew would notice, despite Ella's admittedly very distracting nature. Clove found it nearly impossible to take her eyes off Ella. She was reluctantly charmed by everything she did.

Ella turned her head and winked at Clove. That was their signal. Clove took a deep breath and hurried over to the table. As she did so, Ella knocked over a jug of ale in the middle of a particularly expansive gesture. As the ale splashed over Matthew's arm, Ella let out a shocked gasp, and Clove leant over Matthew's head and carefully grabbed a hair between two fingers. She gave it a hard tug.

"Ouch," Matthew cried, spinning round, one hand raised to his head.

"There was a bee…" Clove said.

Matthew frowned at her, dripping ale. "A bee?"

"In your hair."

"It was enormous," Ella confirmed. "I think it might even have been a hornet."

Matthew looked around frantically. "Where did it go?"

As Matthew was gazing around the kitchen for the bee, Clove dashed out of the room, calling to Mrs Samson that she was going to get some more ale.

She ran up to her attic bedroom. Once there, she followed the instructions on the DNA testing kit. The few seconds the device took to extract DNA from the hair follicle felt like a lifetime to Clove as she waited, hopping from foot to foot. This was the moment of truth.

Roughly two decades later, the top of the box lit up with the results.

<u>Match found in database:</u>
MATTHEW GEORGE GALLOWAY
<u>Gender:</u> M
<u>Nationality:</u> SCO
<u>DOB:</u> 14/5/2021
<u>DOD:</u> Unknown
<u>Permanent address:</u> Unknown
<u>Criminal history:</u> Life sentence for political terrorism. Incarcerated in Wakefield Prison 2039–2040
<u>Threat level:</u> **Highest**

Folios/v1/Time-landscape-1745/MS-9

File note: DNA results for MATTHEW GALLOWAY

So.

There was no denying it. The man downstairs, covered in ale and confusion, was genetically her father. He wasn't just her distant ancestor. He really was her dad. Somehow.

Clove ran her hands through her hair. She didn't know what to think. Her father was here. Was he time-travelling too? Or was he a clone of the man who was her birth father?

"My parents are alive in the past," she said aloud, testing out the idea. "They're really here. In 1745 – or one of them is, at the very least."

She was suddenly filled with longing for home. Now that Spart's theories had been confirmed scientifically all she wanted to do was hide from it all.

"Can we go home now, Spart?" she asked her watch. She had done what she had come to do. She could process the information back home in 2056.

> I recommend staying in the eighteenth century a little longer. We are more likely to determine the source of the anomaly in the subjects here than in 2056. This is where the issue first appeared.

"*'Subjects'? 'Anomaly'?* You're talking about my parents like they are some kind of experiment!" She'd just met her father as a teenager in 1745, and all Spart wanted to do was analyse him.

> They are my data. I have to treat them scientifically. Handling this situation emotionally would only be detrimental at this point. Emotions never help. I've seen enough episodes of *Sherbot Holmes: Robot Detective* to work that out.

"They are real people. Not *data*."

> Irrelevant. You asked me to find your parents. I have found one of them for you. You can't question how I did it.

"Fine," she said, exhausted. "What do you think I should do now, then?"

> Now we've found "MATTHEW", don't you want to know why he is here?

"How can I do that? Just ask Matthew what he's doing here? How he got from 2040 to here?" she said, voice breaking at the thought. "I can't. It's too much."

> You can, and you will.

"I want to go home. I'm so bad at this. I couldn't speak to him – and Katherine isn't even here!"

> You can't go home, not yet. We can't determine what is happening without new data. When you feel less emotionally vulnerable, you will realize how vital this journey is.

"All I'm doing is carrying you around, and making a fool of myself. I'm useless. I'm not helping anyone."

> CLOVE SUTCLIFFE, you are doing things no human has ever done before. You are groundbreaking. You are unique. Do not cease to function due to inappropriate emotional weakness.

She reread the message, trying to work out how he could possibly be talking about *her*, the girl who messed up all her relationships and who couldn't do anything right.

"Groundbreaking?" Her voice was disbelieving. She found herself biting anxiously at her fingernails and shoved her hand behind her back.

> Everyone gets scared. You must not allow it to stop you from
> being incredible.

"You're not my Dumbledore, you don't get to give me inspiring speeches like that," she mumbled, brushing away a tear. She wished she could trap her feelings down somewhere deep inside herself where they couldn't keep leaking out and making her *feel* things. "But ... I'll stay. For now."

> Thank you. I think we're dealing with something more important
> than either of us realize.

"What do you mean? What can be more important than my parents appearing throughout history?"

> *Why* they are appearing there. I have been analysing each of
> the time periods where the subjects appear.

> I have had my suspicions about it for a long time, but I
> have been unable to establish any empirical evidence. Now
> that we know the situation is real, I think I can tell you
> my conclusion.

"What suspicions? What are you talking about?"

> The moments where the subjects appear always seem to be a
> turning point in history. To put it in more metaphorical
> terms, "MATTHEW" and "KATHERINE" appear at a split in the
> landscape of time, when everything could change.

"What?" Clove pulled out her knitting, unable to stand listening to this without something to focus her energy on.

> Whenever your parents appear, something important happens which could have led to circumstances shifting dramatically if a few details were adjusted.

> For example: in the time-landscape 1940, subjects "MATTHEW GALLOWAY" and "KATHERINE FINCHLEY" helped the police catch a murderer at Bletchley Park and saved ALAN TURING's life.

Clove's brain whirred as she realized what Spart was saying. If her parents hadn't caught the murderer, then Alan Turing might have died. If Alan Turing had died, the Allied war effort would have lost a huge advantage.

> Your parents helped win World War II.

"OK," she said, shakily. "That's a little incredible."

> That's only one example. In time-landscape 1854, the diary of the British Army commander LORD RAGLAN notes that during a field meeting in the Crimean War, a journalist named "MATTHEW GALLOWAY" and his servant, who turned out to be "KATHERINE FINCHLEY", raised the alarm about a rocket that was minutes away from hitting them.

> RAGLAN's diary states that if the French and British commanding officers hadn't been alerted, every single one of them would have died during the very first battle of the war. There would have been no one to lead the Allies and they would almost certainly have lost the war.

"My parents helped to win the Crimean War, too?" Clove swallowed. This was unreal. "What else?"

> Before we left 2056 I wasn't able to isolate clear events
> in each time-landscape. However, an obvious conclusion
> can be drawn from the data: the subjects made significant
> contributions which affected the Cold War, the assassination
> of the American president JOHN F. KENNEDY, as well as World
> War I and the Napoleonic Wars.

Spart stopped talking to let Clove process everything. She had never even considered why her parents were placed throughout history – it had been enough that they were. But now it seemed so obvious. They were always present at huge moments, events so big that even Clove – who had never really been interested in history – had heard of them. How had she not realized it sooner?

"The bacteria," Clove said, eventually. "When they stopped the bacteria being released, that was them saving the world again."

> The events of time-landscape 2039 and 2040 seem to be the
> latest in a long series of episodes in which the subjects
> have provided aid to humanity.

She blew out her breath. "Powerful. And I thought human beings were insignificant in the grand scheme of things."

> Apparently these particular human beings are not insignificant.
> I believe the same can be said of you.

Clove ignored Spart's suggestion that she was special. She didn't understand why he kept saying that. "What about now?" she asked. "What's happening now? Why are they here?"

Spart took a second to answer.

> According to the records, subject "KATHERINE FINCHLEY" died
> protecting COLONEL DURAND at a meeting during the siege
> of Carlisle. Subject "MATTHEW GALLOWAY" continued to help
> support the defence of Carlisle after her death. The subjects
> sacrificed themselves to help the cause, once again.

"Why? Why would this time be important to history?"

> They must have contributed enough to the defence to make sure
> that England was not defeated during the Uprising.

"But Matthew's Scottish," Clove said. "Why would he help the English?"

> I presume we will find out imminently.

It was all so unbelievable. Her parents were superheroes.

"But how did my parents know to do this stuff?" Clove sighed, and ran her hands through her hair, overwhelmed. She stared down at the screen of the DNA kit, at the record for Matthew Galloway's criminal history and the words THREAT LEVEL: **HIGHEST**. "Why is this happening to *my* parents? What's so special about them?"

CHAPTER 19

Saturday 16 November 1745

A local woman and volunteer by the name of Katherine Finchley was regrettably killed today in a round of musket fire following a disagreement with the militia, who refused to continue to guard the castle against the Rebels. Her life was given to protect mine, and for that I will never forget her.

Her companion, Matthew Galloway, who was present at the scene, was unable to save Miss Finchley. He was greatly upset by this, and has scarcely left my side since in an attempt to ensure that her life was not given in vain to our cause.

I, being equally affected by the loss of the local woman, of course reassured him that I had no intention of surrendering. We must honour her memory. No more innocent blood will be shed.

```
Folios/v1/Time-landscape-1745/MS-12
```

```
File note: Diary entry of COLONEL DURAND during the 1745
          Jacobite Uprising. The entry concerns subjects
          "KATHERINE FINCHLEY" and "MATTHEW GALLOWAY". It
          was recorded before CLOVE's arrival in 1745. See
          Folios/v1/Time-landscape-1745/MS-12-alt for the
          diary entry as recorded after CLOVE's visit to 1745
```

Carlisle, England, 1745

When Clove finally went back downstairs after testing Matthew's DNA, she was relieved to find that he had gone to change into dry clothes. Mrs Samson scolded her for disappearing halfway through making breakfast and put Clove to work in the wash-house doing laundry.

"Did you find the ingredients which you need for your spell?" Ella asked, as she arrived an hour later with another load of dirty clothes for Clove.

"I did. It's all done. Thanks for your help," Clove said, trying to hide how out of breath she was from the pummelling of undergarments. *Barbaric.*

Ella deflated. "I was hoping you would wait for me. I wanted to watch."

"Sorry."

"Did it work?"

Clove paused a beat too long before nodding.

"It worked, but you aren't happy with the result?" Ella guessed.

Clove shrugged. "It's just… I don't really know what to do now."

"I can help with that." As she spoke, Ella dipped a hand into Clove's bucket of fresh water and flicked her with it.

Clove leapt back, but the freezing cold water still splashed her arm. "Hey!" she said, trying to be serious, but she couldn't help the way her mouth just wanted to smile. She ducked her head, giving in to the urge to grin.

When she looked back up, Ella's expression took her

by surprise. She looked … awestruck. Like she couldn't believe what she was seeing, when what she was seeing was Clove. Just Clove. No one had ever looked at her like that before.

"What?" Clove asked, a little defensively.

"Nothing," Ella said. "It's just… I've never seen you smile before." She sounded winded.

Clove swallowed hard, her laughter dying in her throat. It was true that she had been very stressed recently. But surely she had smiled before? She couldn't remember, right now, when Ella was looking at her like that.

Flustered, Clove flicked her hand into the water. Ella skittered away and let out a giggle.

Clove chased her out of the wash-house and across the lawn. But by the time she had cornered the girl by the kitchen door, all that was left of her attack was two damp palms. She pressed them to either side of Ella's neck as she tried to squirm away.

Ella winced at the coldness of the water on her skin. The two girls were standing so close that Clove could see droplets of water clinging to Ella's collarbone and the goosebumps standing up on her neck. Ella's cap had come off and her hair was falling out of its bun again, messy spirals curling off in all directions.

There was a moment when they just stared at each other, breathing in unison. Clove felt like every molecule of her skin was alert and attuned to Ella's movements. Something had snapped their bickering into a meaningful tension. She parted her lips. If she just leant a little closer, if Ella just tilted her head a little to the right, then—

Ella stepped back. Then she lifted her arm, holding up Clove's bucket of water – which she must have grabbed before running out of the wash-house. Clove didn't have time to react before the water fell through the air in an iridescent arc, splashing Clove right in the chest.

It was so cold that Clove couldn't catch her breath to speak, and when she did all that escaped was helpless laughter. "Ella!" she gasped.

Ella was laughing so hard she nearly fell over. "Yes!" she screeched. "Got you!"

"I'm soaking wet!" Clove's bodice was drenched, and her skirts were rapidly darkening as the water spread. "I'm going to throw you in the pond," Clove threatened, tugging the damp fabric away from her skin.

Ella only laughed harder. "You look like a drowned cat! All bedraggled and furious."

Clove hissed at her, baring her teeth like an angry feline. "If I get a chill and die, it'll be all your fault." Clove held a hand to her forehead, letting out an overly long groan of pain, which turned into laughter when Ella jabbed her in the ribs.

"I think you will recover, Miss Tabbycat," Ella said. "Especially as the last time you were dying you managed to *wander off and escape me*."

"The salad days," Clove muttered, sighing to herself and leaning into Ella's side.

Ella tightened her arm around Clove's shoulder.

* * *

That evening Clove washed the plates from dinner. Outside, bats swooped: dark shadows that ducked and dived as they caught flies. The kitchen was warmly lit by the glowing fire, and still smelled of the bread Mrs Samson had baked for the next day. Clove put the last plate on the draining board and turned away from the sink. As she did so, she noticed Matthew sitting at the kitchen table.

"Oh!" Clove said, backing up until she hit the basin. She hadn't heard him come in.

"I think you need to tell me who you are, Anise," Matthew said.

She took a deep breath, preparing herself for the conversation to come. Then she said, "My name is actually Clove." She sat down at the kitchen table, brushing her hair away from her face, and tried to sound calm. "Clove Galloway."

He frowned, scratching his nose. "We're related?"

"Yes."

"How?"

Clove picked at a flake of something crusty on the table. "I'm the daughter of Katherine Finchley." She watched him carefully, waiting for any sign of recognition on his face. There was none.

"Who's that?" He tilted his head, staring at her with a blank expression.

How could he possibly not know who she was? They'd spent lifetime after lifetime together. "Your wife."

He flinched. "What?"

"You're going to marry her," Clove said, staring him

right in the eye. "You're going to marry Katherine Finchley and have a baby. You're going to call her Clove."

"What?" he repeated faintly.

"I'm your daughter. From the future," Clove said, leaning forwards on her elbows. "I know you know all of this. You don't have to pretend you don't."

Matthew leant backwards. "You have gone mad."

"I'm not mad. I travelled back in time from the future, so that I could meet you. You must ... you *must* know what's going on. It's impossible that you don't!"

"What are you talking about?" he asked, horrified. "You need to see a physician! There is something wrong with you."

"There's nothing wrong with me! I travelled through something called a wormhole, which is a kind of gap in the space-time landscape that connects two points in time. It's made by generating a lot of energy and causing an explosion. It's—" She stopped. She didn't need to explain any of this to him. He knew it already, surely. He must do.

But instead of saying, "Clove, it's so brilliant to meet you at last," Matthew stood up. He was pale. For some reason, her words had taken him by surprise. Had he not expected her to talk about time travel?

"You must know who I am!" Clove said. "You're Matthew Galloway, my father. In a few weeks, when the city is besieged, you and Katherine will ... will sacrifice yourselves in some way to the cause..." She trailed off. Matthew was looking at her as though she was mad.

"I do not understand anything you are talking about,"

Matthew said. "Who is Katherine? What in heavens does the Uprising have to do with me?"

Clove pulled her watch out of her pocket. "It's all here. Spart found out all about you and Katherine, and what you do in 1745." She tapped the screen and it lit up to reveal her locked screen – a selfie of Meg and Clove smiling at the camera. Clove and Matthew watched the large 20:37 tick over to 20:38.

Matthew dropped back into his seat like his strings had been cut. "What – what *is* that?" he cried.

"It's a computer," she said. "You must have seen one before." Why was he being so stubborn about this? Why not just admit that he knew who she was?

"That device sends people back to the past?" he asked, incredulous.

"Yes, exactly," she said, relieved. "Well, a bigger one does, but it's the same basic idea."

A message from Spart popped up on the screen.

> Hello, MATTHEW.

"It's a demon!" Matthew cried. "That thing. It's taken you under its spell, made you believe its lies. You aren't from the future – you can't be. You're just enchanted." Before she could stop him, he snatched the watch from her and threw it into the fire, where it fell between two burning logs and disappeared into the red-hot embers.

"No!" Clove cried out. "Don't!" She reached into the flames with her bare hands. Her mind was blank with panic. She didn't even notice the pain as the fire burned her.

She couldn't do this without Spart – she wouldn't last a day!

Matthew grabbed her elbows and pulled her back before she could rescue the watch. "Let it go," he said, voice cracking with fear. "Let me help you, Anise – Clove. Whatever your name is. You're going to be better now. Trust me. That … that demon was possessing you!"

Her watch glowed white-hot in the flames.

"Let me go, Dad, *please*."

In shock, he released her. "I'm not your father! Can't you see how senseless that is? We're the same *age*!"

Clove fell onto the hearth and grabbed the iron poker. She knocked her watch out of the flames, hands trembling. The computer hit the hearth, sparking on the tiles.

"It had you under its spell," Matthew repeated. "It had you crazed."

"It didn't," she sobbed. "You don't understand."

She touched the screen, frantic to see if it was broken, but it was too hot. Without her watch, she was lost. Without it, she couldn't talk to Spart, or— Oh God. She couldn't get home! If she didn't have the watch, she had no way of contacting Spart-in-the-lab in 2056, and so no way of getting back to the future. Clove burst into frustrated tears. She was stuck here for ever.

For ever.

"That thing still has hold of you," Matthew said. "It's going to kill you. I can see it in your face. You can't let it control you like this."

"You've destroyed it already," Clove said, gasping. She couldn't seem to stop crying. Her whole body hurt, and she couldn't draw breath properly. Her chest felt tight, like she was having a heart attack. She pushed out one long breath, drawing it back in as slowly as she could.

Matthew was still watching her in horror.

"Can you get me some water?" she asked when she felt a bit steadier.

"Water will make you ill. I'll get you some ale." Matthew fetched some from the pantry.

Clove drank it, breathing in and out, until she felt calm again. She wiped away her tears. By then, the watch had cooled enough for her to touch it. Cautiously, she tried to turn it on. The screen stayed black. This had never happened to her before. She had no idea how to fix it. All of those hours she'd spent studying programming were worthless in the face of a problem with the hardware.

Clove tried to remember whether watches could survive high heats, but her mind was blank. She thought that they must be able to – they were solar powered, after all.

"Do you want me to fetch someone?" Matthew asked, touching her forehead as if checking her for fever. "You need help."

Clove shook her head. She was so confused. Matthew seemed to know nothing about the future role he was to play. What if he decided that she was insane and took her to a doctor? By discussing this with Matthew she was risking more than she had realized. Who knew what the doctors here would do to her, if they thought she was crazy? They might even put her in an insane asylum – or burn her for witchcraft, like Ella had mentioned.

"Please," she said. "I promise I won't cause any trouble, or whatever you think I'm going to do. Just – just don't call anyone. I … I just need to rest."

He stared at her for a long time. "What if you hurt yourself?" he said finally. "I can't risk it. You need help."

"I don't! I'm fine!" She tried to lower her voice, which was getting increasingly frantic. "Nothing is going to happen. Please!"

He didn't look convinced.

"If Spart really is a demon, then you've killed him, right?" Clove said. "It should just wear off, shouldn't it? The spell. If there's a demon, you've saved me from it. I don't need help."

Matthew rubbed his forehead. "I don't know what is happening any more. I need time to think. I can't decide anything now."

CHAPTER 20

<u>Clove Sutcliffe</u>'s infamous first journey to 1745 would go on to inspire her later work as a <u>History Revisionist</u>. She ran into issues early on, and struggled to recover command of a situation which very quickly spiralled out of control.

Her actions would later motivate her to create the first and most important of the <u>Cardinal Rules of History Revision</u>, now recited by children in nurseries everywhere:

> *Time and space are complex*
> *and vast,*
> *So to roam freely in the past,*
> *To this one rule you must consent:*
> *Tell no fact to those present,*
> *Or however far you venture,*
> *Never shall you find your future.*

File note: Extract from *An Unauthorized Biography of Clove Sutcliffe*, first published in 2344

Carlisle, England, 1745

Clove turned the dead watch over in her hands, the rainbow strap flopping back and forth. She scrubbed at the blackened screen with her nails, trying to clean off the soot marks. The battery had been charging constantly for over twenty-four hours and her watch was still dead. Clove didn't know what else to do. Nothing she did could make it switch on.

She had always – *always*, for her entire life – had a computer to help her do anything she wanted. Any question she had, she just had to ask and it was answered. Any help she needed, it was given before she had the chance to think about it. Now that she was completely alone, she realized how much she relied on her watch. Worst of all, if she couldn't work out how to fix it, then she would be stuck in the past for ever.

She would never be able to go home.

She would never see Jen or Tom or Meg again.

Her parents would think she had vanished without a trace. They would never find out what had happened to her.

This was such a mess. Especially as she hadn't solved anything with Matthew at all. Did he really not know anything about Katherine or time travel? Would Katherine know more, if Clove ever found her?

Trying to hold back her tears, Clove rested her head on the windowpane and stared down at the garden below. If only she could manage to *think*, just try and work out how to fix her watch – but her brain felt full of syrup. She couldn't wade through the hysteria to find a solution.

She had nothing. Nothing but her own mistakes and failures, weighing her down.

The next day, Clove finally met Katherine Finchley. Her grandmother had died, and Katherine had come to live at the house in Carlisle. She had arrived late the night before and gone straight to bed. Clove only found out she was there when she was told to help her dress for breakfast.

Katherine Finchley was sitting at her dressing table, staring blankly at her own reflection in the mirror. Clove stood in the doorway and looked at the back of her head, trying to slow the frantic beating of her heart. If Matthew's DNA results were anything to go by, then this was her mother.

Clove walked across the room, aware of every movement she made. "Good morning, Miss Finchley," she said. She tried to keep her voice level, but it came out smaller than she had been expecting. "I'm Anise. Your – your maid."

Katherine didn't move. Her hair was a tangle of knots, long left unbrushed. There were dark shadows under her eyes and hollows under her cheekbones. She was aching for her lost grandmother – so much so that she didn't recognize her own daughter, right in front of her. Or at least Clove hoped that was the reason. Surely Katherine had to know the truth, even if Matthew didn't?

Clove swallowed. "Shall I help you dress?"

Katherine inclined her head, just a little.

Clove tried to stop her hands trembling with nervous

energy. She took a dress from the wardrobe and helped Katherine to stand. She moved her limbs wherever Clove pushed them, like a puppet. She didn't even seem to register the touch.

Clove was desperate for Katherine to look at her, but she couldn't see anything past her own grief. Would she recognize her? Clove had already decided that she wouldn't tell Katherine what she'd told Matthew. She couldn't risk getting the same reaction.

When she was dressed, Katherine opened her mouth, lips pulling apart with an audible sound. "Thank you," she said, after a pause.

"It's my pleasure, Miss. Is there anything else I can do for you?"

Katherine shook her head, with a slight delay. "No, thank you." She closed her eyes, opened them again, and Clove saw the visible effort it took to summon the energy to step outside her bedroom.

Clove watched her for a moment and then looked at the strand of hair she'd palmed while helping Katherine dress. Getting it had been a lot easier this time, but she didn't really need it. She already knew what the DNA would tell her: this was her mother.

Later that day, Clove was scrubbing at more of the endless laundry and thinking about Katherine and Ella and her watch and Katherine-and-Matthew and Ella again, when Matthew appeared. Clove could feel him examining her as he leant against the door to the wash-house, and this time he actually seemed to take in how similar they looked. It was the first time since her outburst that he'd acknowledged her. She'd lost hope of him ever talking to her again. But at least he hadn't called the exorcist.

"It's her, isn't it?" he said. "The one you said I—"

"Yes," she said, semi-casually, and not casually at all. "It's her." She tried to keep the hope out of her voice. Maybe now he was finally going to admit to knowing what Clove had been talking about. Clove still hadn't given up hope, although she realized it was ridiculous.

"You have her eyes," he said. His gaze roved over her face. His skin was deathly pale, like he was looking at a ghost. "You have my nose, and her eyes."

Clove pushed her hair back behind her ears. "You've met her?"

He nodded shortly. "Her aunt, Mrs Finchley, took her to the dressmaker's. I drove them there in the carriage. She's beautiful. And sad."

"You should talk to her," Clove said. "If you get the chance. I think she needs a friend."

Matthew didn't reply, just traced the tip of his shoes through the dirt in absentminded spirals. "You seem much calmer today. I'm sorry I upset you, by destroying your S–Spart." He stuttered over the unfamiliar word. "I only meant to help. You really will be better off free of him."

Clove sighed. "It isn't a demon like you think. But it's broken now anyway, so you don't have to worry about it any more. I've been trying to fix it, but I don't think I can. I can't exactly buy a replacement for anything broken."

Matthew's forehead wrinkled. "What do you mean, fix it? Have you been feeding him?"

"I don't need to. It gets energy from the sun – like plants."

"Like plants?" Matthew said. He seemed curious despite himself.

"The watch has plates. Like mirrors. They catch the sunlight and it collects the energy from the heat."

"Oh," Matthew said. "That sounds … very strange. Could the smoke from the fire have obstructed the light somehow?"

Clove frowned, thinking. "I'm not sure what the fire did." Maybe Matthew was right, though. Maybe the solar panels were blocked up with soot. The watch's screen had been black with ash and she'd had to scrape it clean. She hadn't thought to clean the solar panels inside, though. Perhaps that was why the watch wasn't working? Clove made a mental note to clean the solar panels later. She would have to find a way to take the casing off the back of the watch.

"About Katherine…" Matthew said, breaking into her thoughts. "Why do you think it would matter … if Katherine and I did … fall in love?" He said the words quietly, a dull pink curling up his throat.

As a servant, the idea of being in love with a gentlewoman must be close to treasonable for him, Clove realized. But now that he'd met her – and now that Clove had put the idea in his head – he seemed to be actually considering it.

"You both … you help save the world," Clove said.

"I know that sounds ridiculous, but you both help to make sure things work out the way they should. There are some big wars coming up, and you two make sure that they always end in the safest way for humanity."

Matthew stared at her blankly. "That is ... ridiculous. Why would you think that we make any difference to anything? I'm a servant. Is this what that ... that demon told you?"

"How I know is irrelevant." She didn't want him to start talking about Spart again. "You just need to know that you're clever and brave and you fight for what you believe in. And by doing so you save the world."

He frowned, shaking his head. "I don't – I don't understand this. It seems like a fairy tale you would tell small children. Not real life."

"It doesn't matter if you believe me," she said softly. "It's the truth."

Running a hand through his hair, Matthew stared out through the open doorway and across the garden. For a moment, there was a look in his eyes as if he was taking her seriously: a fleeting glimmer of passion as he imagined himself to be the hero she described. Then he shook his head and the look was gone.

"People like me don't save the world," he said, pushing his hands into his pockets as he walked away. "Not even with Katherine Finchley to help us."

CHAPTER 21

File note: Messages on social media, dated 14 December 2058

Carlisle, England, 1745

Any moment she could spare, Clove slipped away to the attic bedroom to work on her watch. Despite the hours she had spent attempting to open up the back, she couldn't get the screws to budge. To her dismay, the casing was completely unmovable. She was close to giving up. Even if she did get it open, what chance was there that she could clean the solar panels? It wasn't like she could get any spare parts. She dropped the watch back into its hiding place behind the pot of lavender and looked out of the window.

Matthew stood on the driveway below. The reins of a mare were loose in his hand as he talked to Katherine. Or rather, they weren't talking. They were staring at each other, not saying a word. His head was ducked towards her, even as she tilted her face to his. They were like magnets, drawn together.

They both seemed to glow around one another. For the first time, Clove could feel in her heart that this was right, that they were meant to be together.

Clove's mother hadn't just been an eighteen-year-old girl who had got pregnant in her first semester at university. Her parents' love story had been going on for centuries. It was inevitable. Together, they made everything around them blur and fade into insignificance. They were always meant to be in love, from one life to another.

The thought made Clove yearn for home even more. She wanted to find her birth parents in 2056, and she wanted to tell Jen and Tom that she loved them.

She had to fix her watch.

Clove heard footsteps in the corridor outside the attic room.

"Good morning," Ella said, coming into the room. She hooked her chin over Clove's shoulder, peering down at the view outside the window. "What do you think you're going to do to reconcile with Matthew, now that your spell has failed?"

Matthew had started showing Katherine how to feed the horse an apple: holding her hand delicately as he rearranged her fingers and placed the apple in the flat of her palm. Even from up here, Clove could tell he was doing a bad job of hiding his crush – but she could also see just how widely Katherine was smiling at him.

"Actually, I think my spell worked after all," Clove said, softly. Whatever she'd said to Matthew, it had clearly made a difference.

"Oh, that's good. Anyway, here, I brought you some breakfast," Ella said.

"Is that bacon?" Clove said, sniffing.

"Of course it is," Ella said with satisfaction.

As Clove ate, she thought about the enigma that was Ella. What could a girl in the eighteenth century possibly be doing, alone in a city? Searching for her family? A runaway lover? Buried treasure?

"Are you ever going to tell me why you're in Carlisle?" she asked.

There was a moment when Clove really thought Ella was going to answer, but then she shook her head. "Not yet."

Clove felt like she'd just failed a test without knowing she was taking it.

"I shouldn't worry about it, Clove," Ella said, tugging her hair out of its bun. "It's not very exciting – not even worth thinking about." She lay back on the bed. Her hair fanned out around her. It looked like it always did, as though she'd pushed her way backwards through four hedges while chasing a badger.

From the back she looked a little like Meg.

Clove missed Meg – except that she didn't, not really. She missed the old Meg, and how easy their friendship had been. She missed that cheerful, relaxed Meg, not the new, embarrassed one who wouldn't even answer her messages.

Clove missed her soft, wispy hair, her wide twinkly eyes, her easy smile. The wishbone necklace she always wore. But she was starting to realize just how much she had idolized Meg.

Now that she had some distance to get over her – centuries of it – she found she had been treating her as a figure of perfection, a dream girl. Clove had needed to take a step away so that Meg's perfection resolved into a real person instead of an angel, so that she could see her properly.

She was always going to wish that none of the mess with the kiss had happened, but at the same time she wouldn't have got over Meg without a catalyst like their kiss. And if there was still a chance for their friendship to recover when she went home – if Clove hadn't lost her best friend completely – then maybe the kiss had been a good thing. Maybe.

"Come on," Ella said. "Mrs Samson has asked us to purchase some flour. She has used up all of her supplies."

Clove nodded. It was a lovely day – perfect for a walk into town.

They walked home from the bakery with butter running down their chins. A boy had been selling steaming muffins from a tray outside the shop, each one glistening with melted butter. When Ella had seen Clove staring at them, she had asked the boy a series of questions about the cooking process, and then apparently satisfied that they were of suitable quality, had bought them one each.

Clove was getting the impression that Ella took food very seriously indeed.

As they walked past the row of shops, taking it in turns to carry the bag of flour, Clove had an idea. Maybe one of the shops here would contain something that could open the casing of her watch. Even just a better screwdriver than the one in Tom's Swiss army knife might be enough to make a difference.

She read the names of the shops off the painted signs that dangled above their doors, looking for anywhere which might sell tools, or... Her brow furrowed as she considered the problem. Would a magnet help? She vaguely remembered something about magnetic screwdrivers being used to open devices. A magnet might help her to turn the metal screws on her watch.

How would she find a magnet, here in 1745?

Didn't they use magnets in compasses? Was that right? She could find a compass, surely? Were compasses household objects? Would she be able to buy one, or did they only have them on ships? Did she have enough money for a compass?

"Ella, do you know where I could find a compass?"

Ella stopped humming what Clove could have sworn was a Disney tune and wrinkled her nose thoughtfully. "I'm not sure. There might be an old lodestone in a curiosities cabinet in a shop somewhere."

"A lodestone?"

Ella looked at Clove, and then grinning, reached over to wipe the butter off her chin. "It's kind of..." She paused, obviously trying to find the right words. "It's a big rock that turns due north if it's dangled from a string. Like a really old-fashioned compass."

Clove felt hope bubble in her chest for the first time in days. It sounded like a lodestone was a natural magnet – a rock that was magnetic. She could use that.

Ella led them to a nearby pawnbroker's. Inside, it was dark, gloomy and crammed full of odd ornaments, lamps and paintings. If Clove hadn't been in such a rush, she would have liked to investigate some of the more intriguing objects, like an intricately carved ivory ball with another ivory ball inside, and a ship in a bottle. There was even a shrunken head hanging from the ceiling above the counter.

Clove cleared her throat to get the pawnbroker's attention. He pushed up a pair of wire spectacles, balancing them on his forehead so he could better frown at Clove. "Yes?" he asked.

"I'd like to buy a lodestone," Clove said.

His wiry eyebrows rose. "A lodestone? Are you going to sea?"

"Not exactly," Clove said. "I just need one. For … reasons."

"Reasons," he repeated, bemused. "What could two maids want with a lodestone?" The pawnbroker's eyebrows didn't seem sure whether they should be raised or lowered.

"It's for our master," Clove said, thinking quickly.

"Well, I believe I have one or two somewhere."

He walked into the back of the shop, returning a moment later with a linen-wrapped bundle, which he unravelled to reveal a rough black rock attached to a piece of string.

When Clove pulled a kirby grip out of her hair and touched it to the rock, a small force tugged on the grip. It was magnetic. She took the string and held the rock up, and it twisted in the direction Ella was standing. Clove could relate. An arrow painted on the side showed that the rock pointed north.

"I'll take it," Clove said, barely able to stop herself jumping up and down in delight. She could use the lodestone to magnetize the screwdriver attachment on her Swiss army knife. It would be easy enough to do – she'd seen Tom do it. Rubbing a magnet up and down along a screwdriver would make it magnetic too.

"Well, he was interesting," Clove said, as they walked down the street.

"I liked him," Ella said, swinging her arms like she hadn't a care in the world. "He reminded me of you."

Clove huffed out a half-outraged, half-amused sigh. "If you say because of the eyebrows, I swear..."

Ella laughed. "No. Because he has the same no-nonsense *I have more important things to do than waste my time here with you* attitude as you."

Clove opened her mouth, and closed it again. "Am I really like that?"

"Not any more," Ella admitted. "You were at first. I think you've warmed to me."

"I'm sorry," Clove said, her words coming out softer

than she wanted. "I was just too focused on other things to pay attention. It wasn't you."

"I know," Ella said, lightly. "I've got your attention now, anyway." Her gaze snagged Clove's. Suddenly there was an intangible tug of tension between them. It made Clove's heart thud so loud that she could hear it in her eardrums.

Ella was so caring and considerate, so boldly interesting. Yesterday, Clove had caught her reading a book in Latin, and when she'd questioned her about it, she'd just said that she was studying classical history, as if it was no big deal. Ella was mysterious and lovely and Clove just wanted to keep her for ever.

She felt the urge to press her fingers to Ella's palm or wrist, cup her elbow, her waist or the small of her back. Clove could write a book of the ways Ella deserved to be touched. Instead Clove folded her arms across her own stomach, and just looked at Ella in the way she wished she could touch her – slow and gentle, never-ending.

After a long moment, Ella broke the eye contact. Clearing her throat, she asked, "What do you need the lodestone for, anyway?"

"Another spell," Clove said, thinking fast.

"Oooooh." Ella smirked. "How shall I know if this one works? Will you disappear in a puff of smoke?"

Clove huffed. "Something like that."

"What – really?"

"Fingers crossed I'll disappear without any smoke."

A sad look crossed Ella's face. "Well, I shall hope for my sake that you aren't a very good witch."

They were both silent the rest of the way home. Thinking about leaving Ella made Clove a little bit less eager to fix her watch. It was ridiculous. It wasn't like they could... This was the *eighteenth century*. And did Ella even want to?

But if Clove left, then she would never see Ella again. She wouldn't be able to message her for a chat at 2 a.m. to see how she was doing with her Latin, or finish teaching her how to knit properly (Ella was terrible at it).

Clove wanted to wrap Ella up like a precious treasure. She wanted to unravel all of her mysteries and decode her enigmas. She wanted so many things when she was around Ella.

CHAPTER 22

From: Ella <ella-is-swell@walker.com>
To: Clove <luckyclover@sutcliffe.com>
Subject: EXAM SEASON BLUES (the title of my first album)
Date: 3 January 2059 17:54:48 GMT

Clove,

Look, I know we're technically ~fighting~ and everything, but my exams start tomorrow and I'm sad and tired and I haven't talked to you in three days and that sucks, so I'm calling a truce. Plus, I only know half of my Latin conjugations and I am so D O N E with revision that I'd rather talk to a Clove-who's-mad-at-me than no Clove at all.

I'm sorry. I should never have forced you to go to the NYE party with me. I *know* you don't like parties. I know that. But I had all of these plans for what I was going to do and say at midnight and it was going to be so powerfully romantic. I thought I could persuade you to enjoy yourself anyway.

I'm really sorry you had a crappy night. I should have listened to you. I'm pushy and bossy and I do things without telling you about them because I think I know best. (Which is so stupid because you're one million times cleverer than me.)

I know you hate it when I do stuff without asking you first. We had enough of that in 1745. I really should have learned my lesson by now.

Look, we're never going to agree on everything. You're always going to find it annoying that I take endless selfies and believe in aliens even though I've never met any (yet). I'm never going to understand how you can spend all your time at a computer without wanting to go outside for a bit, or why you would rather stew in your feelings instead of talking through problems with me. (Or why you bite your nails – it's such a bad habit.)

We're going to argue. That's how this works. That's what makes it real. If it was easy, it wouldn't be us, would it?

Ella xx

File note: Email from ELENORE WALKER to CLOVE SUTCLIFFE, dated 3 January 2059

Carlisle, England, 1745

After they had finished their work for the day, Clove and Ella went up to their room. Clove wanted to start trying to fix the watch immediately, and Ella said she had some reading to do.

Clove sat on her bed with her back to Ella, who sat by the window to pore over something ancient and probably Latin. When Clove had asked why she was learning a dead language, Ella had just laughed, and said that it being *dead* was a matter of perspective. Ella didn't make sense, sometimes.

With Ella intent on her book, Clove got down to work by the light of a flickering candle. She rubbed the lodestone up and down the length of the screwdriver to magnetize the metal. Then she tested it against the watch's screws, using the screwdriver to turn them in their sockets. Slowly, they slid free. It had worked! Clove carefully took out the screws. Holding her breath, she pulled away the back cover of the watch.

The insides looked fine. There didn't seem to be any detached elements, or melted wires on the circuit boards. So why wasn't it working? Clove didn't know what to do. She had hoped there would be an obvious problem – something she would be able to fix easily.

Tears rose in her eyes. She was never going to get home. Sighing, she forced herself to be calm. She was just tired. Maybe she'd be able to see the problem if she looked again in the morning.

As Clove was slotting the cover back into place, she noticed that the reverse sides of the solar panels were covered in soot. She remembered that Matthew had actually suggested that soot might be the problem. If the panels were dirty, then maybe they couldn't charge. Holding the watch up to the candle so that she could see better, Clove scraped at the soot with her nail. She didn't want to risk using a knife in case she damaged the glass. Eventually some of the black sediment rubbed off.

After scratching away as much of the dirt as she could, she replaced the cover. Hopefully when she next left the watch in the sun, it might actually charge.

"What are you doing?" Ella asked, looking over at her. She'd stopped reading and was brushing her hair.

Clove dropped the watch into her lap. "Nothing."

"Well, if you're doing nothing, would you brush my hair for me, please? There's a knot in the back that I can't get to."

"Of course," Clove said and surreptitiously slid the watch onto the windowsill to charge in the sun when it rose the next day. Maybe tomorrow she would finally be able to go home.

The next day, Katherine smiled – actually *smiled* – at Clove when she was helping her to dress. She was blooming, all because of her new relationship with Matthew.

Clove wandered downstairs in a bit of daze. When she'd come to 1745, she had been hoping to find out the truth about how identical versions of her parents seemed to reappear at key points in history. She'd never really considered the idea that they'd been in love in each time period, or that she would be able to *watch them* fall for each other. It was strange, and slightly uncomfortable.

She needed to speak to Matthew again. She needed to make sure that he understood what part he and Katherine would play in saving the city. Clove felt that she'd made some headway the other day, and Matthew could hardly deny a connection with Katherine now. Surely that would help him to believe her?

She found him in the stables, buckling a bridle onto one of its antsy residents. He froze when he saw Clove. Clearly he was still unsure about her. Clove didn't blame him. If he really knew nothing about his reincarnation, then what Clove had told him would be almost impossible to believe.

"You've been spending a lot of time with Katherine recently," she said, after checking to make sure that they were alone. She didn't bother with any small talk. There didn't seem to be any point. She'd already decided that focusing on his connection to Katherine was the best way to get him to at least partly believe what she was telling him about the future.

He swallowed. "I have."

"And? Has it made you change your mind about me?"

Matthew scratched at the underside of his jaw, thinking. "I believe that you speak the truth when you say that I will one day fall in love with Katherine Finchley, which means that you must have some insight of the future, either as a clairvoyant or … or by some other magic. I cannot find a way to believe anything else that you say, however. How could you, a girl of my own age, be my daughter? How could a person traverse time from the future? It's impossible."

Clove decided not to argue. As least he had stopped thinking that she was possessed or crazy. The important thing now was to talk to him about the siege.

"I came to talk to you about the Uprising," she said.

Matthew's eyebrows had risen. "Why do you want to talk about the Rebels?"

Clove took a massive risk. "During the Uprising, you and Katherine are going to help to defend the city."

Matthew's face softened when she said Katherine's name, and then she saw her words sink in. "We *defend* the city? Against the *Scottish*?"

"Yes," Clove replied firmly, realizing once and for all that Matthew had no idea of the part he and Katherine would play in the future of Carlisle. He knew nothing about his other lives. Impossible, perhaps, but somehow true.

"But ... I want Scottish independence," he said, confused. "I'm not going to help the English. I want a Scottish king."

"No," Clove said. "The English win. The English need to win. It wouldn't be good for Scotland to win right now."

"Scotland has to remain under English control," Matthew said, contemplating this. "You believe this is important enough that I should risk my life to ensure it occurs?"

"Not your life," Clove reassured him. "You don't die. Katherine dies defending the city during the siege, but you live longer." Clove had spoken without thinking, and she could tell from the look on Matthew's face that it had been a mistake.

"What?" he said, hoarsely. "Katherine *dies*? No. *No!*"

"She dies for a good cause," Clove said. It was a weak excuse and it clearly didn't make Matthew feel any better.

"She can't die!" he cried. "Not when ... not when..." He trailed off.

He had only known Katherine for a few days, and yet Matthew was already in love with her. Clove realized she had approached this conversation all wrong.

"But Katherine dies *defending* Carlisle," she said, trying to think of a way to make it better. Surely if she explained it properly, he would see that it had to happen? That it was a sacrifice for the future of humanity. "Katherine makes sure that the city doesn't surrender to the Rebels. That's very important. She's a hero!"

"But she's still going to die. Can't you use your powers to save her? She has to survive!"

Clove paused. He looked so determined. She didn't know how to tell him that whatever he did, Katherine would die over and over and over throughout history, and so would he. They met, saved the world and died young. Always. He couldn't change what happened. Even if he wanted to, he shouldn't. "No, Matthew. That's not how it works."

"I can't let her die. Not when she doesn't have to. What do I do? *Tell me what to do!*"

"Matthew – I can't. You absolutely *can't* change what

happened." Clove felt panicked. Had she made a huge mistake telling Matthew about the future? "Katherine dies to protect future generations. If she doesn't, then the world I live in would be completely different. I might not even be *alive*."

Matthew's eyes filled with agony. He turned away from her. Eventually, he nodded. The muscles in his shoulders were tight. "I understand," he said, but Clove could tell that he was lying. He led the horse outside and tied it to a hook on the wall.

Clove followed him, blinking in the bright sunlight. Matthew kept his face ducked away from her, not letting her see his expression. There was a dampness on his cheeks like he'd been crying.

Clove intensely regretted telling Matthew about Katherine's death. He was going to interfere, and who knew what would happen then?

"Matthew, promise me that you won't stop Katherine from helping with the siege. I really mean it. If she doesn't help, it could change everything. It's very, very important that England defeats the Rebels."

Anything could happen if Matthew changed the course of the siege. It could impact the entire future for the next three hundred years. The consequences of a small adjustment would ripple through time like a tidal wave.

"I promise," he replied firmly. "I won't stop her. She can help."

"Good," Clove said. She still didn't quite believe him. She wished that Spart was here to tell her what to do.

Clove paused. Should she tell Matthew any more about the future? She thought for a few moments and then decided that she'd already told him so much, telling him a bit more couldn't really make a difference.

Spart had sent her lots of documents about the war, and she tried desperately to remember what they had said. "It's really important that Carlisle hold off the Rebels for as long as possible. After that, the Rebels will have to fight off the English Army, and they will eventually be defeated at the Battle of … Culloden – but that's still months away. For now, you just need to make sure that Carlisle defends itself for as long as possible."

"When is Carlisle attacked?"

"In a few months. That's the beginning of the Rebels' downfall."

"There is still a long way to go until victory," Matthew pointed out.

"Yes, but the attack is the first step," Clove replied. "After that everything that happens is important."

"What do we do?"

"Nothing, yet. You only need to act when the siege happens. That's when you can change things."

"So we wait?" Matthew asked, sounding a little disappointed. Clove had the impression that he wanted to start fighting immediately, to protect the woman he loved.

"Yes." She was about to warn him again that he couldn't change what happened, but then she caught sight of someone standing in the doorway of the stable. It was Katherine.

Oh, oh *no*. What had she overheard? Katherine was looking at her properly for the first time, and Clove felt her skin heating up. Why was Katherine staring at her? Did she know who she really was? Did she know Clove was her daughter from the future?

"Sorry," Katherine said, her voice trembling. "Did I interrupt?"

Clove stared at her for a second or two. There was nothing on Katherine's face to indicate that she recognized Clove or suspected what they had been talking about. They might have got away with it. But Clove was a terrible liar. She would leave Matthew to deal with the explanations. Without a word, Clove dipped into a curtsey to Katherine, and went quickly back to the house.

She heard Matthew say, "No. It's quite all right. That was my cousin," in a carefully light-hearted voice. Clove was relieved. His voice had sounded normal. No one would suspect that only minutes before, he had heard news that had left him heartbroken.

Clove returned to her chores consumed with worry. Everything she did here had the potential to change the future. What if her conversations with Matthew were never meant to happen at all? Had she made a difference to the past? Had she altered the future?

CHAPTER 23

Voice message left by <u>Clove Sutcliffe</u> **at** <u>13:29</u> **on** <u>4 January 2059</u>:

Hey … I guess you're in a class or something. I got your message. I hate fighting with you too. And obviously I forgive you. I was never really that mad at you.

This was all completely different to 1745 or 2040 or whatever anyway. It's not a big deal. I probably made it sound like I was angrier than I was. I'm sorry if you've been worrying. It was nice, the surprise party.

I just … [loud exhalation] I hate when you make plans without telling me. I like to be in control. You're very impulsive and mysterious – and I like that about you! It just takes a lot of getting used to. Especially when I don't know what's going on.

Obviously I've never, like … I've never done any of this relationship stuff before. I know I can be too harsh. I don't know… I feel like this was my fault.

Anyway… I'm meeting Meg for lunch, so talk to you soon? We can discuss your many, <u>many</u> feelings about aliens then. [brief laugh]

Oh and … I don't find it annoying that you're always taking selfies. It would be pretty hypocritical of me if I did, seeing as I'm using one of your selfies as the lock screen on my watch.

I miss you. Bye.

File note: Voice message left for ELENORE WALKER from CLOVE
         SUTCLIFFE on 4 January 2059

Carlisle, England, 1745

The next day Clove went about her work in a daze. At the first opportunity, she escaped upstairs as quickly as possible. As she headed to her room, she caught sight of Katherine crossing the hall below and was reminded of how oddly she had acted when Clove had gone to her room that morning.

Katherine had been brushing her hair at the dressing table when Clove had arrived.

"You asked for this, Miss?" Clove had said, holding out a package of Matthew's clothes for Katherine to wear at the castle. Katherine had told Matthew the night before that she wanted to help build up the city's defences. Clove had been relieved to hear it. It meant she hadn't accidentally changed the past – at least not yet.

"Oh! Yes, thank you." Katherine had taken the package, smiling at the pheasant feather that Matthew had tucked into the knot.

"Will there be anything else?" Clove had asked, ducking her head to hide a grin. Her parents were so sweet.

Katherine had run her fingers along the feather, deliberately not looking at Clove. "Have you had any news of the Jacobites?" she had asked.

Clove had tried not to frown. Katherine's tone was too carefully casual. Besides, why would she come to Clove for news ... unless she had heard something of her conversation with Matthew yesterday?

"I haven't, no."

"What – what do you think of the rebellion? Do you think it has any chance of success?"

"I don't really know much about it, Miss."

"Oh, really? I thought I heard you discussing it with the coachman." Katherine's voice had turned sharp, fast.

Clove had realized, slightly amused and concerned, that Katherine was suspicious of Matthew. Did she really think he was a Rebel? Clove hadn't known what to say. Every time she opened her mouth she only seemed to make things worse. She had done the only thing she could think of, which had been to excuse herself and run from the room.

She sighed now. She really hoped she hadn't broken the future. As she entered the room she shared with Ella, she caught sight of a flashing light coming from behind the flowerpot on the windowsill. Her heart jumped into her throat. Her watch! It was working again!

Clove almost cried with relief when she turned it on and Spart's typical greeting of HELLO CLOVE appeared on the screen.

"Spart!" she exclaimed, her voice cracking. "I can't even explain how good it is to see you."

> I believe I feel the same in reference to yourself. What has happened since—

> CLOVE, I am picking up a radio signal.

> It's a message. The communication is broadcasting on a loop.

"What? What does it say?"

> It's from me. To be specific, the message is from the copy of
  my program which you left on the time machine's hard drive
  in the laboratory at the University of St Andrews in 2056.

> SPART-LAB must be sending the radio signal through the
  wormhole to 1745 and broadcasting it on a loop to make sure
  I pick up the message.

> Message reads:

  CLOVE SUTCLIFFE COME HOME AM RUNNING OUT OF MEMORY CANNOT
  CONTROL WORMHOLE MUCH LONGER SPART

  CLOVE SUTCLIFFE COME HOME AM RUNNING OUT OF MEMORY CAN NOT
  CONTROL WORMHOLE MUCH LONGER SPART

  CLOVE SUTCLIFFE COME HOME AM RUNNING OUT OF MEMORY CAN NOT
  CONTROL WORMHOLE MUCH LONGER SPART

"We have to go! Now! If you're running out of memory
then I could be stranded!" Just the thought made Clove
frantic. She had to go home. *Now.* She couldn't stay here,
not if it would be for ever. She'd had enough time to
consider the consequences of that happening. She knew
she couldn't do it.

Clove began throwing her belongings into her bag. "Is
the message still running? He's still there?" she asked,
buckling her watch onto her wrist.

> It's still broadcasting. I have sent a radio message back
  to tell SPART-LAB our coordinates, so that he can open the
  wormhole here immediately. I'm scanning for a reply now.

> You should hurry. If SPART-LAB runs out of storage then he can't operate the wormhole to bring you home.

"I'm going. Give him the coordinates for the stables. There'll be enough room for the wormhole to open there without anyone seeing it – and I need to talk to Matthew before I leave." She had seen Matthew at lunch, when she had warned him that Katherine was suspicious that he might be a Rebel, but there was still so much she wanted to say to him.

When Clove burst through the stable door, Matthew was feeding the horses. He looked up at her in surprise, his eyes widening. "Clove? What are you wearing?"

"Matthew, I need to go!" Clove exclaimed, panting from the run and already sweating in the radiation suit.

"Go? Where?"

"Home! I have to leave! It's an … it's an emergency!"

Matthew blinked at her. "Are you coming back?"

"I don't know." Clove checked her watch. The screen was still showing the message:

> … broadcasting to SPART-LAB …

"Probably not. I mean, it's really, really unlikely. I'm so sorry." Clove felt a sudden desperate urge to hug Matthew. "I'm so glad I met you. I wish we'd had longer to talk. I have so much to tell you. You will remember what I said, won't you? About not changing things? I don't know what will happen if you do."

"I promise," Matthew said.

Clove didn't entirely believe him. "I have to go," she repeated.

"Let me walk you to the gate," Matthew said.

"No, *now*, here."

Matthew just stared at her.

"You have to leave," she said. He couldn't be here, not when the wormhole opened.

"What? I thought *you* were leaving…" His words trailed off. The air in front of them had started to tremble.

"You promised me," Clove repeated urgently, watching the shimmering air. "Remember. Don't change anything."

"What *is* that—?" Matthew had gone pale.

"Goodbye," Clove said. The wormhole had appeared, and she could see a glimpse of the lab through it. She swallowed, and took a step towards it. "Promise me," she urged again. "Don't change *anything* about the future. You have to let Katherine die. That's what has to happen."

"I promise." Matthew forced the words out. He couldn't take his eyes off the wormhole.

Taking one last look at Matthew's shocked face, Clove put on the helmet and then stepped through the wormhole. The sky tilted into the ground. Her body was heavy and light and solid and liquid all at once, and then she landed with a crash on the floor of the lab, the air bursting from her lungs at the impact.

Matthew's last words echoed in her mind: *"I promise."* Clove wasn't sure she believed him.

CHAPTER 24

Ella—

I had to leave. I'm sorry, it's an emergency. I didn't have time to say goodbye.

I wish we'd been able to spend more time together. ~~I wish I didn't have to leave you behind~~

Thank you for all your help with everything. I don't know what I'd have done without you. ~~Meeting you was the best thing that's ever happened to me.~~ Don't get into too much trouble without me.

~~Love~~ Your friend,

Clove Sutcliffe

P.S. The scarf is a gift. It will suit you.

Folios/v1/Time-landscape-1745/MS-10

File note: Found in the servants' quarters of subject allocation "KATHERINE"'s home on 16 September 1745

UNIVERSITY OF ST ANDREWS CAMPUS, SCOTLAND, 2056

Clove let out a low groan and blinked away the glowing phosphenes from her eyes. Time travel didn't get more fun the second time around, apparently. Clove reached up to push off the suit's helmet. At least this part was easier, now that she wasn't under water.

Rolling onto her side, she noticed that the lab was empty. The security guard who had been chasing her was gone. How long had she been in 1745?

"What happened, Spart?" she asked the version of Spart that she'd left in the time machine's computer. "How have you run out of memory? Weren't you going to use the lab computer's hard drive for storage?" She wriggled out of the suit and stood up, grimacing. She'd forgotten how terrible the muscle ache was from time travel. She walked stiffly over to the desk to read Spart's message.

> I am unable to gain access to the hard drive to use its
  memory as we had planned. It is encrypted – presumably in an
  attempt to prevent the theft of valuable research.

> I didn't want to risk leaving you deserted if I ran out of
  memory, so I broadcast a radio message through the wormhole
  to SPART-WATCH and waited.

> I'm nearly at the storage limit. I deleted most of my non-
  essential functions.

"What time is it?"

> It has been twenty minutes since you left.

Twenty minutes! If she had only been gone that long in this timeline then she could get home without her parents missing her, even though she'd been in the past for seven days!

> I'm very curious to find out what you learnt. However, you
> should leave immediately. There's still a chance you might
> get caught. The security guard left to radio for help.

Clove blanched at the thought of being arrested. It was definitely not the way she wanted to end her adventure. After folding up the suit, Clove put it back in the trunk, then unhooked the memory card from the back of the computer.

After double-checking the lab for any other signs of her break-in, she opened the door. The corridor outside was dark. She blinked to adjust her vision and then walked up the stairs, listening for any noise. She made it to the ground floor, where the lights were on, and was about to walk down the hallway to the main entrance when she froze. The lights were automatic. If they were on, it meant someone had been walking around here very recently.

She could hear voices coming towards her.

"She just disappeared into the machine!" one said, sounding outraged. It must be the security guard.

"I'm sure she's just hiding, Sir," said another.

Hiding! That was a good idea. Clove looked about for a good spot. If she was quick she might be able to get inside one of the classrooms before they turned the corner and saw her – unless the door was locked. She would have to risk it.

She dived for the nearest door, and got inside just before the police officer and security guard turned the corner. She shut the door behind her and held her breath, listening to their footsteps go down the stairs to the lab in the basement. As soon as she heard the click of the lab door shutting behind them, she hurried out of the room and sprinted towards freedom.

She was finally going home. She was alive and she hadn't been caught. Everything had gone perfectly to plan. Clove tried to tell herself that she was happy about what had happened, but the images of Ella, to whom she'd never even said goodbye, and Matthew, whom she'd abandoned in the middle of everything, wouldn't leave her mind.

CHAPTER 25

> WANTED, two household maids for a small family, to clean part of the house, wash, iron and bake. Must have good Characters from places where they have served in the above capacity, and be good-tempered and cleanly.
>
> Due to the abrupt departure of two previous maids without an official resignation, this position must be filled promptly. Enquire to the Finchley family, Annetwell Street, Carlisle, without delay. No Scottish servants or Jacobite sympathizers need apply, regardless of whether they otherwise meet the above description.

Folios/v1/Time-landscape-1745/MS-11

File note: Advertisement posted in *The Carlisle Courier* on 18 September 1745

ST ANDREWS, SCOTLAND, 2056

Clove jerked awake, sending bath water splashing out of the tub and onto the floor. Someone was trying to open the bathroom door.

After she'd walked home from the university, she'd run a bath while eating a packet of smoky bacon crisps. Even though she had been exhausted, she had to wash before she could even think about going to sleep. She had been deprived of shampoo and shower gel for so long that she could *smell herself*. It wasn't pleasant. She had sunk into the warm water, letting herself drift into a contented doze, and fallen asleep.

"I'm in the bath!" she called out to the person outside. She was shivering. The water had gone cold.

There was silence.

"Who is this?" Tom said.

Clove sat up, bubbles dissolving into nothing around her. Her muscles had all seized up. She was seriously considering never time-travelling again, if she was always going to feel like death afterwards.

"It's me, Dad."

There was another silence.

"I'm sorry, I know it's late. Did I wake you? I have a headache," she explained. "I thought a bath might help." She was desperately trying to calculate what day it was now. Friday? Or wait, no, Spart said she had arrived back through the wormhole twenty minutes after she'd left. That must mean it was the early hours of Saturday.

"What are you doing in my house?" Tom said, and this time his voice was low and threatening.

"Dad?"

"Who is this? Let me in, right now."

"Dad? It's Clove."

Why was he being so weird? Climbing out of the bath, she reached for a towel. But where there was usually a neat stack of folded towels, there was nothing. Clove suddenly felt dislocated in her own bathroom. There were no towels anywhere – and now she was looking, there were none of her other things either.

Where were all her toiletries? Why was there——?

There was only one toothbrush on the sink.

Clove grabbed her clothes from her rucksack and pulled them on, trying not to panic. The room hadn't been like this when she'd arrived. When she'd cleaned her teeth before her bath, everything had been in its place.

She didn't know what any of this meant.

"Come out now," Tom said. "Or I'm breaking this door down. Whoever this is, I want you out of my house. Right now."

What was going on? Had her dad had a stroke or something? Had he forgotten who she was? Where was Jen?

"Dad, it's me, Clove," she said, opening the door.

Tom stood outside, his skin pale. "Whoever you are, you need to get out of my house right now." He sounded hoarse with something that she had thought was anger, but now realized was fear.

"Dad," Clove pleaded again, tears welling up in her eyes. "What's going on?"

"I don't know who you are, but you aren't my daughter. I don't have a daughter."

"Look, I know all those things I said yesterday sounded bad, but you're still my parents, even if I am adopted..."

"I've never had a daughter."

She had a flashback to Matthew, also denying that she was his daughter. It was almost funny that this kept happening to her, in a heartbreaking way.

"You... Where's Jen?"

"Jen?"

"Mum? Your ... your wife?"

"I don't have a wife," he said, flatly. At least he didn't sound angry any more. "I think you've got the wrong person. Do you need me to call the hospital? Are you injured? How did you get in here?"

"No wife?" she repeated hoarsely.

What was going on? What had happened while she was away? Clove wrapped her arms around her waist. She could feel herself shaking.

"Let me call someone for you, OK?" Tom said with concern. "You're clearly ... confused. We'll get you home to your family."

"But ... but *you* are my family..." Clove stammered.

What had happened while she was in the bath? Something had changed while she was asleep. Reality had ... shifted, somehow. Altered.

Clove suddenly had an urge to look outside. What if *everything* was different? Without a word, she pushed passed Tom and stumbled down the stairs. He called after her, but she ignored him.

She pulled open the front door, gasping as she caught sight of what was outside. The street, the one she'd grown up on, was unrecognizable. Everything had changed.

And it was her fault.

She'd destroyed the future.

PART
THREE

CHAPTER 26

The following items are banned on penalty of imprisonment:

• Anti-government propaganda

• Media promoting homosexuality

• Alcoholic and hallucinogenic substances

Folios/v8-alt/Time-landscape-2056-alt/MS-5-alt

File note: Pamphlet found in TOM GALLOWAY's rubbish bin on
          22 July 2056

ST ANDREWS, SCOTLAND, 2056

Clove was in an alien world. It was morning, but the sky was a dark, thick grey. The air was arid – she could feel the dust at the back of her throat when she inhaled. The flower gardens that used to fill her street had turned into dusty yards with barbed-wire fences and snarling dogs. The few trees that remained had brown, dry leaves. Every house was covered in graffiti, with boarded-up windows and security cameras.

And every sign was in Russian.

She could have sworn the world hadn't looked anything like this when she'd first got back to the house. She'd been tired, but surely she would have noticed such big changes? Whatever had happened, however she had messed up time, it must have taken a while for the changes to take effect.

She couldn't believe that so much was different. Surely *she* couldn't have done all this, just by visiting the eighteenth century for a single week? She felt something inside her collapse.

It had to have been her. She'd done this.

She turned back to Tom, open-mouthed. She was glad he still existed. He may no longer be her father, but at least she wasn't alone and adrift in this brutal new world.

"I can't let you walk home alone. The gangs—" He broke off. "It's not safe for a girl."

"I don't..." She stopped talking as she noticed the shrivelled body of a cat in the gutter. She put her hand over her mouth. This world was horrible. Broken glass littered the pavement, and a soldier marching past with his gun raised shouted at her to get back inside. Clove jumped. She swallowed a mouthful of bile. It tasted like dust.

"Come on," Tom said, "come in. It's curfew. We'll get into trouble. Let me call your parents." Tom's anger at finding an intruder in his house had turned into concern, which was somehow even worse. He was acting just like her father, as if he was still the man who had raised and loved her. But he wasn't, not any more. "At least come and have a cup of tea while you calm down. You've had a shock."

She let him lead her back into the house, one arm around her shoulders.

Inside, she noticed more things that had changed. Half the furniture was missing, and none of Jen's things were there – not her books or her paintings or her random gadgets. The walls were painted cream instead of colourfully wallpapered.

It was a ghost house, existing on without its occupants.

Tom cleared his throat. "I don't know where you even got it from, but you ... you should probably take that band off," he said, pointing to her watch strap. It was the rainbow-coloured one which he'd proudly given to her when she'd come out to him and Jen the year before.

"What?"

Tom averted his eyes. "You should know what will happen if you go around showing Pride like that. You'll be arrested."

She gaped at him.

"I don't know how you've survived this long."

Clove felt a hard, ugly knot twisting her gut. She'd never, ever felt ashamed of her sexuality. How had she managed to change the world so much that her own dad thought that she should hide who she was? How was her home now a place where it was illegal to be gay?

She had to fix this. Now. She needed to get away from her not-father, so she had time to think.

"Excuse me," she said, avoiding eye contact. "I need to use the bathroom."

"Well, you know where it is," he said, trying to be upbeat.

She turned her lips up in an imitation of a smile and then went upstairs, bypassing the bathroom to go to her bedroom – which was now apparently an office.

By the time the door was closed she found that she couldn't even breathe through the tightness in her chest. She wasn't going to have a panic attack. She wasn't.

"Spart, what's going on?" Her voice came out stronger and more authoritative than she'd expected. She was going to fix this. She could fight anything life threw at her, and she was going to win.

> History changed after your visit to 1745. I've been searching online, and it looks like the time-landscape diverged completely.

"But how is everything so different?! It looks like Russia has taken control of Scotland!"

> They have. Russia invaded the British Isles in 1855, after defeating the English in the Crimean War.

"What? How has that got anything to do with me? I didn't even go to the nineteenth century!"

> Your visit had a knock-on effect. Apparently, after you left 1745, the Jacobites seized and entered Carlisle almost immediately. I've run a comparison between the Folios I created of historical documents in our 2056 and those in this one. It seems the main difference is that during the siege of Carlisle, instead of subject "KATHERINE FINCHLEY", subject "MATTHEW GALLOWAY" died protecting COLONEL DURAND, the commanding officer of the castle's defences.

Clove swore loudly. "He must have sacrificed himself to protect Katherine. He promised he wouldn't, the liar!" She ran her hands through her hair. She was such an idiot.

> You informed him of the events which would take place in his future?

"Yeah, when you were out of it. What a colossal mistake that was."

> You shouldn't have done that, CLOVE. It changed history.

"But I don't understand! Why did it make such a big difference? I mean, Durand survived, right? It should have all gone exactly the same after that, except that it was Matthew who died and not Katherine."

> DURAND survived, but subject "MATTHEW" wasn't there. Previously he had helped to convince DURAND that he should hold the defence against the Jacobites.

"And Katherine never did that after he died. She must have been too grief-stricken." Clove remembered how in love Katherine and Matthew had seemed. When she'd seen them by the carriage, they had looked so happy. How could you ever get over losing a love like that?

> It is unlikely that the colonel would have taken the advice of a woman, regardless. She might have tried to convince him to hold off the Rebels and been ignored.

> When subject "MATTHEW" died, the support DURAND needed to ensure that he kept holding off the Jacobites wasn't there.

He gave in to the overwhelming pressure of the attacking forces. The Jacobite forces took control of the city.

Clove knew what happened next. "So then they defeated the English Army, because the battle happened sooner, when the English hadn't had a chance to gather their forces."

> Precisely. England lost, and Scotland established their national independence.

"What happened next? How did that affect the nine-teenth century enough for Russia to win the Crimean War?"

> After Scotland achieved independence, there was an economic collapse. According to the data I can obtain, this lead to a nationwide famine in 1765. Millions of people died.

"*No.*" The concept was impossible to grasp. She'd killed literally *millions of people.* Clove was responsible for the deaths of entire generations and Spart was only up to the 1760s. Who knew how many other people were dead because of her?

> The next big change was the Napoleonic Wars. Scotland refused to contribute their numbers to support the English and Allied ones. However, it didn't make much of a difference, and England still defeated France by a margin.

"OK…" Clove felt relieved that there was at least something she hadn't changed, but it didn't seem like much of a consolation.

> But then there was the Crimean War.

"Oh no."

> This time the Russians defeated England and France. Both
  countries lost their commanders early on in the battle when
  a rocket hit a tent. They were defeated and Russia invaded
  both England and France. They took Scotland too.

"You've mentioned a tent before," Clove said. "Ages
ago. Katy and Matthew, when they were in that time, saved
the commanders from the rocket that hit their tent."

> They didn't save them this time.

"Why not? Weren't they there?"

> They were, but subject allocation "KATY" died before the
  rocket attack. She was shot at the Battle of the River Alma.

"What? Was she never shot before, then? That's new?"

> Before things changed from the previous history, one of
  the articles subject allocation "MATTHEW" published in *The
  Times* mentioned that he and his assistant were saved on
  the battlefield by a Highland soldier. The Highlander took
  a bullet and died to protect them. As the Scottish forces
  weren't present at the battle this time, the Highlander never
  protected them, and subject "KATY" was shot.

Clove had killed her mum. And her dad. More than once.
"So they never saved the commanders?"

> Evidently. After the commanders died, the Russians won the war easily. England came under their control, as did Scotland, which couldn't stand up to their forces.

"So I made everything Russian."

> There's more.

"Nooooo, no! How can there be *more*? Isn't that *enough*?"

Clove wiped tears from her cheeks. She felt overwhelmed by guilt. She was picturing everyone she'd ever known and loved being put through the worst kind of hell ... all because of her.

> Nearly everything after 1854 changed from the history we know. During the Second World War, Germany seized England from Russia. Germany won the war.

It was so big that Clove couldn't comprehend it. Germany had won the Second World War because of her. England was German. Scotland was Russian. This was the biggest mistake anyone had ever made in the entirety of human history.

> Then there was the Cold War against America. In this timeline it wasn't a "cold" war. Russia had superior forces to their enemies, even after losing England. They had a large portion of Europe under their control by that point. They fired nuclear bombs at the American continent, and the resulting backlash lead to a global nuclear holocaust.

> At this point in time, most animals and wildlife are extinct, and the global population is at 70 per cent of what it was in the original timeline.

Clove couldn't hear any more. It was too much. "I need to fix it."

> How?

"I ... I don't know." Clove buried her head in her hands. "I don't know."

There was a knock at the door. "I hope black tea is OK. I've finished my week's milk ration," Tom said, as he came inside.

Clove nodded dully, taking the mug. "Black is fine. Thank you."

"You've found my office, then," Tom said, nodding at the computers humming behind Clove, where her bed had once been. His tone was sharp.

"Oh! I'm sorry. I didn't mean to sneak around."

"Right." Tom sat down, rubbing his mug between two palms. "Why don't you tell me who you're working for?"

Clove raised her eyebrows. "Working for?"

"How did you know to come here?" he asked, voice hard. "How do you know about us? What were you really doing in my bathroom?"

"'Us'? I don't ... I don't know who that is."

Tom's gaze roamed over her face. Finally, he relaxed. He put his mug down, bracing his hands on his knees. "You really don't know. You're not with the *politsiya*, are you? You're just a child."

Clove didn't let herself be offended by that. "I don't even know what the police-ia is," she admitted. Clove desperately wanted to ask who "us" was, but she didn't want to ruin whatever was happening here.

"How is that possible? Where have you been, that you don't know that?"

She swallowed. "You trust me? Just like that?"

He frowned. "I don't know why... Just ... there's something about you ... something familiar. Yes, I do trust you. I think."

Clove wondered if a part of him remembered her – or recognized her somehow. She'd changed time so abruptly that perhaps some part of Tom's old memory still existed. Deep in his subconscious, a part of him remembered that Clove was his daughter.

Clove decided she was going to tell Tom everything. She had to try and get him on her side, even if there was only a small chance that he remembered who she was. She couldn't deal with this alone any more. She took a fortifying sip of tea. "I have something to tell you, Tom. It's going to sound like nonsense. But please hear me out."

Tom folded his arms and leant back in his chair, his gaze never leaving her face.

"So" – she scratched her head – "I'm not really sure where to start. You know the time machine?"

Tom's eyes widened imperceptibly. "What time machine?"

"You're not researching time travel at St Andrews Uni?" Clove asked. She couldn't get a hang of all of these changes. Maybe it was best to assume that everything was different here.

"I'm not, no." He frowned at her. "I work with computers. Not time machines. I don't even think there is a time machine at St Andrews."

Clove didn't know what to say. She had used the time machine yesterday, and it had definitely been at St Andrews University. Unless… That couldn't have changed while she was sleeping too, could it?

The realization knocked the breath out of her. The time machine was gone. Her changes to time meant – somehow – that even the *time machine* wasn't in the same place any more. Did it even exist?

"Well. OK. That changes things." She pinned her hand to her thigh to stop it from shaking. She'd had a vague plan to go back to 1745 somehow and stop herself from ever talking to Matthew, to make sure she never changed the future. But if there wasn't even a time machine any more … she was stuck here. For ever. And she was completely alone. If her parents didn't know who she was, then it was unlikely anyone else would either. Not even Meg.

"Well," she said again. "The reason I don't know about the *politsiya* … and the reason I just turned up in your bathroom out of nowhere…" She wished she didn't have to say this. "I'm … I … I travelled here in a time machine."

There was a long silence.

"From the future?" he asked. She could tell from his voice that he didn't believe her, even though he was trying hard to hide it.

"… no. From some kind of alternate version of time, where I'm … I'm your daughter." She took in a deep breath, feeling it rattle around the cavernous nervy space inside her. Clove decided to just blurt information out until he stopped looking like he was about to throw his mug at her and flee the room.

"In my version of 2056, you and my mum work on a time machine at the university. I broke into the lab and used it to travel back to the eighteenth century. But while I was there, I told people things about the future. Information that I should never have shared. It must have changed things, because now everything is different. You don't know who I am, and Scotland is some kind of Russian police state. Nothing from my world was like this. Nothing at all. And I need" – Clove couldn't stop herself sobbing – "I need you to help me get my world back. Please, Dad. *Please.*"

Tom didn't say anything for a long time. He scratched at the nail of his thumb. Then he swallowed. "Right," he said, his Adam's apple bobbing up and down.

"I can prove it. Ask me anything." Clove wondered how many times throughout history she was going to have to try and convince people that she was their daughter.

"You don't need to prove it. I just ... I need a minute." Tom stood up, running one hand through his hair. He walked over to the window and stared at the ruined world outside.

Clove chewed at the inside of her mouth, waiting.

"When you were little, did you hide inside your duvet cover when you were upset?" he asked, without turning to look at her.

What? What did that have to do with—? "Yes?" Clove

said, slowly, and then more quickly, "You – did you *remember* that?"

"You used to call it Cloudland." His shoulders relaxed.

"Yeah. I did." Clove couldn't stop the hope bubbling inside her.

"I … I believe you." Tom's voice was hollow. "The first time I saw you, I recognized you. I ignored it. But I knew. And I remember you. I remember the life we used to have. How is that possible?"

Clove thought about it. There was no way to know what a person would remember, if their whole life was rewritten. It wasn't like anyone had ever created an alternate timeline before. Maybe this was normal. "I have no idea. But I'm so glad you do."

"I'm going to help you. We're going to get your world back," Tom said. "What do you need me to do?"

Clove tried to calm her raging thoughts enough to focus on the problem. She needed to find out whether there was a time machine anywhere in this world. And get to it. There was only one woman who could help with that.

"I need to find Dr Jennifer Sutcliffe," she said.

CHAPTER 27

Saturday 16 November 1745

A disastrous meeting today. A local man and volunteer by the name of Matthew Galloway was killed by a round of musket fire after the militia refused to guard the castle against the Rebels.

A local woman named Katherine Finchley was greatly affected by the passing of the man. I feel responsible for her grief as it was in the act of protecting not only Miss Finchley but also myself that he was killed. His life was given to save my own, and for that I will never forget him.

I find myself persuaded to surrender. His violent and cruel death was seemingly without cause, and it has resulted in more panic and disillusionment amongst the militia.

I see no future where the siege of Carlisle can result in anything but more death. I must choose to surrender peacefully now, before more innocent lives are lost.

I will declare my surrender immediately, to ensure that Matthew Galloway has not died in vain.

Folios/v1/Time-landscape-1745/MS-12-alt

File note: Diary entry of COLONEL DURAND, written during the 1745 Jacobite Uprising. The entry concerns subject allocations "KATHERINE" and "MATTHEW", as recorded after CLOVE's arrival in 1745

As shown in *Folios/v1/Time-landscape-1745/MS-12*, CLOVE's influence on "MATTHEW" during her visit to 1745 was a direct cause of the surrender of COLONEL DURAND during the siege, a disastrous decision which would impact the next three hundred years of British and global history

ST ANDREWS, SCOTLAND, 2056

"A 'J Sutcliffe' works at Cambridge University, in Deutsch-England," Tom said, reading off his watch. "Physics department. Is that who you mean?"

"Is there a picture?" Clove asked, leaning over to look at his watch. It was a much older model than Clove's – she'd changed technology, too, the way she had changed everything else in this timeline.

"Yeah. She's pretty," Tom said, enlarging the photo.

It was Jen.

Clove bit back a smile. "Yeah, she is."

So her mum was alive here. She just lived in another country. Clove wondered if she'd married someone else. Did she have kids?

To Clove's surprise, a message from Spart appeared on Tom's watch. Even though so much had changed, Tom had still created the AI. It was nice to know that some things were clearly constants.

>> DR JENNIFER SUTCLIFFE took over as leading research professor at the university after the recent collapse of the Nazi regime.

"The end of the Nazis was the only good thing to happen this decade," Tom muttered.

>> The professor is working on wormhole creation at the University of Cambridge.

"That's the time machine!" Clove said. "She's still working on it! Even if she is in England..." Clove tried not to think about how she could possibly get there. At least the time machine still existed somewhere.

>> Would you like me to obtain more information?

"See if you can find her contact details," Tom said. "Clove might need to call her."

While Tom's Spart started looking for holes in the university website's firewall, Clove showed Tom her own watch. Along with her clothes, it was the only thing that hadn't changed since she'd arrived. "I have a Spart too," she said.

Tom broke into a wide beam. "No kidding! Look at that. Hi, Spart."

> It is an honour to be your progeny in multiple time-landscapes, TOM. I hope you have no complaints as to the state of my programming.

"Not at all. It sounds like you've been having a bit of an

exciting time. Did you have a hand in Clove's adventures?"

> I must deny such charges. Any and all inappropriate and
history-destroying behaviours are due solely to CLOVE's
instruction.

"Hey!" Clove said, offended. "Unfair, Spart. You are at
least fifty per cent to blame for all of this."

Tom winked at her. "I think I programmed both of them
to have the same sense of pride. Hey, Spart – say hello to
your alternate-universe twin."

>> I … have no previous data about how to deal with this
scenario.

> My own social programming is equally lacking.

>> May I ask the value of your computational IQ?

> You may not. I don't believe that is an appropriate question
to ask a new acquaintance, even with the similarities in our
design.

Clove gleefully followed along as the two Sparts
verbally circled each other like territorial cats. She stopped
when she realized Tom was still staring at her watch and
frowning.

"What? What is it?" Clove said, looking down at her
Spart's latest message, where he was boasting about being
a more advanced model than Tom's Spart.

"Clove…" Tom's voice was rough. "Look at your hand."

When she did, her mind struggled to process what she was seeing. Her skin was *see-through*. She was turning … *transparent*?

Clove couldn't – she couldn't— She pulled up her other sleeve, then her trouser leg. Her veins and flesh were visible where skin should have been. She was fading.

Why?

"Tom," Clove said, voice carefully steady, "do you have a brother?"

What if Kate and Matt had never had a daughter in this universe? What if she had never been born?

"Yes," Tom said, still staring at her hand, at the muscles flexing under her skin. "Matt. He's in prison, along with his girlfriend. They were activists – they were caught breaking into a military laboratory over the border, in Deutsch-England. But what does that have to do with—?"

So Kate and Matt still existed here, but they'd both been arrested. Kate had never escaped and fled to Scotland.

"Your brother. He doesn't have a daughter, then? His girlfriend – she wasn't pregnant when she was arrested?"

"No," Tom said, confused. "Not that I – I don't know! She never had a baby!"

Clove felt like she'd been punched in the stomach. She had never been born in this world. She had changed history so much that she'd erased her own existence.

And if she couldn't fix it … she would disappear for ever.

CHAPTER 28

File note: A sketch by TOM GALLOWAY of the journey from St Andrews to Cambridge, showing the new borders of the British Isles in his universe

ST ANDREWS, SCOTLAND, 2056

Clove wrapped her arms tighter around Tom's waist, trying to ignore the rumble of the engine and how fast the ground was moving beneath them. Clove would have sworn violently that her father was not the kind of person to ever own a motorbike. Clearly she had been very wrong.

The bike was black and sleek and *dangerous*. Tom rode it through the streets with precision. Clove just tried to hold on tight enough that she didn't fly off the back.

When Clove had started despairing about getting to Cambridge before she was erased from existence, Tom had scratched at his beard thoughtfully and said, to Clove's utter amazement, "I guess this is where I tell you I'm a hacker for an underground resistance fighting the government."

In this timeline, Tom was still operating as the hacker Spartacus. Apparently because he'd never met Jen, got married or become a professor, he was still doing the same thing he had as a student: online illegal activism. Jen's calming influence on him must have extended further than Clove had realized. In a world where he had never met her, he had become a completely different man.

Clove couldn't deny she was impressed. It was a bit annoying that her dad was a hundred times cooler than she was, though. Her dad was some kind of action-movie badass in this reality.

The bike turned a corner and nearly touched the ground. Clove swallowed a yelp.

"Where next?" Tom called over his shoulder.

Clove lifted her arm from around Tom's waist just enough to see the map on her watch, which showed the route they should take out of town to avoid running into any of the patrols. According to Tom, there had recently been a lot of rioting by the Scottish resistance.

Tom had got hold of the *politsiya* patrol patterns through an online contact, and his Spart had found a route that they could follow to get them through St Andrews without being seen. It was going to be a close thing. According to the patrol timetable, at one point, they would have barely thirty seconds to get past a guard.

"Next left," Clove shouted in his ear. "You might want to go a bit faster!"

The engine roared. Clove's stomach jumped.

"Second right!" she called, her voice high-pitched. She cleared her throat, and then they turned another corner and she forgot all about the tone of her voice. *"Stop here!"* she yelled. "There's a patrol ahead!"

Tom pulled in behind a line of dustbins, and cut the engine. He ducked over the handlebars. Clove bent down out of sight too, trying to keep an eye on the *politsiya* at the same time.

Two soldiers crossed the road ahead of them, chatting loudly in thick Russian. Clove and Tom stayed frozen as the *politsiya* passed by. As they disappeared around the corner behind a row of houses, Clove let out a relieved breath.

"That was close," Tom said.

"Come on," she whispered. "Let's go before they come back."

"We should be OK as soon as we're out of the city. I can get us to Cambridge in six hours if I go at over ninety!"

"Please don't," Clove said.

By the time Tom pulled up around the back of the Cambridge Department of Physics, it was early evening. In the pale grey twilight, Clove's skin seemed to be disintegrating. Her hands felt soft, like the gentlest brush would tear her open. She wondered if she still had blood, or if that had already dried up, disappearing from her veins until her skin clung to the bones like an ancient Egyptian mummy.

She carefully dismounted from the bike on shaky legs. "We have to hurry," she told Tom, her breath frosting in the cold. "I don't have much time." She took off her helmet but kept on the dust mask that everyone here wore as protection against the polluted air.

"It's a Saturday evening," Tom said. "The building won't be open."

Clove began looking through her rucksack. "Don't worry. I've done this before. You just keep a lookout."

Clove crouched down by the entrance to the physics department and used her Swiss army knife to unscrew the key-card scanner by the side of the door. She pressed the memory card containing a copy of Spart into position on the circuit board. "OK, Spart. Time to work your magic," she said. "Get us inside."

"Did I teach you that?" Tom said, looking hugely impressed.

Clove couldn't help her smug tone. "You've taught me a lot of things, Dad. But this? This I taught myself." Her smile dropped when she saw a new message from Spart on her watch.

> CLOVE, I'm sorry. At the University of St Andrews, I was operating using previous knowledge taken from TOM and

JENNIFER's network. I do not have access to the same
information in this institution.

> The security system is too different to what I am used to. I
can't break it.

Clove told Tom what Spart had said. "We're going to
have to wait until the building opens."

"Can you last that long?" Tom asked, tugging at her
sleeve to check the state of her wrist.

She could see her bones: a vivid, fluorescent white
against the muted colour of her flesh.

"I don't know," she said. She felt suddenly and
completely terrified. "Dad, you have to do it anyway. Even
if I disappear. You have to carry on – to fix things."

"How?" he said, sounding both nervous and determined.
"You haven't even explained... I would have no idea where
to start! What if I make *this*" – he gestured to the world
around them – "worse?"

It had just started to rain. The thick droplets burned
when they hit her skin, sending fiery trails of acid rain down
her cheeks. She brushed them away. "I— I don't know," she
said. "I don't know if it's even possible to fix things." She
realized she was crying. "I don't know *anything*."

"We can't wait." A muscle in Tom's cheek twitched.
"I can't stand here and watch you fade into nothing. We
have to call Jennifer. She might remember you too," Tom
said as he dialled the number Spart had found. "Like
I did."

It only rang twice before Jen answered. "Hello? Who is this?"

"You talk to her," Tom said, holding out the phone.

"Mum?" Clove said, tears welling up.

"Sorry?" Jen said. "I think you've got the wrong number."

Clove cleared her throat. "No, I don't. This is Jen Sutcliffe?"

"Yes," Jen admitted.

"There's an emergency. You need to come to the Cavendish Laboratory as soon as you can."

"An emergency? It's the weekend!"

"I'll explain when you get here. It's about the time machine."

"Who is this? Are you a student?"

"My ... my name is Clove," she said, hoping that whatever kind of memories Tom had retained, Jen would have similar ones.

There was a moment of silence. "I'll be there as soon as I can," Jen said, and hung up.

The first thing Jen did when she arrived was to pull Clove into a hard hug. "I thought it was a dream!" Jen said into her neck. "I thought I'd imagined it all!"

"Mum," Clove said, unable to believe that Jen recognized her. "You *remember*?"

"Of course I remember," Jen said, and when she pulled away, her eyes were bright with tears. "How could I forget my own daughter?" She looked at Tom. "I remember you too."

Tom broke into a nervous smile. "I don't remember as much as you do," he admitted. "But ... but I'd like to."

"I don't remember that beard," Jen said, touching her hand to his cheek. "That's new."

"Do you like it?" Tom raised an eyebrow, and to Clove's surprise, Jen let out a giggle. Were they *flirting*?

"I don't think this is the time," Clove said, exasperated. "Mum, I'm disappearing." She held out her hand to Jen, showing the state of her skin.

Her mother gasped. "What do you need?" she asked.

"I need to use the time machine," Clove said. "I need to fix history."

Jen's eyes widened. "The time machine?"

"You can get us inside, right?" Tom asked. "You have the key card."

"I can get you inside..." Jen said uncertainly, gaze flickering back and forth between Tom and Clove. "But the time machine's not working. It's incomplete."

Clove felt like she'd been punched in the chest. "It doesn't work?" she asked. "At all?"

"Not yet. I was hoping by the end of next year, maybe..."

"But I need it now! I'm disappearing!"

"The software isn't ready," Jen explained. "Clove, I'm sorry. But the program is incomplete. We can't control the size of the wormhole yet. It's too dangerous to risk turning the machine on. It could create a black hole."

"The software?" Clove scrubbed her hands across her face, thinking quickly. Tom had been the one to create the software. In this world he had never been part of the time-machine research team, so the software must be less developed because he hadn't been there working on it.

"Tom wrote the program in my timeline," Clove said. "That means with him here we can – we can try and fix it, right?" She looked at Tom for confirmation. "It's worth a shot?"

"Clove," Tom said, "I've never seen a time machine in my life! I might have written code for it in your world, but here I'd have no idea where to even start. And I definitely don't know enough to do it in a few hours."

"I've seen the software working," she said. "You taught me how it works. I can help you. I'll tell you everything I can remember. *Please.*"

Tom sucked in a breath. "OK. Let's try. We can at least try."

CHAPTER 29

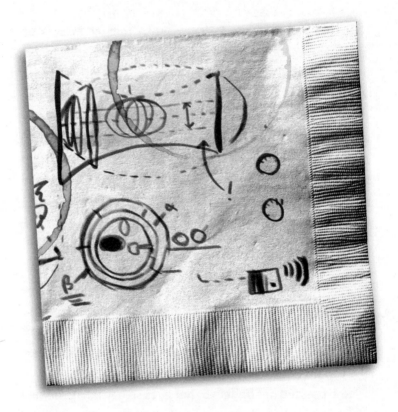

Folios/v8-alt/Time-landscape-2056-alt/MS-6-alt

File note: A rough sketch of the University of St Andrews
          prototype time machine, drawn in Cambridge on 22
          July 2056 by CLOVE SUTCLIFFE during work with TOM
          GALLOWAY on the program

"No, that part is wrong," Clove said to Tom, an hour later. They were trying to make progress on the code while Jen set up the particle accelerator, but Clove could tell it wasn't going to be enough. The time machine was much more primitive and basic than Clove's version, and she felt a huge moment of despair. They would never be able to get this working. And even if they did, she still needed to go to 1745 and stop herself from interfering in Katherine and Matthew's lives.

Clove tapped the screen to point out another problem, but instead of touching the glass, her hand went straight through it. She reared back.

Her hand had just *passed* through the screen, like it was nothing! Carefully, she pressed her hand to the desk. Her hand disappeared through the wood, like it was made of liquid. She was nearly gone. She had faded so much that she couldn't touch anything any more.

She pressed her fingers to her eyes so hard that she saw stars, and let herself mourn her failure. It was impossible. She didn't have enough time.

Her eyes flew open a second later.

She could hear footsteps in the hallway.

"There's someone coming," she hissed to Jen.

Jen jumped up from where she was opening a panel on the particle accelerator. "It must be a security guard! I'll get rid of them."

After she left the lab, Tom and Clove stared at each other,

while listening carefully for any sounds from outside the door.

"We need to get back to work," Tom said.

Clove nodded. "She'll be OK," she told him. "They won't hurt her. She works here." She could see in his eyes that he didn't believe her.

Ten minutes later, the door flew open, hitting the wall with a metallic bang. Jen walked into the lab, a security guard behind her. He was holding a gun to Jen's head. Her hands were handcuffed behind her back.

"I'm sorry," Jen said to them. "I'm sorry."

"Get away from the machine," the guard said. "Or I'll shoot."

"Keep going," Tom said under his breath to Clove. "He can't arrest all three of us."

"But…" She couldn't even touch the screen. She couldn't input any more code, even if Tom held the guard off long enough for her to try. They'd lost.

"GO!" he shouted, and dived for the guard.

Clove didn't stop to argue. She turned to the computer, speaking quickly, and letting the computer type up her words. From behind her came the sounds of yelling and fighting. Clove tried not to think about Tom, or Jen, or the gun. She just ran through as much code as she could, her words tumbling over one another as she spoke. There was a loud gunshot, then in quick succession, another. Every muscle in Clove's body seized up.

She turned around slowly.

Tom was bent over the body of the guard, who was

lying on the floor, unconscious. The gun was in Tom's hand. Clove guessed it must have gone off as Tom was wrestling the guard to the ground.

Dropping the gun to the floor, Tom ran to where Jen had collapsed. He unlocked her handcuffs and rolled her over, touching her cheek as he did so.

"Was she shot?" Clove asked, heart in her throat.

"No," Tom said. "She's OK. She just got knocked out when she fell."

Clove let out a sigh of relief. "Thank God!"

Tom moved Jen into a more comfortable position and then stood up. "We need to be quick. Someone will have heard the noise." He walked awkwardly over to the desk, one hand pressed to his waist.

"Dad! What happened?" Clove asked.

"Nothing, I'm fine."

"But you—" She cut herself off. His hands were bright red with blood. He'd been shot. It must have happened during his tussle with the guard.

Tom sat down, pressing his hand more firmly against his side and blanching at the pain.

Clove tried not to panic. His injury couldn't be too serious if he was still moving about. He would be fine. They just had to fix the past, and then she could take him to a hospital. It was going to be OK.

"What do we do next?" he asked.

Clove let out a shaky breath. "The program is nowhere near being finished and you're hurt. W—we can't... This isn't going to work."

For a second, Clove considered running the time machine anyway, and hoping that somehow their bare-bones program would work. But she knew she couldn't risk it, not even to save millions of lives. If it didn't work – which it wouldn't – then the wormhole would grow out of control and turn into a black hole. It would destroy the whole planet.

It seemed impossible that after all this effort, with so much help, she had still failed. It wasn't supposed to end like this, with Tom bleeding out, and Jen unconscious, and a broken time machine.

If only there was another way. If only she could use time itself to find a way to cheat. Why couldn't she just get someone from the future to bring her the working code? She promised herself that if she ever got the time machine working, she would bring back the code and rescue herself in the past right here and now. She closed her eyes and wished really, really hard.

If she ever managed to time travel from this reality, then the code would appear on the computer screen when she opened her eyes.

She opened her eyes.

There was nothing.

Well, it had been a long shot.

Tom let out a long, moist exhale and wiped away the blood from his mouth. "I'm sorry, darlin'. I tried. I tried as hard as I could."

Clove could only just make out the edges of the bones in her wrist.

She was as good as gone.

When she looked up again, there was a message flashing on the screen.

> To Clove: You're welcome. Love, Clove xx

As she gaped, the message changed.

> Program ready to use

> Please set destination

Clove-in-the-future had come through with the goods.

Clove's elation was cut short as she realized she had no idea what to use the time machine for. She didn't have time to go back to 1745, not any more. She'd have disintegrated into atoms long before she had a chance to stop herself from speaking to Matthew, and Tom was in no state to go there either. She had to come up with a new plan.

The reason everything was falling apart was because Katherine and Matthew had never achieved what they were supposed to in 1745. Matthew had died, sacrificing himself to save Katherine. If Clove could just use the time machine to rescue Matthew before he died, everything would go back to normal. Wouldn't it?

"I'll ... I'll bring Matthew back," she said aloud, on an impulse. All this had happened because Matthew had died. So if she put him where he should have been, it would all go back to normal.

A message from Spart popped up on her watch.

> How are you planning to do that? He's dead.

"I can…" She stopped talking to think. How could she bring someone back to life? And then it came to her.

There were loads of versions of Matthew throughout history, dozens of them. She just had to take one of them and put him where he was needed the most. In 1745. Somehow.

She might be able to take one of the Matthews she knew wasn't needed any more in their time. One who had definitely finished whatever it was he had to do, like the Matthew who had saved the commanders from the rockets in 1854. She could take him and put him in 1745.

That would work, wouldn't it?

She was almost certain that it would.

Probably.

She had to try.

"Spart, open the wormhole to 1854," she said. "After the rocket attack on the commanders' tent. We'll take the Matthew from then and put him in 1745." She tried to ignore the quaver in her voice.

> But he won't survive the—

"Just do it! Before it's too late!" Clove yelled, blind with panic. She couldn't believe Spart was arguing with her. The world was destroyed, Clove was fading into nothing, and Spart didn't want her to fix it. *"NOW."*

> Scanning time thread …

> Subject allocation "MATTHEW" detected in time-landscape 1854

> Initiating wormhole …

The huge particle accelerator began to whirr, and she watched the wormhole appear. Inside, Clove caught a glimpse of the world of 1854 on the other side: blue sky, brown ground, red uniforms, and then Matthew Galloway as he was sucked into the hole, headfirst. He fell into the lab in a tumble of limbs.

"Now open the wormhole again," Clove yelled, "to 1745. Make sure it's exactly when Matthew was killed there."

> But he—

"DO IT!" Clove screamed at Spart.

> Scanning time thread …

> CLOVE, the radiation will—

"Clove…" Tom groaned. He had lost all colour. He dropped to the floor with a rough grunt of pain.

"I'm here," she whispered, crouching beside him. "Dad, I'm here." She tried to cup his cheek, but her hand passed right through him. Behind her, Spart was still operating the time machine.

> Subject allocation "MATTHEW" detected in time-landscape 1745

> Subject allocation "MATTHEW" in time-landscape 1745 timed out

> Initiating wormhole …

The wormhole reopened on the cathedral in Carlisle. Clove could see an elegantly painted ceiling and pews filled with people. Lying on the floor, just inside the wormhole, was Matthew. Katherine was curled over him. Spart had timed it perfectly.

> Intervention in progress …

> Transferring male candidate …

> File loading …

The 1854-Matthew – who had been lying inside the time machine with his head to his knees, groaning – disappeared into the wormhole. He fell onto the floor of the cathedral just as the dying Matthew from 1745 was pulled through time. He arrived in the lab in a rush of wind and a cloud of red.

> … closing wormhole …

An expression of horror and confusion on Katherine's face was the last thing Clove saw, before the wormhole was sucked in on itself and the vision of 1745 disappeared into nothing.

As the whirring of the machinery died down, there was a long second of silence. Blood fell from Matthew's body like rain, spraying the floor with a fine red mist. Clove stared at him, unable to believe what she'd just done. Then she shook herself and turned to see if Tom was OK.

To her shock, Tom had disappeared. So had Jen and the guard.

Blinking disbelievingly at the room, which was empty except for her and Matthew, Clove wondered what this meant. Had they disappeared because she'd succeeded in changing the past? Had she fixed the mistakes she'd made to the future? Or had she made everything worse?

She held her hands up to the light, bracing herself. She could no longer see her bones, only the pale pink of her skin.

She wasn't fading any more. She was saved.

And Tom and Jen – they would be at home, wouldn't they? If they weren't here, they must be in St Andrews. It was so hard to make sense of everything, but they had to be. Unless she'd somehow erased them from existence completely.

She called Tom's watch, bracing herself for new changes.

"Hello?" he said when he answered, voice sleep-thick and quiet.

"Dad?" She tried to hide the tremor in her voice.

"Darlin'?"

She couldn't hide her sob of relief. He was alive, and he knew who she was. She'd got her dad back.

"Clove, are you OK? Where are you? Why aren't you asleep? Where are you calling me from? Are you *out*? At this time of night?"

"What is it?" She heard Jen say in the background.

"Sorry," Clove said. "I'm in bed. I rang you by accident. I'm fine. Go back to sleep. I love you."

"I love you too," he said automatically. "Don't stay up too late."

He hung up, and Clove ran her hands through her hair, trying to decide whether to curl up and cry or dance with glee. She'd done it. Tom was alive, and still her dad. She had saved the future.

But she was stuck in Cambridge, in the empty basement of a physics department, without even a time machine any more, because for some reason that had disappeared too.

It took Clove a second to realize why: because it hadn't been built in Cambridge in her version of time, it had been built in St Andrews.

Before Clove could even begin to work out how she was going to get home, the eighteenth-century version of Matthew Galloway let out a long, low groan.

CHAPTER 30

The diary of Katherine Finchley

Carlisle, Cumberland, England

<u>Sunday 17 November 1745</u>

I can't understand what I saw yesterday, nor how it could even be possible. Matthew was in my arms, bleeding from his chest and close to death. Then, only seconds later, there was a gust of wind like we were standing outside in a storm, and suddenly the body in my arms had changed. It was the same, but different, in a monstrous, horrific way.

I know the vision I saw was not the delusion of a hysterical woman. Matthew really was shot with a musket. He really was passing into death, there in my arms.

However, somehow my Matthew was replaced – by himself. By an uninjured, healthy, DEMONIC version of himself.

The creature claims to come from the year 1854, from a war in Europe. It says that it is Matthew Galloway. This being mistook me for a woman called Katy, who it claims looks just like me.

The creature is older than my Matthew, with no working man's calluses nor muscles. It has a different hairstyle and talks with a different accent. It is Matthew but different. A twin of him, raised in a different time and place.

I do not believe it can be possible. No part of me understands what kind of Witch's Magicks have caused this to occur, nor how such a thing could happen.

However, if this is truth, then where on earth, or in Heaven or Hell, is my Matthew?

Whatever could the Witch want with him there?

<u>Monday 18 November 1745</u>

Circumstances have evolved. This twin of Matthew's truly has been brought to this time from the year 1854. He was sent here from that distant time to help me, I believe. He has knowledge of the future that has been invaluable in the fight against the Rebels.

We have come to realize that if the City of Carlisle surrenders to the Rebels, then England will be defeated in the Uprising. It seems that this would be disastrous for future events. With this

Matthew's help, I have persuaded Colonel Durand
to maintain defences against the Jacobites. Hopefully
we can prevent the Rebels from seizing the North.

If this is the reason the Witch brought Matthew's
twin to me, I hope she knows what she is doing.
He suffers greatly from a mysterious illness, and
becomes sicker with every day that passes. I worry
for his Life and Soul. I still have no knowledge of
my own Matthew.

Thursday 21 November 1745

Matthew Galloway, born 1833, passed away sometime
in the early hours of 21 November, the year of
our Lord 1745, of a fever and sickness I still do
not understand.

At least I may rest assured he achieved
whatever he was sent here to do, as Colonel
Durand has agreed to maintain defence of
the City.

May Matthew rest in peace, alongside my own
Matthew Galloway, wherever he may now be,
born 1728.

CAMBRIDGE, ENGLAND, 2056

Clove sat in the hospital waiting room, staring at a mauve wall and trying to process everything that had happened. The version of Matthew she had pulled from 1745 had been in surgery for two hours, and she hadn't heard anything. She'd had to pretend that she was his sister so that the nurses would let her stay – but that lie was the least of her worries. She had no idea how he would react when he woke up. He'd have no idea where he was.

He was used to the old-fashioned world of carriages and candlelight – what would he do when he found himself in a hospital bed, surrounded by beeping machinery? If he hadn't been able to handle seeing Clove's watch, how would he react to the modern world?

Clove itched to run into his hospital room to reassure him, but she wasn't allowed. Instead, she had to sit in the waiting room, doing nothing. She'd been here for hours, exhausted and full of adrenalin, all at once. It was hard to believe so much had happened in what was, here, only one night. It was now early on Saturday morning. At eleven the night before, she had been breaking into the physics department at St Andrews University. That Clove felt like a different person.

Earlier, Clove had messaged Tom, telling him that she'd gone to Meg's house first thing to try and make up with her. He hadn't sounded worried. He didn't seem to remember anything that had happened in the alternate 2056.

"Spart?" she whispered.

> Yes, CLOVE?

"Did anything change? Have you looked?"

> The future has reverted back to its original state. You were very lucky.

> The subject allocation "MATTHEW" from 1854 worked with the subject allocation "KATHERINE" in 1745 to persuade DURAND to maintain the city's defences against the Jacobites, as required. It worked.

Clove closed her eyes. "Phew." The world was back to its healthy and mostly flourishing self, with no sign of Russian soldiers or nuclear holocausts in sight. She'd fixed everything.

> However...

"Yes? What?"

> According to medical records, the subject "MATTHEW" from 1854 died within days, of symptoms that resembled radiation poisoning. As I tried to tell you in the lab, it's not possible to travel in the wormhole without a suit for protection.

"I killed him?" she asked hollowly. The knowledge didn't hit her the way it should. She seemed to be killing everyone recently.

She rested her head in her hands. She was too tired.

"Clove Sutcliffe?"

A doctor was standing in front of her. "Your brother has come out of surgery. His condition is stable, although one of his lungs had collapsed. He's sedated, but he should wake up in the next few hours."

"Thank you," she said in relief. "Thank you so much."

"There's just one thing... Do you know of any reason why Mr Galloway might have radiation poisoning?" the doctor asked, frowning at her notes.

Clove tried to look like someone who didn't have any knowledge of time-travel-related transportation devices that might possibly give someone radiation poisoning. "No?"

"Well, we're treating it, and he should survive, but ... it's very strange. It's got everyone flummoxed. We have no idea where it could have come from, short of a nuclear bomb."

"Is he going to be OK?"

"I'm sorry to say that he's going to be infertile for the rest of his life. But apart from that, he should be healthy enough – once the short-term symptoms are treated."

"That's good news."

"But the bullet he was shot with" – the doctor scratched her forehead – "it looks like an antique. Like a musket ball. It's..." She trailed off, at a loss.

"That's really strange," Clove agreed. "I just got a phone call from him telling me that he'd been hurt. I called for an ambulance when I got there. He was unconscious by then. I have no idea what happened to him."

"Well, when he wakes up, the police will want a statement about the shooting. I'm sure they'll need to talk to you too."

"That's absolutely fine," Clove lied. "No problem."

This was a huge problem. Matthew couldn't talk to

the police, not in England in 2056 – where Matthew Galloway had broken out of Wakefield Prison in mysterious circumstances sixteen years earlier. The police would arrest him immediately.

When the doctor had gone, Clove rested her head on her knees, trying to decide exactly how much trouble she was in. At least Tom was still alive, and the future was saved. That was a relief. And she was no longer slowly fading away like a ghost. Those were the positives.

On the negative side… 1745-Matthew had been shot because of her, and he might still die from his injuries. If he did survive, he was hours away from being imprisoned for a crime 2039-Matthew had committed. 1854-Matthew had died of radiation poisoning and his body was stuck in 1745. All because she hadn't stopped to think through her time-travel plan properly before she'd gone ahead and done it.

Keeping all of these different versions of Matthew straight was giving her a headache.

Everyone knew that if you travelled back in time you'd end up stepping on a butterfly and somehow killing your grandad by accident. Clove had apparently cut out the middleman and just killed her own father. Twice. It was too terrible to think about.

Another problem occurred to Clove. When – *if* – 1745-Matthew recovered, and if she managed to break him out of the hospital before the police found him, then she would still have to deal with having brought an eighteenth-century coachman to 2056. Somehow.

She had several options, she decided. She could tell Tom and Jen that she had found Matthew – who was currently in a hospital in Cambridge being treated for a gunshot wound, over a decade younger than he should be, and spoke like he was from the very distant past – and then suffer the inevitable fallout.

Or she could wait until Matthew was better, and then send him back to 1745 without Jen or Tom ever knowing. She thought she could probably pull off another lab break-in if she really had to.

So sending Matthew straight home to 1745 seemed like the less complicated option. She would take her time, though, and not panic and do something crazy again, like go into the past and bring someone back with her.

But first, she needed to have something to eat, clean her teeth and have a nap. Urgently.

When Clove woke up from an uncomfortable but much-needed doze in a waiting-room chair, she was told that Matthew was still sleeping. Clove was desperate to talk to him, but at least the police hadn't managed to take his statement yet. Too impatient to sit still and wait, she started looking through the messages on her watch. To her surprise, there was one from Meg.

Nuts_Meg 12:56:03   Can we talk? I miss you

Clove's mouth felt dry. "Spart, call Meg. Audio only." She didn't think she could handle looking Meg in the eye just then.

"Hello?" Meg sounded tentative, but at least she'd answered.

Clove was suddenly hot all over. After everything she'd done in the last week, talking to a girl shouldn't be this terrifying. "Hey," she said, and then cleared her throat and straightened her shoulders. "I wanted to apologize for the other day. I was being an idiot."

Clove heard Meg shift position before she replied. "It's OK," she said.

"I made everything into more of a deal than it was," Clove added. She really had, she realized. What had happened with Meg was nothing compared to destroying the universe. She had completely overreacted to the kiss.

"That's ... good?" Meg said, sounding surprised, which made Clove feel even worse. She must have acted like a real monster the last time she spoke to her.

"Yeah. Meg, you know ... I'm not upset that you didn't kiss me back. I know you're straight." Clove thought of Ella, and pushed the image away. "I was just panicking about losing you to Alec."

"Y–yeah," Meg said quietly. "I know. I'm sorry too, for not replying to your messages. I didn't know what to say."

There was an awkward silence.

"So, how was work experience?" Clove asked eventually, trying to keep her voice bright. "Did the kids behave?"

Meg launched into an excited anecdote, which would usually have had Clove in half-hysterics. Instead she found her mind drifting to Ella, wondering what she was doing. It was almost a physical ache, how much she missed her.

Ella was so challenging, so in-your-face. She had always wanted Clove's attention, always forced her into bickering and messing around. Clove missed her obnoxious teasing, her sharp, slightly pointed chin and the blurred quality it lent the rest of her face. She missed Ella.

"So I had to wear one of the teacher's shirts!" Meg said, giggling. "Mum still hasn't got the paint out of mine."

"Powerful," Clove said, switching back into the conversation. "That's a lot more exciting than my week. I've just been—"

"Programming, programming, programming," Meg teased. "And you loved every minute of it."

"I did love it," Clove agreed, smiling. "So ... did you hear from Alec?"

"Are you sure you're OK talking about him?" Meg asked, a little cautiously.

"Yeah. I'd like to know."

Meg drew in a huge breath, ready to update Clove on an entire week's worth of Boy Interactions. Clove settled in to listen, looking through her rucksack for a toothpaste tablet as she did so. She pulled out all the things she'd taken to the past: the old-fashioned clothes, Tom's Swiss army knife, her first-aid kit. And there, at the bottom of the rucksack, was a dried flower, browned and a little worse for wear.

It was the violet Ella had given her the first day they met, as they were walking by the river. Ella had been teasing her, drawing her out of her shell, and she'd picked a flower and handed it to Clove.

The sight of it made tears well in Clove's eyes. Ella was *dead*. She was nothing but a long-forgotten gravestone somewhere, with no one alive now but Clove to remember her, and nothing more than a flower to show for her life.

"I met a girl," Clove found herself saying.

Meg paused, took in a breath, and immediately squealed, *"WHAT?!"*

Clove sighed. "She was ... powerful."

"Have you fallen *in love*, Clove Sutcliffe? Without *telling me*?"

"I think I have," Clove admitted. "But I've lost her."

Ever the romantic, Meg said confidently, "True love is never lost. We can figure this out."

"I think in this case it might be."

"Is she from the university? Is she a student? Wait, is she a *professor*? Is she an *older woman*?"

Clove laughed, remembering Ella declaring that she was in charge, because she was older. Clove had been furious with her. "Yeah, she's older. She's eighteen."

"Tell me all about her!" Meg said.

Clove laid the violet down on her knees and tried to find a way to describe Ella.

CHAPTER 31

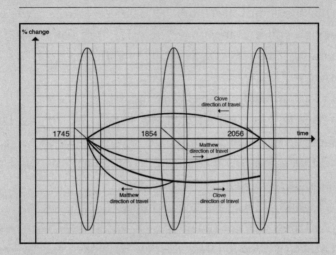

The diagram shows the universe shifts due to Clove Sutcliffe's initial time displacement activities. They are represented in circular coordinates where the axes indicate *time-landscape* versus *% displacement* from the baseline universe. The universe distortions are the result of a metaphorical wobble in the space-time landscape.

File note: Extract from *The Comprehensive Guide to History Control*, first published in 2351

After Meg and Clove had finished talking, a nurse came over to tell Clove that Matthew had woken up. He led her to Matthew's hospital room. "He's been awake for a while, but he's still a little woozy," he said. "He's hallucinating some stuff about a castle? Talking with him might be a bit weird."

Clove grinned. "I think I can handle it."

"But he's recovering well. He hadn't had any of his childhood vaccinations for some reason, so we've had to give him a few. His injuries are healing well, though. He should be fit for release later today."

"Thanks," Clove said, and let herself into the room.

Matthew was hooked up to an IV and several machines, all of which beeped intermittently. He looked exactly like she imagined a corpse would look. She touched his hand, just to check he was actually alive.

"Clove," he said, squinting at her. His voice was low and hoarse, and it sounded just how he looked: ashen.

"Matthew. Listen, Matthew. Don't panic. But you're in the future."

"I had guessed as much," he said dryly. "The Sparts everywhere made that easy to deduce."

Clove tried very hard not to laugh. "Computers. They're called computers. Only mine is called Spart. It's a nickname."

"Right." He coughed, and winced. "Thank you for saving me."

"No problem." She frowned at him. "Why aren't you freaking out?"

"I've had a while to come to terms with the idea of travelling to the future. I did see you disappear through a hole in mid-air quite recently. This is actually *less* strange than I had imagined."

"Well." Clove was desperate to know what he had imagined. "Anyway, the only reason you're here at all is because you *broke your promise*, Matthew Galloway. You said you wouldn't stop Katherine from sacrificing her life, and you did!"

He frowned. "I wasn't going to let her *die*."

"But you were perfectly happy to die yourself? You got shot!"

"But Katherine survived. Didn't she?"

"Yes," she said. "She survived the siege." Clove decided not to tell him about the second version of Matthew now keeping her company. When this Matthew went back to 1745, they could sort it out between themselves. "But you should never have interfered! You destroyed the future! I nearly *died*! I had to fix your mess!"

"It was worth it," Matthew said resolutely.

She gaped at him. *"'Worth it'? 'Worth it'?!"*

He nodded.

"You're insane! You're actually insane! You destroy the entire world and it was 'worth it'."

"I love her," he said, and his face broke into a smile. "I love her. She loves me."

Clove exhaled angrily. "What a mess."

"So – can I go home?" he asked, meekly.

"You've still got a bullet wound in your chest," she said, scowling. "You idiot."

"When I'm better," he amended.

"You can go home. When the doctors say you are better, I'll take you home. If you promise to never ever do anything else that could in any way affect the future."

He nodded. "I've learned my lesson. No more doing things."

"Good," she muttered.

"What year is this?" Matthew asked. "Everything is very ... white. I can't imagine living long enough to see the world look like this."

"You would never have seen this," she admitted. "It's ... it's 2056."

"*What?* How? If you are our daughter? Surely we can only have travelled a few decades into the future, despite all of these advances in science? When does Katherine arrive?"

Clove sighed. She wasn't going to tell Matthew about the reincarnation. "Nope. I'm not telling you anything else about the future, Matthew. I'm not a total idiot."

He looked wounded. "I wasn't going to *do* anything!"

"I don't trust a single word you say. Katherine has sent you crazy. You're a loose cannon."

"You have to tell me something!"

"I'm sorry, but this is your punishment for breaking your promise. You don't get to hear any more secrets."

Matthew sighed. "That's reasonable, I suppose."

"Good. Now, how do you feel?"

"I feel … not as terrible as I would have expected. Your doctor is really good. I always knew women could study like men."

Clove grinned. "It took a while, but gender equality got there eventually. Anyway, be ready to leave this evening. We're going to have to break you out of here."

Matthew's eyebrows raised. "Uh … how?"

"Trust me. The police are waiting to talk to you, and we can't risk them working out who you are."

"Shouldn't we tell them the truth? Won't they understand?"

"That would definitely not help. I don't know what you think the future is like, but time travel is a new thing. No one would believe you."

Matthew nodded his agreement, even if it was reluctant. "I'll trust you, then."

"Do you need anything?"

"A drink?"

"I'll be right back," she said, and stood up. "Try and rest."

When she returned, Matthew was asleep. She left a cup of water by the bed and told the nurse she'd be in the waiting room. Apparently he was scheduled for regeneration of his wounds in two hours, and after that he would be free to leave. There was plenty of time for Clove to nap before then – and plan how she was going to get Matthew out of the hospital. Everyone seemed to do it in films all the time, so it couldn't be that hard. She could probably just wing it. She would have to do it soon, though, before people thought he was well enough to start filling out health-insurance forms and making police statements.

1935

1938

Folios/v1/Time-landscape-1745/MS-12

File Note: Sketches found on the back of the newspaper *The Carlisle Courier* dated 15 September 1745. They are believed to have been drawn by subject allocation "MATTHEW", showing how he thought clothes would look in the future

CAMBRIDGE, ENGLAND, 2056

Clove was walking back to the hospital eating a burger and fries, while listening to Spart lecture her about the things she was and wasn't allowed to do when breaking Matthew out of hospital and sending him home. Apparently she wasn't allowed to do anything at all until he'd told her it was OK. That seemed fair, after the chaos she'd caused so far.

"I know I messed up, but technically it wasn't my fault," she said, brushing her hair back. "I mean, it was Matthew's. It was definitely Matthew's."

Ahead of her on the footpath was a girl, all curls and eyeliner. Her neck was wrapped in an enormous green scarf.

Clove shifted to the left, to give her room to pass. "Spart, I promise I'll—" Clove broke off, staring at the girl. The girl had walked right up to her. The girl—

The girl—

—who Clove realized she'd seen around St Andrews University, back before she'd ever decided to travel back to the past—

The girl was Ella.

It was Ella.

It was *Ella*.

"Ella?" Clove said, certain she'd made a mistake.

The girl hooked her chin over the top of her mountain of a scarf – the very same scarf that Clove had stress-knitted, then left in 1745, she realized, stunned – and quirked an eyebrow at Clove. "Hey."

Clove gaped at her, gaped some more, and then abruptly sat down on the pavement.

CHAPTER 32

34 likes

Ella-is-swell Happy anniversary, boo! 3 years today by my count [citation needed].

view all comments

Nuts_Meg You guuuuys! 😍

LuckyClover We should go to Cambridge next year, take a trip down memory lane.

Ella-is-swell By memory lane, do you mean sitting in the street while you refuse to look at me, **LuckyClover**?

LuckyClover Isn't that how all of our dates end, **Ella-is-swell**?

Like • Comment • Share

File note: Interactions on social media between CLOVE
           SUTCLIFFE and ELENORE WALKER from 22 July 2059.
           Included in the fictionalized biography *Ella &*
           Clove: A Love Story

CAMBRIDGE, ENGLAND, 2056

Ella sat down on the ground next to her. Clove turned her head away, not quite able to look at her.

"What are you doing here?" Clove asked. *"How?"*

"I'm a time traveller. Hey."

"You're a— *I'm* the time traveller. Not you!"

"What, you wanted me to stay in the past and let you leave me?" Ella laughed. "I'm not letting you get away that easily." She shifted position, trying to get Clove to look at her, but Clove didn't turn her head. She couldn't bring herself to look at Ella, not quite yet. She felt too overwhelmed.

"I can't believe you never worked it out," Ella added. "It's not like I blended into the eighteenth century."

Ella had been a time traveller, this whole time. How had Clove not *realized*? How had Ella not told her?

"What year are you from?" Clove asked.

"The future," she replied easily. "Your future."

"What year?"

"I don't know if I should tell you that. But you know one of my ancestors. Megan Walker?"

"Meg is your ... your *ancestor*? *What?*"

"I think she's my ... great-great-great-grandmother? Something like that?"

Clove tried to stop herself from spluttering and failed. "You can't— I can't— What? I mean, *what*?!"

Someone walking past said, "Excuse me," and Clove shuffled back against the wall, out of the way. She was still looking anywhere except at Ella.

"Sorry I never told you sooner. I didn't want to interfere with what was supposed to happen."

"What does that mean? Interfere?" Clove asked.

"Your first trip to the past was known to go a certain way, and—"

"My *first trip*? What do you mean? Do I go again?"

Ella was quiet. "That's up to you."

"I don't understand," Clove said. "How do you know anything about me? Why were you even there? Did you go to the past knowing I would be there?"

"You're famous. I wanted to meet the real person, behind the textbooks."

"*TEXTBOOKS?*"

"Yeah. Look, we should talk about this somewhere more private. People are staring at us."

"But you just—"

"In a bit, OK?"

"Fine! Let's go!" Clove stood up.

Ella stood up too. "Clove, look at me. The world isn't going to end if you look at me." Ella touched Clove's cheek.

Clove felt her skin go flaming hot. She finally, finally turned to meet Ella's gaze.

"Hey," Ella said, a little breathlessly. Clove's cheeks were hot, and every movement suddenly felt meaningful.

"Hey," Clove repeated. Now that she was looking at Ella, she couldn't look away. The make-up couldn't hide her features, and it only brought out the colour of her eyes and her long eyelashes.

When Ella smiled, it lit up her entire face.

A lump rose in Clove's throat. She couldn't ever remember seeing anyone the way she was seeing Ella. She was a supernova, an explosion. She made everything else seem insignificant.

"This is why you were so good at lying," Clove realized, suddenly annoyed. "You were lying about everything the whole time!"

Ella shrugged. Her eyes never left Clove's lips. Clove had always thought her lips were too plump for her face, but now that Ella couldn't look away from them, she didn't mind them so much. "It's my job."

"Job?" Clove asked.

"Let's go somewhere and talk. We have a lot to cover."

Ella handed Clove a mug before sitting down opposite her in a quiet corner of the hospital cafe. It was so strange to see Ella in a modern environment, and under fluorescent bulbs rather than candlelight.

"OK." Ella clapped her hands. "So, let's start from the beginning. You're famous."

Clove made a noise that was the audible equivalent of question marks.

"You're the first time traveller. Of course you're famous. You established a whole new area of scientific study: History Control."

Clove prodded her cream and chocolate sprinkles with her spoon. She had? "What is History Control?"

"It's a way of adjusting history, of changing minor events

to try and improve the quality of life for humans as much as possible. You've saved more lives than any other person in all of history."

"I have?" Clove said, aiming for nonchalant but ending up closer to uncertain.

"You will. And I'm training to follow in your footsteps, to be a History Revisionist. I'm only in my first year of uni, though. I've still got loads to learn." Ella scraped the cream off her drink and then licked it off the spoon.

"So you, what, you choose a point in history and change it? I did that by accident and nearly destroyed the world. I was fading away! I nearly disappeared!"

"It does have its risks. But if you do it right, you can improve everything."

"And you think I invented this?" Clove shook her head. "I'm never travelling in time again. It's too dangerous."

"You will." It was hugely annoying that Ella seemed to know stuff about Clove's future that Clove didn't. "And students in the future will study your life."

"That is insane." As Clove drank her hot chocolate, she tried to wrap her head around the idea of being a *role model* for anyone. Let alone a role model for *time travellers* who helped *revise history*. It was impossible.

Ella unzipped her rucksack, rummaged inside and then pulled out a battered textbook.

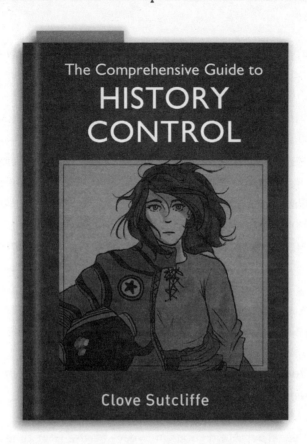

The Comprehensive Guide to

HISTORY CONTROL

Clove Sutcliffe

File note: Cover of textbook *The Comprehensive Guide to History Control* by CLOVE SUTCLIFFE, first published in 2351

It was written by Clove. In the future. Clove carefully looked away from it. That textbook could tell her everything about her life. She didn't want to know. "You still use paper books?" she asked, casting around for something to say.

"No, of course not. It's a tablet. It just has a skin on it, to make it look like a book, so it blends into historical environments. See?" Ella turned a page, and suddenly the textbook was moving: a clip of film played on its pages.

Clove examined the new technology, intrigued, and then realized she was getting distracted. She shouldn't be looking at her future. She closed the cover. "You change history, then. Were you in 1745 to change something about the Jacobite Uprising?"

Ella looked shy for the first time. "Er, no. I actually study the Romans."

Clove remembered Ella sitting in the attic bedroom and pouring over a Latin text. Clove realized with a jolt that Ella was telling the truth. Ella was a time traveller, and had been this whole time. If Clove had just paid more attention, she might have worked it out for herself. "That's why you can speak Latin," she said.

"Yeah! Our current mission is to save the Library of Alexandria."

"I've heard of that. Didn't it burn down?"

"Yes, around two thousand years before your time. All the books, and all knowledge of their civilization, was lost for ever. If we could save it ... humanity might develop its technology centuries earlier. It could save so many lives. Civilization would progress loads faster."

"That's ... powerful," Clove said, stunned. Ella was *literally a superhero.*

"It's going to take a long time to do it. I probably won't even get permission to go to the first century A.D. until after I graduate. It's harder to travel that far back in time – it takes a lot more energy. For now, I'm stuck sifting for evidence in the eighteenth century, which is as far back as I can go until I qualify." Ella sighed. "It's all red tape."

"So that's why you were in Carlisle," Clove said, amazed. "Well, I'm glad you were. I would never have met you, if it wasn't for your paperwork."

Ella ducked her head. "That wasn't the only reason I was there. I wanted to meet you too."

Clove was thrown off guard by the nervous look in Ella's eyes. Her reply caught in her throat. "Because I'm in your textbooks or whatever?"

Ella fiddled with her spoon. "Uh. Yes?"

"Why don't you sound sure?" Clove asked, suspicious.

"Well. Mainly it was because you're hot." She looked up at Clove from under her eyelashes, and smirked.

Clove coughed. She was blushing again; she could feel it. "What's time travel like for you in the future?" she asked quickly. "Is it still the most painful thing you could ever experience?"

Ella held out her arm. Some sort of panel was embedded into the skin of her wrist. It glowed luminescent as it lit up with messages: a screensaver of stars spiralling across her lower arm. "This is my Skim. It picks up signals from an electrode in my brain, so it's run directly via mind control."

"Powerful," Clove said, awestruck. "Tell me everything. How does it charge? Where is the processor?"

"Well, I don't know any of that stuff. I'm more of an arts student. But anyway, that's my time machine."

Clove blinked at her. "What, that?" It was tiny. It couldn't make a wormhole, could it? That little thing?

Clove wondered when exactly in the future Ella was from, if technology had progressed that much.

"Yeah! You have to travel with a certified historian until you're twenty-one. I forged a permission slip to come on my own." She looked extremely self-satisfied.

This was so surreal.

"So you broke the law, just to see me?"

Ella nodded. "It was worth it."

Clove frowned doubtfully. "It seems like a crazy reason to travel back in time." Ella had spent so much time and energy trying to find Clove. She'd even seen her in St Andrews the week before. "Why were you in the physics lecture?" It felt like ages ago. It couldn't be, though, because it was when she'd been on work experience, which was chronologically only yesterday.

Ella grinned. "I was in that lecture about an hour ago. I time-travelled to here straight after it. I went to the university after you left Carlisle, because I was trying to find you, but I arrived in 2056 a day or two early. You were *crying*, Clove. What happened?"

"I was having a bad day," Clove mumbled, remembering how terrible everything with Meg and her parents had been. "So why didn't you talk to me then?"

"It had to be in 1745."

"Why?" Clove asked. Based on Ella's smug expression, she wasn't sure she wanted to know the answer.

"Because I'm in the textbooks. I know we met in 1745."

"You're ... you're in your *own textbooks*?"

"Well, the textbooks just refer to an Ella, but I was

pretty sure it was me. When I got to 1745 and there was nobody else called Ella standing near by ready to fish you out of a river, I was certain it was me."

"I *knew* I hadn't imagined someone rescuing me!" Clove said. She'd thought it had been a hallucination from lack of oxygen. But it had happened. "That was really you? You saved my life?"

Ella slurped her drink. "Be grateful I actually do the assigned reading for school."

Clove was affronted. "What happened to '*I wanted to meet you because you're hot*'?"

Ella laughed in delight. "Oh, you're definitely still hot."

Clove bit her lip, trying to hide a smile. Then she frowned down at the table. "So you went to 1745 and saved my life because you read in a textbook that you were going to?" Clove rubbed her temples. "Surely there's a paradox in that."

Ella shrugged, one-shouldered. "I suppose the first time I met you – which was presumably in a timeline before I read the textbooks – I was only there to find information about the Library of Alexandria. I would have met you totally by accident. After that first time, I always knew I was going before I went there, because I got the idea *from* the textbooks. The current hypothesis for when things like this happen is that time is lots of little loops, repeating themselves until there's an equilibrium – but that's still hypothetical."

Clove exhaled loudly. "You're enjoying this far too much."

"You won't believe how hard it was to not tell you everything! Watching you talk to your father for the first time! I was bursting at the seams."

"Well," Clove said, sulkily, "I wish you had told me all this earlier. That was a giant mess. I should never have spoken to Matthew. It nearly destroyed the universe."

"That point in time is locked. I couldn't interfere in your conversations with Matthew. It's illegal for time travellers to make unrecorded contact with you. Your life is too important to risk changing unless you initiate it. You're a set point in history. There are some things which are just too major to risk changing – it would create a completely different timeline, one that might be unrecognizable."

"Like the motorbike universe," Clove said, thinking of how different everything had been there.

"The what?"

"Never mind. So why was what I did in 1745 so important?"

"Your work spawned the entire theory of History Control. Everyone in my class – every historian in the *world* – would kill to be in 1745 to witness you in action. There were probably time travellers hiding in every bush for miles around trying to eavesdrop. The cook, Mrs Samson, is originally from the twenty-second century, or someplace ancient."

Clove blinked. Was everyone she'd met in 1745 secretly a time traveller? She thought about the way nobody had ever seemed to question her odd slang or faux pas. Suddenly everything was starting to make a lot more sense – especially given the rule that said they couldn't reveal themselves. Clove had already messed up history quite enough. Imagine if Katherine or Matthew had known the whole house was full of time travellers!

"If my past is ... 'locked', then why were you allowed to

get involved?" Clove asked. "You interfered with everything I did, constantly! You never stop interfering!"

Ella smirked. "Yeah, but I don't count. I'm special."

"Why? Why are you special?"

"I'm the love of your life."

"The" – Clove could feel her eyes bulging – "the—"

"The love of your life. Historically speaking."

"I..." Clove had no idea what to say. What was the correct response, when someone told you that they were your soulmate? She should probably ask Matthew. If anyone knew, he would.

"I know," Ella said, when Clove still hadn't managed to speak thirty seconds later. "It took me a while to get used to it too."

"I..." Clove sighed. "This is really weird." She traced shapes on the table.

"It's amazing, isn't it?"

Clove dropped her head on the table and knocked it against the wood a few times. "I'm not sure yet."

Ella rested a hand on the top of Clove's head.

Clove stilled. "I can't decide whether this makes you a stalker or just very determined."

"Probably both." She could hear Ella's smile in her voice.

"So what happens next?" Clove said, sitting up.

"Well, haven't you got a parent from the eighteenth century who needs to get back to his one true love?" Ella gestured to the Skim on her wrist. "Need a lift?"

CHAPTER 33

Clove Sutcliffe has given frequent interviews about her time in Carlisle since that first experimental History Control mission, and one constant appears in them all: she would not have been able to achieve half so much during her time in 1745 if it were not for a fellow time traveller referred to only as Ella.

> **Elenore Walker Comment:** Homework due next Fri: 1k words on C.S in 1745

Ella had more experience of surviving unnoticed in historical periods, and her guidance to Clove, an amateur trying to find her feet in the as-yet-unexplored field of History Control, would have been invaluable. Not only that, but Ella saved Clove's life upon her arrival in 1745, when she landed in a river and nearly drowned.

> **Elenore Walker Comment:** Is it creepy that I can't stop imagining this Ella being me?

The identity of Ella, whom Clove has more than once described as "the love of her life", has never been revealed. Both travellers value their privacy, so little further information is known. However, it has been hypothesized that Ella must originate from some point in the six centuries after Clove Sutcliffe's birth, as after the year 2678 time travel became much more highly regulated and no unlogged journey to pre-internet eras would have been possible.

> **Elenore Walker Comment:** The dates fit and everything. Huh.

File note: Extract from *An Unauthorized Biography of Clove Sutcliffe,* annotated by ELENORE WALKER on her Skim during a history lesson

CAMBRIDGE, ENGLAND, 2056

"The *maid*?" Matthew said later that day, as he stared with wide eyes between Ella and Clove. "She's not my daughter too, is she?"

"No, I'm Clove's girlfriend," Ella said, before Clove could reply.

Clove whipped round to stare at Ella, who straightened her shoulders and stared right back. Clove grimaced but said nothing. There were more important things to deal with than Ella right now. Also Clove didn't want to start trying to explain the word *girlfriend* to Matthew or give him an abridged political history of homosexuality. Not when they were about to perform a highly illegal patient break-out. She had to hurry this process along, before a nurse came.

"She's going to get you out of here," Clove said, finally.

"Are we going to find Katherine?" Matthew asked, immediately starting to get out of bed.

"Wait! Let me take out your IV first," Ella said, wincing. "It's very admirable how much pain you are willing to go through for love, but some of it isn't necessary."

Matthew suffered the indignity of Ella helping him remove the medical equipment, which started beeping until Ella pressed the screen and shut it down.

Clove found Matthew's old clothes under the bed, neatly laundered, and he got dressed. Apart from a scar across his chest and a lack of colour in his cheeks, he was almost better. She could send him on his way with a dose of penicillin, and he should be fine. Hopefully.

Ella was fiddling with her Skim. Clove had never seen someone control a computer with mind control. It made Ella look a little cross-eyed.

"We're going to Katherine?" Matthew asked, with impressive single-mindedness.

Ella took Matthew's hand, and Clove's in the other. "Kind of," Ella replied.

Before Clove could question what that meant, a familiar sucking sensation spread through Clove's hand, and she was tugged into a vacuum.

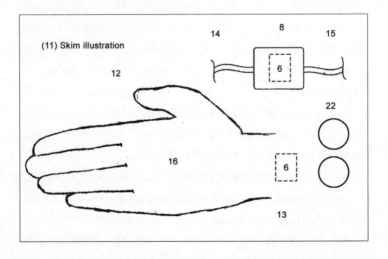

File note: Diagram of the "Skim", as enclosed in the original patent application

* * *

When the spinning stopped, Clove was so dizzy she couldn't work out which way was up. "Didn't we need a suit?" she asked, gasping for breath. She spat out one of Ella's curls and blinked away the phosphenes. "For the radiation?"

Ella shook her head, apparently unaffected by the wormhole. "Built into the Skim."

They were standing in the rain on the side of a road. The white van driving past definitely wasn't an eighteenth-century carriage.

"This isn't 1745! Where are we?" Clove asked, confused. "I thought we were taking Matthew home?" Perhaps Ella had used a wormhole to break them out of the hospital and would create another one to take them to 1745. It seemed an awful waste, though. Wormholes gave Clove a really bad headache.

"I had a better idea," Ella replied, as Clove realized she was still holding her hand and let go abruptly. "We'll take Matthew home later. Right now we're in 2040, on the Scottish border. In about thirty seconds, there should be…"

Ella broke off as a bus swerved out of the traffic and pulled to a stop in front of them. The door slid open with a squeak. Ella climbed on board, gesturing for Clove and Matthew to follow her. She paid the driver and then headed straight for the back row of seats.

Clove stared after her in furious shock. She couldn't believe that Ella was taking them somewhere without even explaining what was happening or asking Clove how she felt about it. It was beginning to seem like Ella enjoyed making Clove feel lost and off-balance.

"Ella, what's going on? What are you doing?" she hissed, dropping into an empty seat opposite her. Matthew sat beside Clove. The bus was almost empty, but Ella had chosen to sit down next to the only other passenger – an old lady with a shawl wrapped around her head. She had her head down, and her arms were wrapped around a large rucksack. She didn't look up at her new companions.

Ella stared meaningfully at the old woman.

"What?" Clove hissed, and then she realized.

That wasn't an old lady at all.

It was Katherine Finchley.

Clove gaped. If they were in 2040, and that was Katherine Finchley … then this must be her actual mother: the Kate who had given birth to Clove in Scotland, before leaving her with Tom so that she could break Matt out of an English prison. If they were on a bus, on the Scottish border, then Kate must be going to the prison right now.

Kate had given birth to Clove only days before. This was her mother.

"Excuse me," Clove said, leaning forwards, buzzing with excitement.

Kate's whole posture stiffened. She must be terrified of anyone discovering her identity. She was considered a terrorist in England: the number-one most-wanted criminal.

"Excuse me," Clove repeated, and this time Kate looked up. Her gaze flickered warily from Clove to Ella, and then to Matthew, where it stopped.

"*Matt?!*" Kate asked, her voice hoarse.

Matthew, who had been staring with fascination out of

the window at the countryside speeding by, spun around to stare at Kate. "Katherine?!" he spluttered. He stood up and then abruptly sat back down to grab Kate's hands. "How did you get here? What happened to you?"

"*Me?*" she said. "What happened to *you?* How did you get out of prison?"

"Hi," Clove said, interrupting them both. They turned identical, amazed expressions on her. "Sorry to interrupt, but I can explain. This isn't your Matt, Kate. Matthew, this isn't Katherine. Not the version you know, anyway."

Kate seemed to understand instantly. "When are you from?"

"1745," Clove replied for him.

As Kate threw herself at Matthew and pulled him into a hug, her rucksack fell to the floor. "Matthew," she said. "The coachman. I remember you."

"You remember him?" Clove and Ella both asked together.

Kate nodded. "I remember all of my lives. I remembered months ago."

Ella's eyebrows raised. "I didn't know that," she said, confused.

"What's happening?" Matthew asked.

Clove didn't answer. She realized that she should have asked Ella sooner what she knew about Kate and Matt. Ella could probably have explained everything, but Clove had been too overwhelmed to consider it before now.

"I don't understand," Matthew said, still holding Kate tightly.

"You're reincarnated," Clove said quickly. "For some reason that I never worked out, you and Katherine keep being brought back to life, throughout history. Kate is one of the newest versions."

"I know why," Kate said. "It's because we needed to have a child. My daughter, Clove. That's why we keep coming back."

Clove broke into a nervous smile. Kate thought the reincarnation was because of *her*? "Er, that would be me. Hi." Clove waved at Kate.

"My daughter is a baby," Kate said. "She's only three days old."

Clove shrugged. "Time machine."

Kate's expression turned serious. "Clove?"

"Hi, Mum."

Kate stared hard at Clove. There was a long silence, and then she abruptly burst into tears. "I left you," she said. "I had to leave you, I'm sorry. I'm so sorry."

"It's OK," Clove said, touching her arm and trying to sound reassuring, even in such a strange situation. "Tom was a great dad."

"Tom *raised* you? Matt and I *never come back*?" Kate gasped.

Clove nodded, unwillingly. She didn't want to upset Kate, but she couldn't lie to her. For Kate, this was all new and raw – especially as she'd given birth only days before. Clove had had a lifetime to get used to the idea of Tom being her father. She couldn't imagine it any other way.

"That's why we're here," Ella interrupted. "To make sure you get Matt home."

"You're going to help me rescue Matt?" Kate said, sniffing, just as Clove said, "We are?"

"We're going to get him out of prison," Ella confirmed. "And take you both home to your family."

Clove was gobsmacked. They were going to take Kate and Matt *home*? After all these years? How could Ella bring her here and suggest something so life-changing as if it was no big deal, without even *asking* Clove if she wanted her parents to come home? What would it mean if Kate and Matt came home? Would Clove have to leave Tom and Jen and move out?

She couldn't believe Ella was doing this to her.

Kate's emotions clearly weren't so mixed. She'd grabbed Clove's hand like she never wanted to let go, tears of joy running down her cheeks.

"I have absolutely no idea what is happening," Matthew said. "What do you mean when you say I'm ... reincarnated?"

Clove took a deep breath and pushed her feelings aside. She had brought Matthew to the future, and she had a duty to make sure he didn't go crazy because of it – which, judging by his frenzied eyes, and the way he was holding tightly to Kate's arm, was very close to happening.

"OK. Matthew, you and Kate are born over and over again, throughout history. Every time you are born, you get together and do something important, like what you did at Carlisle to help stop the Jacobite Uprising. In the early twenty-first century you were born again, and when you were trying to do your big thing – which in this case was stopping a biological weapon being used in warfare – the version of you here was arrested and taken to prison. Kate escaped to Scotland, where she gave birth to me. So I guess I'm technically not actually your daughter? I'm the daughter of another version of you. Are you with me so far?"

Matthew shook his head. Clove persevered. Even if he didn't understand, at least he looked a little calmer.

"After Kate gave birth to me, a few days ago, she decided to try and break Matt out of prison, so they could finish their task of stopping this biological weapon from killing millions of people. She left Me-as-a-Baby with your – Matt's – brother. He raised me, because Kate and Matt disappeared for ever after that. We had no idea where they went, for sixteen years. So Ella here decided that Kate probably needed our help, and brought us here – to a time before they disappeared."

"That sounds about right," Kate said, in a tiny, over-whelmed voice.

"Forgetting all of that," Ella said to Kate, "you just said you thought you were reincarnated *because* of Clove? How did you know?"

"Sorry, who are you again?" Kate asked.

"This is my friend Ella," Clove said quickly, before Ella could make another unsubstantiated claim about their relationship status. "She's the one with the time machine. She's from the future."

"Oh!" Kate said, and let go of Clove's hand to take Ella's. "It's great to meet you."

"It's lovely to meet you too," Ella said. "So, you were saying about Clove…?"

"Right," Kate said. "Clove is the reason we were

reincarnated, I think. I worked out that in every other life we never had any children, so I figured we kept being reborn until we did. Clove must grow up to do something really important." Kate took Clove's hand again, smiling at her proudly and affectionately.

Ella snorted. "That's a good theory. You've got it a bit backwards, though."

"What do you mean?" Clove asked. "I thought you said I do end up being important! You said I saved millions of lives."

"You do. But your parents aren't somehow magically reborn to make sure that you are alive to do that. They are reborn *because* of you doing that."

"What?" Kate and Clove asked together.

"You change history using your parents," Ella explained. "That's how it works, your History Control. You make sure that there is a version of your parents alive in every time period where they could be useful. You put them there and make sure they meet. Together they act like white blood cells for the universe. They isolate issues and fix them, and make sure things happen the way they should. In the last beginning, back in 2040, Kate gave birth to you."

Clove's brain switched itself off, then turned on again. She couldn't process what Ella was saying.

"Dropping people into pivotal moments of history is a crude prototype for the current system of History Control in my time," Ella continued. "But it worked for you. You thought it would be less intrusive to history to use existing people, rather than to send in loads of agents from the future, who might mess things up beyond repair. I think you'd been burned by your first mission and by all of the changes you made in your visit to 1745."

"You put us here?" Kate asked Clove, trying to catch up. "But why? How?"

"I have no idea," Clove said. The idea was unbelievable… But Ella wouldn't have any reason to lie, surely. That meant Clove was going to use her parents to change history. *She* had been the one planting them in the past. This whole thing was Clove's fault. "Why would I do that, Ella? It doesn't make any sense."

Ella pulled a face, clearly trying to work out how to explain it. "You thought that Kate and Matt had the … *instinct*, you called it, in your book. They could sense what needed doing better than any computer."

Clove shook her head. "That's ridiculous. There's no way I'm going to do that."

Ella shrugged. "You will."

Clove glared at her and folded her arms. "I think I know my own mind." She was annoyed at how cockily certain Ella was of everything. It made her feel like she had no control over her own future.

"I *know the future*, Clove. I *literally* know *exactly* what is going to happen. I promise that you will do this."

"Oh, you can't just use the fact that you 'know the future' to win every argument, Ella!" Clove retorted. "How is that fair?"

"If you'd just listen to me—"

"Stop telling me what to do!" Clove burst out.

Before Ella could reply, Kate cleared her throat. She looked between the two of them. "Uh, how did you two meet?"

"Ella stalked me," Clove replied at the same time as Ella said, "I saved her life."

Kate sighed. "I think we've all got a lot of catching up to do."

"Yes, please," Matthew said. He pressed his forehead to Kate's, sighing loudly.

CHAPTER 34

<u>History Control Assignment</u>

Name ...Elenore Walker.....................

Form ....7!.............................

Fill in the gaps in the time loop diagram below. Identify the main paradox intrinsic to Clove Sutcliffe's life.

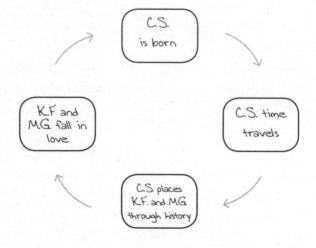

This is a paradox because Clove would never have time-travelled if her parents hadn't been placed throughout history, but they are placed throughout history because she travelled.

File note: Homework assignment submitted by ELENORE WALKER for her history class

LEEDS, ENGLAND, 2040

After the bus had deposited them in Leeds, Matthew, Kate, Ella and Clove checked into a hotel. It had been nerve-racking, seeing as the group was comprised of a terrorist and three time travellers, none of whom had legitimate identification, which was an issue during the political tensions in 2040. They ended up in a disreputable motel on the outskirts of the city, because nowhere else would take them.

To Clove, this time looked old-fashioned and sparse. The streets stank of exhaust fumes, and everyone seemed wary and suspicious. To Matthew, it was all a miracle. It was almost impossible to get him up to the motel room, because he wanted to inspect everything, from bus stops to carpets to light fittings.

"Excuse me for a minute, will you?" Kate said, throwing her rucksack onto one of the twin beds and pulling out a breast pump. "My body still thinks I've got a baby to look after." Her gaze drifted to Clove. She shook her head. "I still can't believe you're her. You're so grown up. You look just like Matt."

"She has your eyes," Matthew said.

Kate's own eyes brimmed with tears. She brushed them away. "I miss you so much," she said to him. "I know you're here, but it's not … you're not…" She sighed. "I miss my You."

"I miss my You too," Matthew echoed.

They stared at each other with an intensity that made Clove look away. "Shall we go and get some food?" she asked Ella.

Ella nodded and pulled out a few banknotes, before passing them to Clove.

Clove was suspicious at how prepared Ella seemed to be for this trip. Had she been carrying money from 2040 around the whole time because she had been planning to bring Clove here? She must have done so much research about this time to know exactly where Kate would be and when. Why had Ella never mentioned her plans to Clove?

When they were on the street, Ella stopped and turned to Clove. "Go on then."

"What?" Clove said, surprised.

"Didn't you bring me out here to fight?"

Clove squirmed under her steady gaze. "No."

"Yes, you did." Ella crossed her arms defensively, and then uncrossed them and tucked her hair behind her ears.

Clove blew out an exhale. "Fine. I don't know what you're doing, Ella. I asked you to help me take Matthew to 1745, and instead you brought us to 2040, completely out of the blue. You obviously had it all planned out in advance because you *brought money with you*, and you knew exactly where Kate would be."

Ella tried to speak, but Clove pushed on. She needed to get it all out.

"And anything could happen while we're here! I've destroyed the future once. I don't want to do it again! We've already made things worse by showing Matthew even more of the future. It's getting so complicated! You should have told me what you were planning. I really, really don't want to be here, Ella."

"I'm sorry," Ella said, blinking quickly, tears filling her eyes. "I wanted to help, but I didn't think things through. I can be really bossy sometimes, I know. I'm really, really sorry. I messed up."

"Just ask me, will you, next time? I feel like you're … I don't know…" Clove pushed her hair back from her face. She still felt annoyed. "You're enjoying that you've got this leverage over me, because you know everything that happens. You're marching ahead with all this confidence, doing everything according to your textbooks. But you can't tell me what to do and then expect me to do it. Surely that's not the way it works! If you make all the decisions for me, then I will never do any of the things you think I'm going to do. *You* will have done them all."

"You want me to pretend I don't know what happens?"

"*No!* I want you to work with me, so we can decide together what the best thing to do is, regardless of what your textbook happens to say. Ella, you *study* History Control! Your entire life is about finding the best path of history, the most optimal version of events! Why is this any different?"

Ella's frown disappeared. "Oh. I can do that." Ella held Clove's hand, swiping her thumb along the sensitive skin of Clove's wrist. "I really am sorry."

Clove could feel Ella's heartbeat thumping against the skin. It sent shivers through her. Her breath came out too sharp. She wanted to cradle Ella's cheek, to push her fingers into her hair. "I didn't want to have to regret becoming emotionally invested in you," she said in a whisper.

Ella laughed quietly.

There was an unfamiliar low-level thrumming under Clove's skin. Clove took a step closer to Ella, forcing the space between them into nothing. Ella's hand was on the small of her back, her gaze on Clove's lips.

Clove drew a breath in, and then all of a sudden they were kissing, softening together like wax. Ella's hair felt like silk when Clove pushed her hand through it. When she touched Ella's scalp, Ella made a small hitching sound that went straight to the base of Clove's spine. Clove had never felt anything as good as the brush of her tongue against Ella's, the slow exploration of each other's mouths, the soft warmth and catch of her teeth on Ella's lips.

Clove remembered Ella's declaration, "I'm the love of your life," and the thought shot heat right through her. Her mind went deliciously blank of anything that wasn't Ella – the viciously bossy girl wrapped up in her arms.

This was the polar opposite of her kiss with Meg, and of the fear and panic that had followed it. Clove felt safe. She could fall without worry, knowing that Ella would catch her.

When they finally pulled apart, Ella blinked dazedly. "That was my first kiss," she said, touching a finger to the swollen pink of her mouth, which was the same colour as her bright cheeks.

Clove took her hand. "I wish it had been mine."

"It wasn't?" Ella asked, her look sharpening.

Clove grinned. "That's not in the textbook, then?"

She pulled Ella down the street, telling her about Meg while they searched for a chippy, and restraining herself from dropping kisses on Ella's lips more than once a metre.

When they finally got back to the motel room with bags full of food and grease, Kate was curled up beside Matthew on one of the beds, her head on his shoulder.

They all sat on the bed, pulling flaming hot chips out of the paper and comparing details of each of their timelines.

Clove couldn't remember ever feeling so happy.

CHAPTER 35

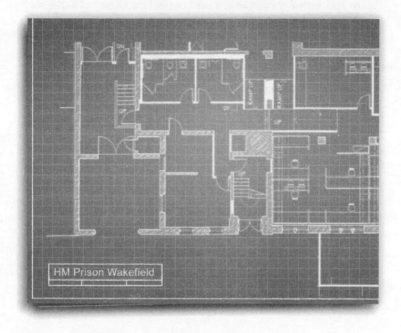

File note: Blueprint of Wakefield Prison

LEEDS, ENGLAND, 2040

"So what are you doing here?" Kate asked when they'd finished eating and explaining the joint phenomena of hot showers and Harry Potter to Matthew. "Are you going to help me break Matt out of prison?"

Ella looked at Clove, who was leaning against the headboard, chewing on a toothpaste tablet. Clove was pleased that she was actually waiting for her to make the decision, and she smiled at her. Clove wanted to think about it carefully before deciding. She was reluctant to mess with the past again. What if breaking Matt out of prison here in 2040 changed something in 2056? It might be too much of risk, however immoral it was to leave him there.

Although he really *did* break out of prison in 2040. It was a fact: something that had always happened. Surely she wouldn't be changing history so much as helping it on a bit? Besides, what if they had *always* come here to break Matt out of prison?

"I think we should, yes," Clove said, slowly. "I think we're supposed to. Nobody could ever work out how Matt had escaped. It must have been the Skim that got him out, all along."

"Thank you," Kate said, looking hugely relieved. "I had no idea where to start, honestly. But if you can use your Skim thing, that'll be loads easier. I had a vague plan to, like, dig a tunnel or seductively bribe a guard or something. I have an old Victorian floor plan of the prison that we could use to find him, once we know what cell he's in. It might be out of date by now, though. We might end up in an ancient slurry pit." Kate began flicking through files on a tablet that looked slow and clunky to Clove. Between Kate's tablet, Clove's watch and Ella's Skim, they had almost the entire history of computers in one room.

Ella's hand was resting on the bed next to Clove's. Clove moved her little finger so that they were just touching. "Spart, any chance you could find a newer map?" Clove asked, enjoying the tingle of Ella's skin against hers.

> I can certainly do that. The prison won't have any security protection against AIs in this time period. We won't be widely used for another decade.

> I should also be able to stop the security cameras from recording during your visit.

"I can open a wormhole in his cell, but at least one of us will have to go through to bring him back," Ella said. "It should all be super easy if I have the coordinates. We'll need to find out exactly which cell is his, of course."

Matthew cleared his throat. "Er," he said. "If you don't mind, I would really like to go home before you do any of this. I don't think I would be of much use to you, and, as pleasant as it has been to meet you all" – he cast a goofy look at Kate, which made Clove wonder what the two of them had been up to while Clove and Ella had been outside snogging – "I am ready to return to my own time."

"I was wrong to bring you here," Ella said, looking apologetic. "It's too confusing for everyone. I should have taken you home to Katherine, like Clove suggested."

"It was very … interesting to come here. However, I believe I belong in Carlisle. This time is impossibly strange for me."

Clove nodded. She'd put him through enough. He deserved to go back to Katherine. She was grieving for him, after all. "Let's take you home. Kate, we'll be back in a sec."

"You're getting awfully cavalier about time travel, aren't you?" Ella whispered in Clove's ear as Matthew said goodbye to Kate. *"Just travelling back three hundred years, no biggie, save me a biscuit."*

"Oops, gotta pop home. I left the oven on three thousand years in the future!" Clove replied, laughing.

"It was an honour to meet you, Kate," Matthew said.

A lump rose in Clove's throat at the sight of them together. They treated each other so tenderly, like the other person was the most valuable thing in the world.

"I never would have imagined that my Katherine could be living somewhere like this," Matthew continued. "I can't wait to tell her how incredible she is – you are." He touched Kate's cheek.

Kate kissed Matthew carefully, eyes closed and hands curling around his elbows. "I love you," she murmured against his lips, pressing their foreheads together. "I always have, and I always will."

Matthew's fingers followed the line of her jaw, and he kissed the side of her mouth and then her temple. "Look after our daughter. She's very special."

When they kissed again, Clove looked away. She started helping Ella to choose when to arrive in 1745.

"Are you ready?" Clove asked Matthew after a moment.

He nodded. "Thank you for bringing me here," he said. "It's the greatest gift you could have given me."

Ella took Matthew and Clove's hands, and activated her Skim. Kate waved goodbye, wiping tears away, as the wormhole pulled them in again.

Carlisle, England, 1745

They landed in the attic in the house in Carlisle. Only days before, Clove and Ella had slept in this very room. It was neat and tidy now, ready for the next maids to use. Clove wondered whether the new servants would be time travellers too, on a sightseeing trip to Clove's history.

Matthew seemed to visibly relax. "Home," he said, and smiled. "At last."

Clove suddenly wished she was dressed more time appropriately. It felt unnatural to be here in jeans and a T-shirt, when she'd spent so long blending in with a dress.

"Shall we go and find Katherine?" Matthew asked, smiling hard enough to split his face.

Clove led them down the servants' staircase to Katherine's bedroom. Winter had arrived since Clove's last visit, and through the windows she could see that the garden was white with frost.

"The Jacobite siege is happening right now," Clove told Matthew before she knocked on Katherine's door, remembering what she had read in the Folios. "But the house is empty. The family fled the city, and Katherine is here alone. A few days ago she saw you die in the cathedral and then come back to life, only it wasn't you. It was the Matthew from 1854. I used the time machine to bring him here to try and get this timeline back on track – but he didn't have a suit and the radiation killed him. Katherine will be very sad and confused at the moment."

Matthew ran a hand through his hair, a little nervously.

Clove went on, "I should go in first. Wait further down the corridor. We don't want to give her a heart attack when she sees her dead boyfriend." Clove knocked on the door. "Miss Finchley?" she called.

"Who's there?" Katherine asked as she opened the door. She was wearing a nightgown, with a shawl wrapped around her shoulders. Her eyes were red from crying. "Anise?" she said, surprised. "What are you doing here? Have my aunt and uncle returned to the city?" She gasped as she took in Clove's appearance. "What are you *wearing*?"

"I have something to tell you," Clove said carefully. "I'm not really a maid. I'm actually from the future."

"What?" Katherine gasped, falling back against the door frame. Her face went white. "You mean, you … you're the witch! The one who … who brought Matthew from the future after my Matthew died in the cathedral!"

Clove opened her mouth, and then closed it again. She'd had a whole speech planned out, but Katherine was quicker to pick up the intricacies of time travel than she'd expected. "That was me," she said instead. "I'm sorry. I know it made everything so much more complicated for you. But I had to do it. I was saving the world. The future would have been destroyed otherwise."

"We suspected as much," Katherine said, voice fierce. "We thought there must be a reason for it. It seemed impossible for anyone to be so cruel otherwise. He *died*, Anise. You brought Matthew back to me, and then let him die right in front of my eyes, and there was nothing I could do!"

Clove flinched. "I know. I'm sorry. I'm so sorry. Everything was going wrong in my time. I was dying, and my father had just been shot! It was a nightmare, and I panicked. I tried to fix things as best I could. I'm sorry you had to live with the consequences."

Katherine squared her shoulders, wiping away her tears. "Was it worth his death? Did everything become better, for you?"

Clove nodded. "It did. And … I have some news. I took Matthew – your Matthew, your coachman – to the future. I healed him. I saved his life."

Katherine stared at Clove, uncomprehending. "You *saved* him?" Her voice cracked.

Clove met her gaze unblinkingly. "He's alive, and he's well."

"Where is he?" Katherine said. "I'll do anything, just please give him back to me!"

"I'm here." Matthew appeared from where he had been standing just out of sight down the corridor. Katherine's face crumpled with joy. She and Matthew fell on one another, kissing desperately.

"We should leave them," Clove said to Ella, after watching them for a moment. She was torn between joy and guilt. "They don't need us any more. Let's go back to 2040. We have to track down my father."

Before they could leave, Matthew spoke. "I just wanted to say … thank you. Thank you for everything, Clove."

"Thank you," Katherine echoed. "Thank you so much for bringing him home to me. I don't understand any of

what you have done, or why, but I am so, *so* grateful that you brought him back to me."

Clove smiled. "You're welcome. I'm sorry again that it was so overcomplicated and messy. I tried my best." To Matthew, she said, "Don't forget to take your penicillin."

Matthew grinned. "I promise. I hope you find me – I mean ... er ... Matt."

"Are we ready?" Ella said.

"Take us to the future," Clove confirmed, and waved to her parents, instantly feeling foolish.

They waved back as they fell out of sight, and then Matthew and Katherine were left together in 1745, where they belonged.

CHAPTER 36

A story by Ella Walker, age 11

Clove Sutcliffe
& the

* *Regency* * *

* * *Cyborg* * *

Found this in your drawer when
I was looking for headphones.
Totally not judging, but did you
write fanfiction about me when
you were little? – C ×

NO, NO, NO! I THOUGHT I'D
DESTROYED THIS. I have to go
and have a very angry discussion
with my mum. If you hear the sound
of screaming, don't worry, I'll just be
murdering her. Ella ××

File note: Messages between CLOVE SUTCLIFFE and ELENORE
          WALKER

LEEDS, ENGLAND, 2040

Kate jumped in surprise when Ella and Clove arrived back in the motel room. "You're back *already*? You were only gone thirty seconds!"

"Time travel," Ella explained. "I had a great time sneaking up on Clove before she knew I had a Skim."

"*That's* how you were always so quiet in 1745!" Clove said, with dawning realization, thinking of the time Ella had found Clove in the stables and interrupted her when she'd been trying to get Matthew's DNA. It seemed so much longer ago than a few days. "This makes so much more sense."

"You two have a very ... confusing timeline," Kate said, squinting at them.

Ella smiled. "It isn't that complicated really. Clove and I are in love in the future, just like you and Matt are in love in the past."

"That isn't simple *at all*," Clove interjected. "And stop telling people that we're in love! We're not!"

"Not *yet*," Ella said with a cheeky grin. "And – speak for yourself." She shot Clove a salacious look.

Turning red, Clove let out a loud sigh, hoping that it conveyed the heavy weight that all of Ella's drama was adding to her life.

"Do you know my grandmothers?" Kate said, clearly eager to change the subject. "In your time?"

Clove shook her head. "I didn't even know you and Matt were my parents until a few weeks ago. I don't know anyone at all from your side of the family."

"Oh," Kate said in disappointment. "I wonder if they're still alive in 2056. I hope they are. You would like them."

"Maybe you can introduce me to them?" Clove said. The question made her nervous, but Kate just broke into a brilliantly bright smile.

"Of course! But ... I think we should rescue Matt first. He's been in prison for nine months now, after all."

"Right," Clove said, and turned on her watch. "Spart, have you managed to find out anything from the prison's system?"

> I have successfully obtained access to the Wakefield network. Subject allocation "MATT"'s prison cell is number 345.

Kate lit up with joy. "That's on Spart's map! I knew my ancient one would be out of date by now. We can Skim right into the room! Is Skim a verb?" she asked Ella. "Can you Skim through time? It should be. It sounds magical and scientific all at once."

Clove grinned to herself. She liked Kate a lot, especially now she wasn't so sad. Instead, she was almost giddy with relief that they were so close to saving Matt.

> 345 is a single occupancy cell, so you should be able to gain access and remove "MATT" from the premises without being observed.

> The CCTV network was also decidedly simple to access. If I were more morally inclined, I might update the system for them.

"You're just used to technology decades more advanced," Clove pointed out.

> You are correct. By comparison, their vintage software is almost prehistoric.

Ella choked, and everyone turned to her in surprise. "Nothing!" she said. "Nothing. It's just ... 'vintage software'. There's a human/cyborg Regency romance novel called that in my time. Not that I ... er ... read those kinds of things." Ella flushed red and suddenly became very interested in the design of the curtains.

"I definitely want to hear more about that later," Clove told her. "But now is not the time. Kate, do you think this is going to work?"

Kate nodded. "We should set the wormhole to arrive at night, so we know he'll be in his cell."

Clove agreed. She sat down with Kate to make a plan, reluctantly looking away from the attractive shade of pink that Ella's cheeks had turned.

By the time their strategy was ready, it was midnight. They decided to wait until tomorrow, because Clove couldn't remember how long it had been since she'd last had a proper night's sleep, and Kate was still recovering from childbirth.

Kate took one of the twin beds, so Clove and Ella were left with the other bed, which made Clove feel a little awkward. In the end, there was nothing to be nervous about. Ella kissed the tip of Clove's nose, then fell asleep in seconds.

Clove watched her for a few minutes, taking in the long

curl of her eyelashes against her cheeks in the dim glow of the streetlights through the curtains. She didn't think she was in love with Ella, but then she didn't have much of a comparison. She did like Ella a lot, and she liked the thought that one day they might be a couple, as in sync with each other as *KateandMatt* or *TomandJen*.

CloveandElla. EllaandClove. She liked the sound of it.

There was still so much she didn't know about her, though. Besides, how would it even work, having a girlfriend who lived in the future? You couldn't get more long distance than that. Would they be able to message each other when Ella went back to her own time? Could the Skim send emails through time?

"Matt," Kate mumbled sadly in her sleep, and then rolled over and snorted out a dream-laugh. "My delicate flower," she said affectionately.

If Kate and Matt could make it work over all of the years they'd been together, then maybe Clove and Ella wouldn't have a problem.

Clove let herself drift into sleep.

The next morning, Kate woke Clove up before six. "Can we go now?" she asked, as Clove blinked sleepily and tried not to breathe morning-breath all over the place. "I've been lying awake for *hours* and I know it's still early, but I need my Matt back. Please."

Clove let go of Ella's waist, which she'd somehow wrapped her arm around during the night. "All right," she said, sitting up. "We can go. I need something to eat first, though."

Kate pushed a bowl of cereal into her lap.

"Is this *apple juice*?" Clove asked, staring into the bowl.

"Tell me about it!" Kate said, looking vindicated. "Matt doesn't think it's that weird, even though it's *so gross*. But there's still milk rationing because of the war."

Ella, who was somehow still asleep, rolled over and pushed her arm over Clove's stomach, mumbling something incoherent. Clove patted her consolingly on the head and began eating.

When they were ready to leave, Clove held Ella's waist, then took Kate's hand. Ella had entered the exact coordinates of Matt's prison cell into the Skim, along with the time they wanted to arrive – about 1 a.m. that night. All the time jumps made Clove's head spin.

"Ready?" Ella asked.

Clove took a deep breath and nodded.

Ella pressed the Skim on her wrist, and they were all sucked into the wormhole in a mess of limbs and sparks of phosphenes.

HM PRISON WAKEFIELD, ENGLAND, 2040

Clove opened her eyes tentatively. Wherever they were, it was very dark.

"No prison security against wormholes," Ella whispered, shaking her head. "Amateurs."

Once Clove's vision had adjusted to the light, she could

make out a door in front of her. As Clove touched the handle, an alarm sounded – a harsh klaxon that echoed all around them. A beam of scalding bright light shone down from the ceiling to reveal a long hallway lined with rows of metal doors. Prison cells, Clove realized. Somehow they had arrived in the corridor instead of in Matt's cell.

"We're on the wrong side of the door!" Clove had to yell to make herself heard over the blaring of the sirens.

Ella grabbed Kate's hand and dived for Clove. Then they were gone, twisting around in another wormhole. Seconds later they reappeared somewhere else dark. The alarm was still screaming.

"Where are we now?" Kate shouted.

"On the other side of the door!" Ella replied. As she was speaking, the alarms cut out, and she found herself yelling into a sudden silence. "Oops," she whispered.

Clove checked her watch, hoping Spart would have an explanation. "Spart, what's going on? Can you shut down the security system?" If he didn't, they would have only a matter of seconds to get Matt out before the guards arrived.

She read his response off the screen.

> I have succeeded in gaining control of the security system.
I have cut off the CCTV feed for this floor. You're not being recorded.

> I have also adjusted the records to state that the alarm was activated in a different cell block, so no guards should investigate here.

"Spart's in the system," Clove whispered to Kate and Ella. "We're safe for now."

"Kate?" said a voice from the darkness.

Clove turned on her watch's torch. A sparse prison cell became visible, with a narrow bed along one wall, and a sink in one corner. There was a figure sitting up in the bed.

"Matt!" Kate dived for the bed and the figure, wrapping her arms and legs around him. She pulled him into a kiss. Matt grabbed the back of her top in his fists so tightly that Clove could see the skin on his knuckles turn white. She widened her eyes in embarrassment at Ella, but Ella didn't notice. She had her ear to the metal door of the cell, presumably listening for any sounds of movement outside.

When Kate eventually let Matt go, he looked at Clove and Ella.

"Here we go again," Ella muttered, as Clove braced herself. She didn't know if he would remember her or not. Kate remembered her past lives, but that didn't mean Matt would.

"Oh, this is—" Kate said, gesturing to Clove.

"I know who you are," Matt interrupted. He swallowed nervously. "Hello again, Clove. I haven't seen you in three centuries."

"Hi," she said. "It's been a long time, Dad."

"You know who she is?" Kate asked. "How?" She couldn't seem to stop running her hands over his arms, shoulders, through his hair.

He kissed her again. "I've been waiting for you since the alarms went off," he said. "It took me a couple of months to sift through my memories from 1745, but eventually I remembered Clove, and how she took me – me in 1745, I mean – to the future. I knew you'd come for me, eventually. Or I hoped, anyway. I knew you were trying to find me."

The idea of remembering a plan you'd been told three centuries earlier was so incredible that Clove wanted to ask a dozen follow-up questions, but this wasn't the moment for a tearful reunion. "We should go, before the guards find us. Spart sent them on a wild-goose chase, but we don't want to hang around, just in case."

Ella immediately began setting up the coordinates on the Skim to take them back to the motel. "Everyone, come over here!" she called when she was ready.

Clove wrapped an arm around Ella's waist again, leaning against her side. Kate took Ella's free hand and Matt held onto Kate. Clove closed her eyes, preparing herself for the tug of the wormhole and savouring the joy of finally finding both of her parents.

After a few seconds, she opened her eyes. "Ella?" she asked. "Why are we still in the cell?"

Ella prodded at the Skim. "It's not working…"

"Crap," Kate said.

"What? Why?" Clove leant in to look. Despite the tension of the situation, she was desperate to get her hands on the Skim and find out how the intricate technology worked.

Ella pushed her forehead away. "Let me see."

"Is it broken?" Matt asked, less curious and more intensely worried.

"Quiet," Ella said, her voice strained. Everyone held their

breath while she pressed her wrist, trying to make something happen. The Skim's glow had dimmed to a weak shine.

"It's out of battery," Ella said, eventually. "Shit."

"Ella!" Clove said, horrified. "Didn't you charge it?"

"I didn't realize how much power it would take to transport so many people. I don't have enough charge to get us all home."

"What do we do?" Matt asked, a tremor of panic in his voice. "There aren't any plug sockets in here."

"Is it solar powered?" Clove asked.

Ella nodded. After pulling a solar-powered battery out of her pocket, she showed Clove how it worked. It wasn't that different to how Clove charged her watch.

"So we wait until dawn," Clove said firmly, squeezing Ella's hand. "It can charge when the sun rises, then we'll be ready to go before anyone wakes up."

"I don't know how long it will take to charge," Ella admitted. She looked wide-eyed and terrified. "It could be hours."

"We'll manage," Clove said.

"It's hours and hours until dawn," Matt said.

"We can start now," Kate said. She shone her tablet's light on the solar panels of the battery charger. "It's not much, but it's better than nothing. Clove, use your computer's light too."

They all waited in silence. After what felt like an eternity, the battery percentage flicked up a single per cent.

"It's working!" Ella said.

"We'll be OK," Clove said, reassuring herself as much as

anyone else. "This will work. It's going to be OK."

"Only six hours to go," Kate said, trying for a feeble smile.

"What a great escape plan you lot came up with," Matt said, and sat down heavily on his bed. *"Let's get ourselves trapped in there with him, that'll work!"*

Eventually, when Clove had started to feel like time was standing still, the sun began to turn the sky a light grey. When Ella saw the light trickling into the cell, she hopped onto Matt's bed to put the battery on the lip of the window, angling it towards the rising sun.

"How long do you think it's going to take?" Matt asked. His arm was around Kate's shoulders, fingers tangled in her hair. Much like Ella and Clove, they'd sat close together all night.

Ella shrugged. "At least twenty minutes."

"What time does everyone wake up, Matt?" Clove asked.

"Half seven."

"Thirty minutes away." Ella's expression tightened. It tightened even more when they heard a noise from the next cell: a cough followed by the sound of feet hitting concrete. A moment later came the noise of the toilet being flushed. Matt's neighbour had woken up.

"Be very quiet," Matt said, the words barely more than a breath. "Noise travels."

Returning to sit next to her, Ella took Clove's hand.

They all waited, trying not to move or rustle or even breathe.

It was still barely light enough to make out each other's faces. Despite Matt telling them to be quiet, Ella kept standing up to look at the battery. She was too nervous to sit still. After the third time, Ella shook her head. "It's charging so slowly," she mouthed. "Another ten minutes at least."

Noises came from the other cells around them as more inmates woke up. When the lights in the corridor flickered on, Matt whispered, "We have to go. Now."

"Is it enough?" Kate hissed. "We don't want to get stuck somewhere between here and there."

"It has to be," Ella said, taking the battery from the windowsill. She tapped it to her wrist, letting the charge transfer into the Skim.

"Leave me here if it can't transport all of us," Matt said. "Leave me here, and get yourselves to safety."

"No way!" Kate said. She grabbed onto his arm, her expression indicating that she would have to be physically removed from his side.

Ella turned on the Skim, her inhale of anticipation loud in the silence. As she was setting up the coordinates, footsteps could be heard outside the cell door, followed by the noise of a key turning in a lock.

"Ella!" Clove yelled, but it was too late.

The door slid open, and a guard stared at them from the doorway.

"Stop!" he yelled, and made a move to grab Matt's wrist.

Clove acted without thinking. She stuck her foot out and tripped up the guard. They were all sucked into the wormhole as he fell to the floor. He was left staring in surprise at the empty space where they had been.

CHAPTER 37

newsbreaking.com ×

newsbreaking.com ★

Home > News

Prison break confirmed

14 Comments

European terrorist Matt Galloway's escape from Wakefield Prison yesterday was assisted by three unidentified females, it was revealed in a police statement earlier this morning. The whereabouts of all four people is currently unknown.

The police have issued warrants for the arrest of Matt Galloway, now 19, and the other suspected terrorists. A prison guard who witnessed the breakout, and wishes to remain anonymous, told this newspaper that they were "a blonde, a brunette and a redhead".

No images of the prison break were available due to an apparent malfunction with the prison security cameras. However, this correspondent suspects that the redhead in question may be none other than Katherine Finchley, Galloway's accomplice and fellow student at the University of Nottingham.

Finchley, 19, fled across the border into Scotland after Galloway's arrest, aided by Matthew Galloway's brother, Tom Galloway. Tom, 23, is also known by his infamous hacking alias Spartacus. Their location for the last nine months has been unknown.

Police gave no information about how the escape occurred or whether they have any leads in their investigation.

Follow @newsbreaking for more updates as the story develops.

LEEDS, ENGLAND, 2040

Even before the raging hurricane of the wormhole had disappeared, depositing them in the motel room, Ella was laughing. "Did you *trip* the guard?" she asked Clove, between giggles.

"Oh my God," Clove said, resting her hands on her knees and trying to catch her breath. She felt sick. "That was terrifying."

"It was really hot," Ella told Clove, fluttering her hand by her face as if she was swooning. "Seriously. Do that again."

"She got that ridiculous bravery from you," Matt said to Kate.

"I know," Kate replied, looking proud and a little smug.

All Clove could think about was having a long, peaceful nap. Her head was spinning as fast as the phosphenes under her eyelids. The constant time travel was taking its toll on her. "Can we go home now?" she asked. "I never want to time travel again. This is *painful.*"

"I'm sorry," Kate said. "I have some bad news."

Everyone jerked around to stare at her, except Matt, who already had been.

"We still have to get the bacteria," she said.

"*What?*" Clove said, and dropped down onto the bed. "When will you all just *let me rest?*"

"This is the last thing we need to do, I promise," Kate said. "You know how we stole a vial of bacteria from a government lab to use as evidence that the English government was planning to undertake biological warfare in the war against the EU? Well, we lost the bacteria when Matt was arrested, because it was in his pocket. And so nobody believed me when I told the press. The English government still has a massive quantity of it, and if we don't make people believe us, there is nothing to stop them from releasing it and destroying the entire world."

"You want us to steal another vial," Clove guessed. "From the lab?"

"We need to stop it from being released," Matt confirmed. "Thankfully you have a *time machine* to help. That would have made things so much easier the last time, by the way."

"You'll have to give me a few minutes to plug in the Skim and recharge it properly," Ella said, and then she looked guiltily at Clove. "I mean, if doing another break out is all right with you, Clove? It's your decision."

Clove smiled at her, then nodded.

CENTRAL SCIENCE LABORATORIES, WEST MIDLANDS, ENGLAND, 2039

They landed in the deserted car park outside a huge derelict building, covered in green mould.

"This is the secret location of the English military's supply of bacterial weapons of mass destruction," Kate said. "They made me and Matt create the bacteria – the versions of us in 2019, I mean. We worked here then."

"We didn't know what we were making," Matt added.

"We thought it was a pesticide for crops. We would never have worked on it if we'd known it was a weapon."

"And they still have it. If it's ever released, it could kill billions of people," Kate added.

Clove looked up at the building, amazed. She knew the events from the movie *The Bacteria Conspiracy*, but it was hard to believe it was really real. Just inside those doors was a substance lethal enough to wipe out the entire human race. It wasn't just a story. It was real, and it was happening right now.

Following Kate's lead, they tentatively approached the entrance. The door had been smashed and glass scattered across the floor.

"I did that," Kate said, kind of proudly. "Last time we were here."

"This is the same day as your break-in," Ella said. "If I timed it right, you're still here."

"What if we run into ourselves?" Matt asked.

"We'll just have to make sure we don't. I didn't want to risk changing things by coming earlier," Ella explained. "If we had broken in first, the lab might have increased security, which would stop you from getting in. That would start a time loop."

"And we couldn't come after we left that first time," Matt said thoughtfully, "because they'd have set up guards then, too. It could only be today."

"We'll just have to be careful," Kate said. "Come on." She led the way into the laboratory, glass cracking under their feet. The foyer of the building had a curved reception desk and a small waiting area. Everywhere was dusty but neat, as if it had just been abandoned at the end of a working day.

"We need to go down to the basement," Matt whispered. "Through that corridor, then down the stairs. There was no one here last time. It should be easy."

Clove wanted to disagree – in her experience, going into the past was never easy – but she bit her tongue. Maybe this time everything would go right. Maybe this time they wouldn't destroy the future.

Ella took Clove's hand as they followed Kate and Matt down the corridor. Clove was nervous. They had to get this right. They needed a sample of the biological weapon, so that they could prove its existence and alert the world to the fact that the English government was planning to use it in the war against the EU. If they couldn't, then Clove might return to 2056 to find a desolate wasteland, with every plant, animal and human destroyed. The thought sent a shiver down her spine. She knew now how easy it was for the future to change.

Ahead of her, Matt and Kate had paused in front of one of the office doors. The derelict building was like a time capsule. Everything was half-finished: experiments were laid out on benches, lab books still open.

"Holy crap, that's us," Kate said, peering through the glass window of the door. Matt shushed her while Clove stood on tiptoes to stare over Kate's shoulder. Inside the office, watching a projected video play on a blood-splattered wall, were Kate and Matt. The very same Kate and Matt that Clove was with *right now*. The sight of them made her head spin.

The Kate in the office was holding a small ornament of a fox in one hand. Clove's heart jolted. That ornament was on her desk at home. It had been in the box that Kate had left for Clove as a baby – the box that had started this whole thing for Clove. This must be where it had come from, then – the science labs where another Katherine had worked in 2019.

"We should go," Ella whispered. "It never ends well when time-displaced versions of people meet each other."

They carried on down the hall, trying to walk as quietly as possible, and then went down a flight of concrete stairs to the basement. It was lit with a narrow line of fluorescent bulbs on the ceiling. At the other end was a heavy metal door. Spray-painted on it in yellow were the words: BACTERIAL STORAGE ZONE. DO NOT ENTER.

In front of the door, head down and playing a game on his tablet, was a soldier. Everyone froze.

Without speaking, they all started back up the flight of stairs. At the top, they stopped.

"He must be guarding the supply of bacteria for the army," Clove whispered. The military clearly didn't trust that the quarantine warnings outside the building would be enough to keep people out. They must have set up a guard as an extra precaution. "Ella, is there a way you can Skim inside the freezer and pick up a sample without him noticing?"

Ella shook her head. "I don't have the exact coordinates, so I'd probably end up opening a wormhole inside a wall. Besides, he might hear me. It's too risky."

"I don't understand," Kate said. "There wasn't a guard

when we came last time. We just walked right up to the freezer."

"Then we need to get rid of him," Matt replied. "Quickly! Before the past versions of us walk up and get themselves shot."

"I'll distract him," Clove said. "I can go to the other side of the building and make some kind of noise so he has to go and investigate it. While I'm gone, you can get a vial."

"I'll come with you," Ella said immediately, to Clove's relief. Her stomach was already tying itself in a knot at the thought of somehow evading a trained soldier with a gun. At least Ella had an exit strategy built into her arm.

"We'll meet you by the main entrance," Clove told Kate and Matt. "Try not to get killed or captured, or run into yourselves and destroy the universe."

"We'll try," Kate said, and saluted her.

Clove pulled Ella back down the corridor. As they passed the office again, Clove peered in. The past versions of Kate and Matt were still inside, watching the video recording. They had no idea what lay ahead of them: Matt would be arrested the very next day. Kate must already be pregnant with Clove, even if she didn't know it yet.

Clove made herself look away.

Once they were back in the foyer, Ella pushed open a door, revealing another flight of stairs. It must lead down to the other end of the basement. "Lucky guess," Ella said, starting down them. "So what's the plan?"

Clove hadn't given it any thought. "Make a loud noise, draw him close, run away?"

Ella half laughed. "Sounds reasonable."

At the bottom of the stairs was another door. Clove slammed it shut behind her. The loud thud as it hit the doorjamb sounded deafening in the quiet. "He definitely heard that," Clove said. "Let's go."

"Wait."

"Ella, he's got a gun," Clove said. "Let's *go!*"

"Hang on a minute." Ella was staring intently down the dimly lit corridor, waiting for the soldier to appear in view. After a few more heartbeats, there was the noise of running, and the soldier came sprinting out of the darkness, gun raised.

"Come on. *Ella!*"

"Not yet."

Clove's heart felt like it was beating ten times as fast as normal. She didn't know if she was more scared or angry. "*Ella!*"

"Stay where you are," the soldier called. "Don't move!"

Clove tugged on Ella's wrist. "Come on. They've had enough time to get a vial. We need to go."

"He'll follow us," Ella said, voice tight. Then she jerked out of Clove's grasp and ran at the soldier full speed.

They collided.

And disappeared.

Clove stared, open-mouthed, at the space where they had been.

"I told her to *tell me* stuff before she did it," Clove said aloud, to no one.

She waited a few seconds to see if Ella or the soldier

would reappear, and then ran back up the stairs. Ella had said to meet at the main entrance. Clove could shout at her there, if she reappeared at all. Clove wouldn't let herself think about that.

When she reached the ground floor, the foyer was deserted. She stood still, at a loss as to what to do next. Should she leave? Should she go back to the basement, to see if Ella had reappeared? What if everyone had found each other and they were all looking for her?

Before she could make a decision, Kate and Matt came sprinting down the corridor, holding hands. *Her* Kate and Matt. She could tell because Matt was still in his prison uniform.

Almost breathless with relief, she asked, "Did you get it?"

Matt leant his hands on his knees, panting. "Yes."

Kate held a glass vial out to Clove. It was filled with a creamy gel-like substance and there was a black skull-and-crossbones printed on the label. Clove's momentary happiness was erased as soon as she remembered that Ella was still missing. "Ella's gone! She took the soldier somewhere!"

"What do you mean, 'took him somewhere'?" Kate asked.

"With the Skim," Clove explained. "They just disappeared."

"Where did they go?"

"She didn't tell me, *like always.*"

"What do we do?" Matt asked. "We can't just wait here and get caught. More soldiers are going to arrive any minute. That's what happened last time. We stole their car."

Clove ran a hand through her hair. "We're stuck here without Ella. We need the Skim."

As she spoke, she heard a military vehicle drive up to the building.

"Hide!" Kate said. She and Matt dived behind the reception desk. There was no room for Clove, so she hid behind a sofa in the waiting area.

What was Ella doing? If she left it any longer, they would be caught for sure. There would be no way to get out unseen once the building was filled with soldiers.

Had the Skim run out of battery? Was that what was stopping Ella from returning? Surely she could just spend a few hours recharging it, and then return here, to this point in time. Unless she'd been killed by the soldier, or caught. If he'd arrested her, he might have taken her Skim away. She'd have no way of escaping at all. Clove was developing a terrible migraine. *Where was Ella?*

The car had pulled up outside the building. Its door opened, closed.

Clove held her breath.

A man's voice said, "The door's smashed in. This isn't a false alarm this time – there are intruders on site."

"Miller hasn't responded to messages for twenty minutes, Sir," said another voice.

"He was in the basement?"

"Yes, Sir."

"Goddamn. He must have been taken out. Call for backup. I'm going inside."

Glass shattered beneath the feet of the soldiers as they

entered the foyer. The hair on the back of Clove's neck stood up. She wished she could see what they were doing. She wished she could warn Ella that there were people here, in case she did manage to come back. It seemed to take for ever for the soldiers to cross the reception area, but finally their footsteps receded as they took the stairs to the basement. Clove let out a long breath of relief.

"Clove?" Kate called, voice pitched low but still echoing.

"Here," Clove said, standing up. There were cobwebs in her hair. She repressed a shudder.

"We need to go *now*," Matt said. "They're about to find us – the other us – at the freezer, when we were there getting a vial the first time round. Then they'll chase us up here. We can't be here for that."

"We need Ella," Clove said, frustrated and worried. "We can't go without her. And if we leave the building, she won't know where to find us."

As she spoke, Clove heard more glass breaking. Heart in her mouth, she spun round, expecting to see more soldiers with guns raised. Instead Ella was standing in the doorway to the building, looking sheepish.

"Misjudged it," she said.

The sight of her settled something deep and terrified in Clove's chest. *"Ella!"* Clove shouted, and ran towards her. "What the hell did you do?"

Ella actually stepped back, although it seemed more like a tactical relocation than fear. "I was getting rid of the guard?"

"Where did you *go*? Why didn't you *tell me*?" Clove barely resisted the urge to shake her.

"You can have this argument later, but now we need to leave," Matt said.

LEEDS, ENGLAND, 2040

As soon as they were back in the motel room, Clove rounded on Ella. "You promised not to do things without telling me!" she shouted.

Ella folded her arms defensively. "It was a spur of the moment thing."

Clove didn't believe her. Ella basically had a reference manual telling her what needed to be done for the whole of Clove's life.

"Oh, as if it wasn't in your textbook!" Clove said.

"It wasn't, actually," Ella said stiffly. She glanced at Kate and Matt, who were looking awkward. "Can we talk in the bathroom?"

Once they were inside, Clove shut the door behind them. "I didn't mean to snap at you in front of them," she said. "It's just I never know what you're going to do and it ... it drives me crazy!"

"I really didn't mean to keep you in the dark this time. It just occurred to me, as the soldier was running at us, that there was no way we could get away from him. He'd just follow us to the entrance. So I took him forward two hours into the future."

Clove's anger abated slightly. She hadn't been upset with Ella, not really. She was just worried and scared. She touched

Ella's hand. "If you hadn't done that, we would all be in a jail cell right now."

Ella took Clove's hand. She immediately felt herself relax.

"Is it going to change the future?" Clove asked. "That you've done something different?"

"I guess we'll find out." Ella tugged Clove closer, resting her forehead against hers.

"We did it," Clove said. She nosed across Ella's cheek, tracing the line of her cheekbone. "We found my parents, saved my dad."

"Saved the world," Ella added, her hands gliding over Clove's shoulders and down her back, then up again, as if she just couldn't stop herself. "You've had a busy day."

Clove kissed her, deep and slow, and then pulled away to drop a series of smaller kisses on her lips.

"Are you sure you want to waste time kissing me?" Ella asked against Clove's mouth, fingers wrapped in her hair. "Don't you have to go and save humanity again?"

When Ella started to snicker, Clove kissed her again to shut her up, sweeping her tongue over her lips. Ella's laughter turned into a sigh.

CHAPTER 38

Angels among us?

A soldier at Central Science Laboratories, West Midlands, UK, claims to have "travelled in time" during a routine security mission.

The soldier says that a "blonde girl" took him to the future and then disappeared into "thin air".

Could this be the first sign of the Rapture that we've all been waiting for? Are our governments once again trying to hide evidence of what we all know in our hearts to be true: that angels are real, and coming for us all?

We are all sending our prayers to you and your loved ones in these dire times.

Leave a comment | 134 comments

10 Ways
To Make Sure That YOU Get Abducted By Aliens This Christmas – And What To Take With You!

21 Things That Only Ancient Multidimensional Beings of Universe Prehistory Will Understand

Get Excited, Shippers: These Boyband Members Are Definitely Dating ... VAMPIRES!

Angels CONFIRMED!

Our most avid readers will remember the angel sighting by a soldier last year. Today we have more information about Earth's latest CONFIRMED celestial guest – and she has friends!

A prison guard at Wakefield Prison, UK, has said he saw three angels at the jail in the early hours of yesterday morning. He described them as "horrifyingly attractive", "angry" and "good at tripping people up". He told UltraTopSecretSeekers.net that the fierce, angelic beings took one of the prisoners away in a "whirling vacuum of smoke and flames".

I'm sure I'm not the only one who can freely admit to being jealous of that foursome!

Sign up here to receive priority booking for the Rapture.

Leave a comment | 97 comments

Folios/v8/Time-landscape-2040/MS-17

File note: News articles posted on conspiracy theorist
website UltraTopSecretSeekers.net, November 2039–
July 2040

LEEDS, ENGLAND, 2040

When Clove and Ella left the bathroom, Kate and Matt were sitting close together on the bed. They jumped apart, looking guilty, when the girls appeared.

"What do we do now?" Clove asked.

"We have to take the bacteria to NATO," Kate said. "So that they can see what the English government is doing and stop them."

Clove nodded. "That's what happened after you escaped in the film – I mean … er … in all the … um … newspaper reports."

"Film?!" Kate asked, sounding delighted, just as Matt said, *"Film?"* in the strained voice of a man who was already bracing himself for a horrifying ordeal.

"It was a really faithful adaptation of your lives," Clove said, trying not to laugh at such a blatant lie.

Ella snorted.

Clove cleared her throat, avoiding everyone's eyes. "Anyway. Spart, what do the records say happened after Matt was broken out of prison? I know that NATO seized control of the English government once they had evidence of the bacteria – but how did they get it? What do we do with the vial?" She looked mistrustfully at the bacteria, which Matt was holding.

> According to the NATO report, a vial of bacteria was dropped off in an anonymous package at the NATO headquarters in Brussels, Belgium, the day of subject allocation "MATT"'s escape.

> Also in the package was a DVD of the evidence taken from CSL that proved the English government had created a weapon of mass destruction.

> Within four hours, the sample was in a laboratory being analysed, and emergency action had been taken against the English government.

"If Ella can help us get to Brussels, it should be easy enough to leave the package at NATO," Matt said.

"I've got the DVD in my bag," Kate said in surprise. "I was planning to send it with the bacteria anyway."

"Spart, can you send the headquarter coordinates over to the Skim?" Clove asked.

Matt wrapped the vial in several layers of bubble wrap, to be absolutely sure it wouldn't break and contaminate the NATO headquarters. He put it in an envelope along with the DVD Kate had brought with her. In a marker on the outside, he wrote WARNING: OPEN IN A SECURE LABORATORY, DANGEROUS EVIDENCE INSIDE.

It took Ella about thirty seconds to open up a wormhole to the inside of the NATO headquarters in Brussels. She'd timed it to be around 8 a.m. there, so the office was empty. Matt carefully placed the package on the reception desk.

"Done," Kate said, looking like a huge weight had been lifted from her mind. "It's finished!"

"We did it!" Clove said, amazed. "We actually did it!"

"We can go home," Matt said, beaming, his eyes bright.

Kate hugged Matt and Clove, one arm around each of their shoulders. After a second, she pulled Ella into the hug too. For a moment the four of them just stood there, unable to believe what they'd achieved. The bacteria was with NATO. Matt was out of prison, and he and Kate would now be cleared of all terrorism charges. And Clove had found her parents – the search which had started this whole thing off.

It was finally time to go home.

"I think I need to eat an entire pizza right now," Kate said.

Clove laughed, feeling a pang of hunger in her stomach too. "Agreed. But … can we do it at home, please?" Now that this was all over, she really wanted to see Tom and Jen, to make sure they were safe as well.

"Where *is* home, exactly?" Ella asked. She looked at Kate and Matt. "Should I take you to Scotland in 2040, to when Clove was a baby?"

"No!" Clove said, more loudly than she meant to. "I mean … I don't want you to go back to then."

Kate looked hurt. "What do you mean?"

Clove bit at her nails. "I just… I…"

"What is it?" Matt asked.

"I don't want to lose my parents," she burst out.

"We *are* your parents," Kate said, not understanding.

"No, you're not. I mean … you are. But Tom and Jen, they—" Clove sighed. "If you go back to 2040, then Tom and Jen won't be my parents any more. They'll just be my aunt and uncle who I only see every now and again." Clove didn't want to lose Tom and Jen once more. It would be like when she'd destroyed the future. She couldn't go home to 2056 and find it *changed*. Not again.

"Clove, I—" Kate said.

"Kate, look. Can't you both come to 2056, with me? We can just say you escaped and made your way home. Then I can have both of you *and* Mum and Dad."

Kate was hesitating. "But, my baby…"

"*Please*, Kate. Please don't take my parents away from me."

Kate looked to Matt.

"It's her life," he said softly. "And besides, if we raised her, would she have gone back to the past? Would any of this have ever happened?"

"It's a paradox," Ella said. "It could create a time loop. You might erase this whole journey from history."

Kate sighed. "I'll lose my baby."

"I'm right here," Clove said. She pulled Kate into another hug. "I could have never met you at all. This is better than nothing."

Matt wrapped an arm around both their shoulders. "She's right. But what about our ages? By the time you're sixteen we'll be – what, thirty-five? Thirty-six? We only look nineteen."

"We'll think of something," Clove said. *"Please."*

Kate held onto Clove like she never wanted to let her go. "OK," she murmured. "OK."

Clove sighed happily and squeezed Kate even tighter.

CHAPTER 39

● ●
North Atlantic Alliance (NATO)

INTERNATIONAL LAW VIOLATION REPORT 24 AUGUST 2040

CRIME: MILITARY POSSESSION OF WEAPONS OF MASS DESTRUCTION

ACCUSED STATE: ENGLAND

Abstract: On 29 July 2040 at 08:43 a package was discovered by ███████████████ in the reception of NATO headquarters, Brussels, Belgium. Initially believed to be a terrorist attack, the Belgian Bomb Disposal Unit (DOVO) was called by ████████████████.

Preliminary analysis showed that the package, labelled ██████████, contained a chemical substance in a sealed vial, as well as a DVD of data. The vial was taken to a secure laboratory for analysis.

Files on the DVD claimed that the vial contained a bacteria similar to the chemical ANTHRAX. This assertion was corroborated by analysis of the sample by ████████████████████ at DOVO. The sample was found to be a mutation of the bacterium ████████████████.

Instructions for an antidote to the bacterium were included on the DVD. Preparations of the antidote were immediately begun by biologists at ████████████████ in case of accidental release or otherwise.

The DVD was also found to contain incontrovertible evidence that the weapon had been created at the behest of General ██████████, who was acting on behalf of the English government. Biologists ████████████ ██████████ and ████████████████████ were instructed to design and make the bacteria at ██████████ Laboratory, England. According to evidence contained on the DVD, they were unaware of its planned end usage.

The DVD also contained evidence implicating the highest ranking officials in the English government in the form of ████████████████ and emails between the English military, ██████████ and the prime minister ██████████. (See Section 5.4.3 for more details.)

As the creation of any weapon of mass destruction is a breach of international law, both ethically and morally, control of the English military and ▮▮▮▮▮▮▮▮▮▮ Laboratory was seized without delay by ▮▮▮▮▮ Regiment on 30 July 2040 at 05:13.

Many complicit individuals fled the country to evade capture. All except ▮▮▮▮▮▮▮▮▮ have since been found and given life sentences at ▮▮▮▮ Prison.

All sources of the bacteria were safely destroyed by trained DOVO officials ▮▮▮▮▮▮ and ▮▮▮▮▮▮▮.

Folios/v8/Time-landscape-2040/MS-19

File note: Report filed by NATO on 24 August 2040, detailing the events of 29 July 2040. Following the dissolution of the English military by NATO, the English shadow cabinet declared emergency rule and peace talks with the EU began

ST ANDREWS, SCOTLAND, 2056

The four of them landed with a thump in Clove's bedroom on the evening of the day after Clove had first used the St Andrews time machine. Rubbing the phosphenes out of her vision, Clove decided she was not travelling in time for at least the next few weeks. Her head felt like lead.

"Clove?" Jen called from downstairs. "Is that you?"

Her stomach dropped. Jen was home. They were going straight into this, then.

Clove's parents thought she'd been at Meg's all day – probably assuming that she was hiding from them after their fight. It had only been two nights ago that they had told Clove she needed therapy, and Clove, in her anger, had said "Jen" instead of "Mum".

"Yes, Mum!" she shouted and then turned to Ella, Kate and Matt. "Stay here."

Clove went downstairs. She stood in the kitchen doorway, watching her mum cook dinner. For a while there, she really had thought she would never see her again.

Jen turned and caught sight of her. "Hello, love. You're home early."

Clove ran over to her, and hugged her, hiding her face in Jen's shoulder. "I'm so sorry, Mum. I never meant to call you 'Jen'. I know you're my mum. I was an idiot. I love you."

Jen wrapped her arms around her, wooden spoon still in one hand. She pressed a kiss to Clove's forehead. Clove squeezed her eyes shut.

"I know. I love you too," Jen said.

"I promise I'll be better, now. I promise I won't—"

"You don't have to be *better*. You just have to be yourself. Your father and I will love you whatever you do."

Clove thought of all the mistakes she'd made, and wondered if that was really true. "Thanks, Mum. You're incredible, and I couldn't have asked for a better parent."

Jen squeezed her tight. "I love you so much, Clove." When she pulled away, she wiped a tear from her eye. "You seem much calmer today. Did you make up with Meg?"

"Meg?" Clove repeated, surprised. "No – I mean, yes.

We talked about everything. We're friends again now."

Jen broke into a smile. "That's good. That's really great. I knew the two of you would work everything out." She turned back to the hob to stir a pan full of Bolognese sauce. Then she spun around and hugged Clove again. "I'm so proud of you," she said. "You've really grown up recently. Work experience has done you good."

Clove grinned over her mum's shoulder. Work experience. That was definitely what it was.

Tom walked in from the garden. "Ah, my girls have made up," he said, beaming, and patted Clove's shoulder. "How was Meg's?"

"Dad!" Clove let go of Jen to hug him too, unable to resist. The last time she'd seen him, he'd been *dead*. And now here he was, alive and well, and holding a handful of fresh basil leaves for the pasta.

"Everything OK, darlin'?" he said, stubble rubbing against her cheek when he kissed the side of her head.

"Perfect," she said, trying to calm her smile. "I love you, Dad."

"I love you too." He blinked at her, and then smiled back, the lines around his eyes crinkling. "Hey, I've decided to grow a beard. What do you think?" He rubbed a hand over his jaw. "It just occurred to me last night."

Clove laughed, remembering how in the alternate universe Jen had commented on Tom's beard. Some part of him must have retained the memory, even if it was subconscious. "You should get a motorbike too," she suggested. "You could teach me to ride it."

His mouth twitched. "Now *that's* an idea."

They grinned at each other, both ignoring Jen, who was muttering about midlife crises. Then Clove ducked her head. She had to get on with this. "Actually, I have something to tell you both. Can you sit down?" Her voice wavered, coming out thin and nervous.

Jen's expression changed from relaxed to slightly terrified. "Are you OK, Clove? What's going on?"

"Stay calm," she began – which was a mistake. She could see them both start to panic. She decided to just bite the bullet and go for it. "I found Kate and Matt."

Tom turned so pale that Clove thought he was going to faint. *"What?"*

"They're upstairs."

"Here?" Jen said.

"Shall I ... er ... go and get them?"

Neither Tom nor Jen spoke, so Clove made her own decision. "I'll go and get them."

In her room, Kate and Matt were sitting on her bed. Matt was looking through Clove's pot of pens, while Kate was holding the fox ornament and rubbing her thumb back and forth across its head – a movement Clove had done herself dozens of times over the last week. Ella sat at the desk chair, with Clove's knitting in her hand. When Clove came into the room, they all jumped up.

"They're freaking out," Clove said. "I don't know what to do."

"Er..." Matt said. He blinked rapidly, and dropped a fountain pen back in the pot.

"Let's go and talk to them," Kate suggested.

"No, they're properly panicking! You can't just... I actually think my dad – Tom, I mean – might faint."

"Tom," Matt repeated, voice cracking like he hadn't really believed his brother was here until she'd confirmed it. He paced two steps across Clove's room before turning and pacing in the other direction. "OK. OK. OK. Let's just ... let's go. Let's go."

"Oh my God," Clove said, and realized she was trembling. Matt stared at her, his eyes as wide as hers. They both ran a hand through their hair in unison. "Oh my God. What are we doing?"

"OK," Matt said again. "This is all absolutely fine."

"Everyone, just calm down!" Kate said loudly. "Matt, shut up." Matt stopped pacing and grabbed her hand. She patted him reassuringly on the shoulder. "Let's go downstairs and talk to them, instead of having panic attacks in Clove's bedroom. OK?"

Clove nodded. They were going to do this. It was going to be fine. Nothing terrible would happen, and nobody would faint. Probably.

After a moment when nobody moved, Kate prompted, "Shall we go then?"

"OK," Clove said, and took a deep breath.

They went downstairs.

"I should be recording this," Ella said to herself, trailing after them.

Tom and Jen were sitting at the kitchen table, staring at each other and communicating silently, in the way Clove always used to hate. Now it just made her think of Ella. They both stood up when Clove and the others entered, chairs scraping loudly across the floor.

When Tom caught sight of his brother, his eyes filled with tears.

By the time Tom and Jen had been told the whole story, and recovered from the resultant shock, it was dinnertime. Clove served up the spaghetti Bolognese, not even trying to stop herself smiling at the sight of everyone sitting around the dining table, arguing over garlic bread.

"Thank you for raising my daughter," Kate said to Jen, once they'd all begun eating. "She's turned into a wonderful person. I think you deserve the credit for that."

Jen smiled brightly, tears shining in her eyes. "I'm very proud of her."

"So, what happens now?" Tom said, looking exhausted. It had taken Clove quite a long time to explain everything, and she knew there would be more questions to come, and definitely repercussions. Jen's lips had thinned when she'd heard how Clove had broken into the lab and used the time machine. "We'll talk about this later," Tom had said sternly, before going back to asking Matt about the prison breakout. The two of them had spent a long time hugging.

"I don't know about you," Kate said to Matt, "but I'm going to be spending so much time getting to know our daughter that she'll be sick of us."

Matt wrapped an arm around Clove's shoulders. "That's definitely first on the list. Then we declare ourselves no longer missing, I suppose. Find a job, now we're not supposed criminals. Find a house. Do whatever else people do when they become an adult. Get one of those cool time-travelling watches."

"That's from the future, actually," Clove said. "Even *I* don't have one of those."

"No more time travel," Jen said firmly. "I'm absolutely not having this turn into some sort of family competition to see who can become a fugitive the youngest."

Clove nodded frantically around a mouthful of garlic bread, trying to look like she meant it.

Ella blinked mutely. She didn't seem able to do anything else but stare wide-eyed at Tom and Jen. "I can't believe I'm eating dinner with the *actual creators of time travel*," she had whispered to Clove at one point. *"Oh my God!"*

"We'll get you both declared legally undead in the morning," Tom said, smiling widely. "Although I don't know how we're going to make anyone believe you're thirty-five, Matt. Can you even grow a beard yet?"

"All right, grey hair. Are those wrinkles or laughter lines?"

Matt punched Tom's arm, and then they were wrestling, and Jen was yelling about watching out for the wine glasses, and Kate was grinning like she'd never been so happy, and Ella was holding Clove's hand under the table, rubbing circles into her skin.

Clove just sat back and watched them all through half-closed eyes, trying very hard not to give the impression of a sunning cat.

* * *

> CLOVE, are you awake?

>> Shhhh, Spart, Ella's sleeping. Let's talk by text. What's up?

> I would like to discuss the situation regarding subjects "KATHERINE" and "MATTHEW" with you.

>> I guessed as much. Are you thinking what I'm thinking?

> I am not fitted with a telepathic unit, so it is subsequently impossible for my system to undertake the reading of minds.

>> It's a turn of phrase. You must not be fitted with a colloquial semantics unit either, huh?

> If we may return to the matter raised. I now understand the repeated appearance of subjects "KATHERINE" and "MATTHEW".

>> Same. I think it's us. It is, isn't it? The ones bringing K and M back to life?

>> I didn't believe Ella when she told me, but the more I think about it, the more sense it makes.

> I concur with your hypothesis. All evidence indicates such a prediction is likely to be accurate.

>> In every time-landscape, K and M do something to save the world. They must have saved so many lives.

> According to the evidence, for every version of subjects "MATTHEW" and "KATHERINE" that meet and fall in love, at least 4×10^6 human lives are saved.

>> 4 million? That's. Wow. That's more than I was expecting.

> It would not be an exaggeration to say that the quality of existence of all humanity is improved vastly each time subjects "KATHERINE" and "MATTHEW" fall in love.

>> But why them? Ella told me that they have some kind of "instinct" for knowing what needs doing and when. How is that possible?

> The human mind is not something within my capacity to understand. Perhaps subjects "KATHERINE" and "MATTHEW" simply have a particularly humanitarian perception of the world.

>> I guess it doesn't matter why they help, as long as they do.

> Indeed.

>> If they really do help the world, then it makes sense to make sure they have as many lives as possible. Right?

> It would do much good. As long as we choose the time-landscapes carefully, so they are best positioned to aid mankind. For example, the Moon Colony Riots of 2043 would be a good choice of landscape in which to place the subjects next.

>> Do you think it's moral? To use them like that?

> I do not see why not, as long as we have the subjects' permission to proceed.

>> I don't know if Kate and Matt will agree to it. It's a lot to ask, to have them live again and again.

> I do not anticipate that being a problem. Both subjects are inclined towards helping others, and as previously stated, this is the most efficient way of achieving such a goal.

>> And you're OK with it? And everything it means?

> My programming values human life above all else. To ensure that, I have no other choice but to bring together the subjects as frequently as possible.

>> We can find parents who can't conceive and ask if they would like help having children. Use IVF to implant them with cloned embryos of K and M.

>> We obviously wouldn't call it IVF, though - at least not before it was invented. People in the eighteenth century will probably just think it's some kind of witchcraft.

> That does seem the most suitable course of action.

>> Do you know anything about cloning?

> I will begin to research.

>> We shouldn't rush into this. We need to think about it to make sure we know what we're doing.

> I will take no further action at this time.

> I have four recently aired episodes of *Sherbot Holmes: Robot Detective* to watch, anyway.

>> We're going to have to keep an eye on them, to make

sure nothing goes wrong. We can't just leave them to themselves, like in 1745.

> I would be willing to monitor their progress in each time-landscape, to ensure that the subjects do ultimately interact with each other in a positive manner. I could file reports for you.

> We would have to be prepared to intervene in the event that the subjects don't operate correctly.

>> Absolutely.

>> Ella's waking up, got to go. Let's talk about this tomorrow.

> I await your command, CLOVE.

File note: Chat log, dated 16 January 2057

EPILOGUE

INT. TV STUDIO – NIGHT

Camera focuses on female presenter sitting on an orange sofa. Bright stage lighting shines down at her. The camera pans over a smiling audience to the presenter.

SARAH
(smiling)

I'm Sarah Phillips and welcome back to *The Shipping Forecast*. Today on the show I've spoken to celebrity vlogger Caistat about his new line of hover-boards, and Blue North has been in the studio talking about her upcoming film *Sense, Sensibility & Cyborgs*. We've also had a special broadcast all the way from 'the loneliest girl in the universe', Romy Silvers.

But I've saved the best for last. Now we have someone who I've been trying to get on the show for a very long time. The famous Clove Sutcliffe, the first ever time traveller and founder of the era-defining History Control. You don't need me to say any more. You all know who she is – most of us had a poster of her on our wall as a kid, didn't we, folks?

The crowd roars with excitement.

SARAH
So without further ado, all the way from the year 2058, please welcome ... Clove Sutcliffe!

CLOVE enters, waving to the crowd.

SARAH
Miss Sutcliffe, it's an honour to have you with us this evening.

CLOVE
It's a pleasure to be here.

SARAH
Is this your first time visiting our year?

CLOVE

Actually, I've been to visit my girlfriend here a few times. She's from this time period.

SARAH

So you're in a long-distance relationship?

CLOVE

(grinning)

Centuries long distance, yep.

SARAH

How's that working out?

CLOVE

(ducking her head, smiling)

Great, thank you for asking.

A voice in the crowd is heard yelling, "TELL US WHO ELLA IS!"

SARAH

(chuckling)

Well, I'm sure you want to keep the identity of your mystery lady private, so let's move on. I want to talk to you about your famous work in History Control. Firstly, how do your parents feel about being used throughout history as tools?

CLOVE

They are happy to help and gave their DNA willingly. It took a bit of getting used to, I think, knowing that there are lots of clones of them out there, but they would do anything to help save one life, let alone millions of them. Of course the Katherines and Matthews ...

(pausing as the crowd cheers)

... the Katherines and Matthews throughout history don't know that they have been created by the DNA of people hundreds of years in the future. But my parents are so kind – they naturally want to help no matter when they are born. The choice to save the world is always theirs. I just give them the means to do it, by placing them at the right moment in history.

SARAH

Your work has saved countless people and their descendants. But how did you first decide that putting your parents in the past was the best way to ensure History Revisions? What inspired you?

CLOVE

I never came up with the idea. I just started doing it, because I saw that's what was happening and realized it was a good idea.

SARAH

So it's a paradox? You do something, because you've already done it...

CLOVE

Right. Somewhere out there, someone must have started the whole thing, but I don't know who. I just carried on their great idea. Time travel is like knitting. You have to build on what's come before, and weave the strands together until it becomes something beautiful.

SARAH

Well, that's something for us all to think about. Now, I have one last question for you. What are you going to do next?

CLOVE

I'm about to start a computer science degree, so right now I'm frantically trying to learn how to cook something that isn't beans on toast. It's an adventure.

SARAH

Thank you, Clove.

(Turning to face the camera)

That's all from us for tonight. Stay tuned next for the much-anticipated season finale of *Sherbot Holmes: Robot Detective*!

File note: Transcript from the first public appearance of
        CLOVE SUTCLIFFE, on popular talk show *The Shipping
        Forecast*

ACKNOWLEDGEMENTS

The most important thanks go to my agent, Claire Wilson, and my editor, Annalie Grainger. As always, I couldn't have written anything without you both. You two encourage me to write all the wild and weird things my heart desires, while simultaneously making sure that at least *some* parts of it remain slightly plausible. Annalie, I'm truly sorry for making you edit all those alternate universes and time-travel paradoxes. Your patience is never-ending.

Thank you to Arts Council England, without whose support I couldn't have been a full-time author. That would have sucked.

Thank you to Alice Oseman for all of the enthusiasm of the "#SOON!!" variety, and for drawing the stunning cover for Clove's textbook. (IT'S IN THE BOOK! IT'S CANON!!!!)

Cat Doyle, you're always the fastest, most eager reader of my writing. Thank you for being so endlessly cool.

Sarah Louise Barnard, thank you for sending me messages from the very beginning telling me how desperately you wanted to read more about Clove and her ladies. I'm glad to have written something that meets your approval. The next one will have more murders in, I promise.

Thanks to The Turtles, whose song "Elenore" was my continuous soundtrack whilst writing this book. One day someone will record the female cover that the world (and Clove) needs. Taylor Swift, I'm lookin' at you.

Thank you to Christopher Banks James for the suggestions of futuristic slang. You're *powerful* too.

And, obviously, thanks to Rachel and Keith James, my mum and dad. I'm so, *so* glad you've never made me chase you guys through time.

Enjoyed this book?
Tweet us your thoughts.
#TheLastBeginning @WalkerBooksUK
@Lauren_E_James

HOW MANY TIMES CAN YOU LOSE THE ONE YOU LOVE?

THE
NEXT
TOGETHER

LAUREN JAMES

"A FUNNY, GRIPPING, AND INCREDIBLY IMAGINATIVE
STORY OF TRUE LOVE AND REINCARNATION."

LOUISE O'NEILL AUTHOR OF *ONLY EVER YOURS*

Katherine and Matthew are destined
to be born again and again.
Each time they fall hopelessly in love,
only to be tragically separated.
Maybe the next together will be different...

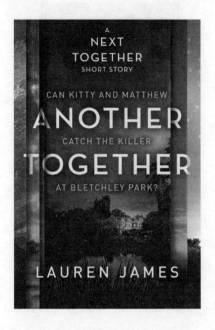

DIGITAL EXCLUSIVE

Download the standalone short story *Another Together*,
set in the world of *The Next Together*

"Are you absolutely certain this is safe?"
Matthew Galloway asked.

Winter, 1940: there is a murderer on the loose at
Bletchley Park. Can two young codebreakers Kitty
and Matthew catch the killer?

LAUREN JAMES was born in 1992. She started writing during secondary school English classes, because she couldn't stop thinking about a couple who kept falling in love throughout history. She sold the rights to the novel when she was 21, while she was still at university.

The Next Together series has been translated into five languages worldwide, and was longlisted for the Branford Boase Award, a prize given to recognize an outstanding novel by a first-time writer.

Lauren graduated in 2014 from the University of Nottingham, where she studied Chemistry and Physics. She is a passionate advocate of STEM further education, and all of her books feature scientists in prominent roles.

Lauren lives in the West Midlands and is an Arts Council grant recipient. You can find her on Twitter at @Lauren_E_James, on Tumblr at @laurenjames or on her website: laurenejames.co.uk.